KA[...]
YOU'RE
KILLING
ME!

KARACHI, YOU'RE KILLING ME!

SABA IMTIAZ

RANDOM HOUSE INDIA

Published by Random House India in 2014
Second impression in 2016

Copyright © Saba Imtiaz 2014

Random House Publishers India Private Limited
7th Floor, Infinity Tower C
DLF Cyber City
Gurgaon 122 002, Haryana, India

Random House Group Limited
20 Vauxhall Bridge Road
London SW1V 2SA
United Kingdom

978 81 8400 460 1

Typeset in Sabon by R. Ajith Kumar

Printed and bound in India by Repro India Limited

A PENGUIN RANDOM HOUSE COMPANY

For Rubina Imtiaz and Mansoor Saeed

'I am a child of Cosmopolitan culture, have been traumatized by supermodels and too many quizzes and know that neither my personality nor my body is up to it if left to its own devices.'

—Helen Fielding, *Bridget Jones's Diary*

CHAPTER 1

Friday, December 31, 2011

Headline of the day: 'Seoul protests North Korean bootlegging in Islamabad'

So I'm re-reading the review I've written of Love At First Bite, Karachi's latest cupcake bakery, not checking it for typos so much as wondering if my boredom, disdain, and self-loathing shine through a little too much when Kamran pops his head out of his door and yells 'GET IN HERE NOW, AYESHA!' It's 4 p.m. and I am itching to go home. I'm supposed to hear back about a fellowship in New York I applied for, a fantastic three-month stint at a think tank writing about religious parties in Pakistan. It's all-expenses paid, I'll get to finally explain developments in Pakistan in more than 600 words—our bloody word limit at the paper—and it'll mean that more people will actually get to read my work, other than my father and my friends. I had a fantastic phone interview with one of the associates at the think tank—despite the loud argument going on outside my flat between two shopkeepers—and I have a really good feeling about this one. Surely I can leave the office even though it's only 4 p.m. I must be the first reporter today to have filed their copy—there's no one else about in the dungeon-like reporter's room affectionately known as Anne Frank's attic—what could I possibly have done now? Kamran's office used to be upstairs where there are windows and natural light, and not down here in the basement with the wretched of the earth—me and my colleagues—till he decided he wanted to keep a closer eye on everyone so now he's in a large glass-fronted room adjacent to the newsroom, and he keeps popping out of it like a particularly disturbing jack-in-the-box.

I walk in and he's about to say something when the phone rings, 'Oh, for fuck's sake,' he says, answering, 'Sana, sweetheart, I'll call you in a bit. Yes, I know, Adil's house tonight.' Kamran's wife Sana is possibly the only human being Kamran has ever shown any consideration towards, at least from what I've overheard in his office. Also, last month when he found out we'd been out-scooped by the *Morning News* on the legislators discovering surveillance equipment in their homes story, he swept everything off his desk in a fit of rage except for their wedding portrait. Looking at it, him in a sharp, dark suit with a boyish grin and JFK Junior hair—every inch the scion—smiling down at fragile, willowy Sana decked out in fat emeralds and a green, pink, and gold gharara that must have cost as much as a small flat, you'd not be able to tell my boss was basically a maniac.

'Check these e-mails out,' he says, tossing me his phone.

E-mail from sub-editor: Sick today. Won't be able to come in.

E-mail from city pages head: Have to take my aunt to the doctor's. Won't be at work today.

E-mail from sub-editor: I have typhoid. Will be on leave till the 10th.

E-mail from page-maker: I have dengue fever. Please grant me leave till the 5th.

'You can't get dengue fever in winter,' I point out in a futile effort to stave off the inevitable.

'Whatever.' Kamran says. 'You're staying late.'

'It's not my fault everyone has taken the day off to celebrate New Year's. And I stayed late yesterday too.'

'You did?' Kamran asks suspiciously, clearly having forgotten that he spent all of the last evening loitering by my desk complaining bitterly about a big rival news network being taken more seriously than his paper. I didn't want to say at the time but it struck me that it could have something to do with his industrialist father buying him a newspaper five years ago on his twenty-sixth birthday following a giant tantrum.

'You're staying till nine, and you need to edit whatever

copy comes in today,' Kamran counters, and begins glaring at the front page of the *Morning News*.

I check my e-mail.

'Thank you for submitting your application for the position of independent researcher at USPak Associates. We thank you for your interest, however we regret to inform you that you have not been selected for the position.'

The rest of the e-mail is a blur of 'many qualified candidates' and 'do apply next year' bullshit. Again, that's what comes from being an actual reporter, not some douchebag sitting in Islamabad gleaning all my insights from the newspapers. Why does the world hate me?

There's no time to even cry over this. I have to edit. My inbox is full of copy that needed to be done an hour ago: Five tortured bodies found near the motorway, two people shot dead as they tried to escape muggers, nine people killed after a bus collided with a train.

I stick my head into Kamran's office at ten to tell him I've had enough and he waves me away without looking up from his phone call—'Sana, I'm telling you, wear the black Armani, not the red...'

Make it home at 10.45, longing for a shower and my pyjamas and in no mood to dress up and party, and head directly to my room without even saying hello to my father, whose TV I can hear through his bedroom door. I briefly consider taking a hotel room for the night and letting everyone think I've been kidnapped or something when Zara texts, 'there in 5'. 'No', I respond, adding 'Need 20 minutes'. I light a cigarette to try to relax a bit and open my cupboard in the hope that something chic I've overlooked will magically jump out at me. Nothing jumps out, but I do notice after a while that I'm seeing double.

I'm about to give up and mourn for the lost fellowship when Zara bursts into my room. She's had her hair cut in that Natalie Imbruglia circa *Torn* crop and looks drop dead gorgeous. I tried that cut a few years ago and looked like a sad street urchin. Though her job is even more stressful than mine, Zara always looks like she just stepped off the pages of a fashion magazine and would be so easy to hate if she wasn't so, well, fantastic. 'Are you still not dressed?' Zara perches on the edge of my bed and pulls a couple of beers out of her handbag. 'Chug this, and get ready.'

I take a long sip, and as the cold beer hits my stomach I realize I forgot to have lunch and dinner and I'm running on a stale packet of chili chips I found in my desk drawer. 'Kamran made me call every single photographer to tell them he'd fire them if they filed photos of 2011's last sunset. It was not fun,' I say, pulling a black jumpsuit out of my cupboard. It's slightly faded but it'll be dark and everyone will be drunk soon enough.

Zara comes over to inspect it, tripping over an extension wire and then a spiral notepad lying on the carpet. My room looks like an installation piece titled 'Where Journalism Goes to Die'. There are notebooks, piles of old newspapers, and shawls seemingly growing from every surface, and I spilled some Diet Coke on the bed sheets last night. I wish I could crawl under the bed sheets, stains and all.

'So can't we just stay in and watch *The Hangover* or something?' I say, so tired she has to tell me I'm trying to stick my foot through an armhole.

'Absolutely not,' Zara says, 'It's New Year's, for the love of god.'

Sometimes I wonder how Zara managed to graduate from business school and become a kick-ass investigative reporter. Zara parties like her life depends on it and knows absolutely everyone, and if she doesn't, she'll find a way to get their entire biodata; how many As they got on their O-Levels and a list of their last five exes.

I met her two years ago at the PPP office waiting for a press conference to start forty-five minutes after the time it was due to kick off. Zara emerged from nowhere just as I headed out for a smoke—though she swears we'd met at a party three years before that that I don't even remember attending—and exclaimed, 'Thank god there's another woman smoking!' Three hours, five boring speeches that I forgot the minute the speaker stepped off the dais, and half a pack of cigarettes later, Zara and I were exchanging numbers and making plans to meet up for coffee. Three months later, she was headhunted to *Morning News TV* after she produced an expose on the public hospital's procurement department and how it was injecting children with water instead of the polio vaccine. I, on the other hand, am still stuck at my low-paying job at the *Daily*

News where I report on everything from cupcake bakeries to clashes between warring gangs.

'Hurry up,' Zara says. 'We have a lot of places to get to.'

'How you can care about New Year's is beyond me,' I say, memories of horrible New Year's Past, Present, and Future flashing in front of me. Last year I was drinking ORS till the 3rd of January after getting through a bottle of local vodka at a party where they ran out of the good stuff early on.

I say goodnight and happy New Year to my father who's standing over a chopping board slicing chicken for the cat's dinner. 'Stay safe,' he calls out.

As we get into Zara's car, I realize I have no idea where we're going.

'So this is the plan for tonight,' Zara says, after she's explained what sounds like a very complicated address to her driver. 'I've made a list of every single house party we've been invited to and ranked them in order of boring, will serve crappy booze or expect us to bring our own, to those where they may actually play music we recognize. I've also looked up all of the addresses on Google Maps and figured out how we can avoid those stupid road blocks.'

'Or not,' I say, pointing ahead. There's a cop frantically waving at us to turn back.

'Oh seriously, what the hell,' Zara says. 'Clearly the cops have run out of containers. They've closed off this road with concrete blocks.'

Zara rolls down her window to ask the cop where we can

pass through from, but a guy jumps out of the Land Cruiser behind Zara's car and starts screaming. 'This is my fucking house!' He's pointing to a massive three-storey mansion just behind the roadblock that looks like a copy of an ancient Greek temple. There are towering columns, more white marble than in the Taj Mahal, and the boundary walls are layered with barbed wire. The guy, who couldn't be much older than Zara and I, is raving at the cop to 'move those motherfucking blocks' or he's out of a job.

The cop looks terrified and starts trying to lift one. Zara groans. 'Let's just take another route,' her driver suggests. We pass by similar mansions, each one's walls higher than the next. 'Hey look,' Zara nudges me. 'Isn't that Saad's house?' She points to the only house in the neighbourhood that still has a low gate. It was built in the 1950s, when one could potentially talk a thief out of robbing the house by reminding him that he could do better things with his life, when instead of barbed wire, people put broken glass on the walls so they'd hear someone trying to jump over. I cut my foot on that glass when I was seventeen, trying to win a bet with Saad that I could jump over even in a dress.

'Yeah,' I say, craning my neck to see if there are any lights on. 'Hey, did you tell him where we're going? You do remember he's joining us, right?'

'Yes, yes, I told him. Just tell him not to hit on me tonight, ok? I know he's your friend but I hardly know him and he keeps giving me the glad eye. I really want to meet someone NEW. Like, someone I don't feel ashamed about fucking.'

As we mull over this, the holy grail of casual sex in Karachi, in silence, the driver makes a turn, and we pass by the park where Saad and I did yoga for a full two days before we gave up and resumed our diet of kebab rolls and fries. It doesn't feel like New Year's. There are no street parties or fireworks. All I can see are a few cars on the road. When I was younger, everyone I knew would camp out on the public beach road. It was like an actual carnival: kids rode camels, guys in too-tight t-shirts and jeans blared hits from Indian films on their car stereos, and the cops would always try to make a quick buck by harassing couples. I remind Zara of this and she looks a bit wistful. 'Yeah. It was nice, wasn't it? Though you know—and I hate to say this, because it sounds like one of those tales our grandparents tell us—but sometimes I feel like that didn't happen at all, like I'm trying to remember some sort of previous incarnation, like in a Bollywood film.'

The street lights go off while we wait at a traffic light and within a minute, the roar of generators kicks in. 'Power cut on New Year's,' the driver mutters. Just as well. It goes with how gloomy I feel anyway, though I'm sure it'll be better once I have a drink in hand and see Saad. I realize that I still have no idea where we're going.

'So whose party is this?' I ask Zara.

'Faryal's,' she says flippantly, checking her reflection in her compact.

'I'm not going to Faryal's. I ran into her at Agha's the other day and she said she was impressed people could shop there on reporters' salaries. It's a different issue altogether that I can't really and only went there because I was having an uncontrollable craving for Bonne Maman jam.'

'Oh come on,' Zara rolls her eyes. 'She's not that bad. And I think Zain—that really cute cousin of her husband's who I danced with at their mehndi—might be there.'

Faryal's house is a smaller version of the Greek temple-styled mansion and as we walk in I instantly hate my clothes. The women look like they belong on the pages of Vogue: I can spot someone wearing a floor-length dress that looks eerily like the one Angelina Jolie wore to last year's Oscars. The bar runs the length of the garden and there are about a dozen bartenders whipping up drinks. People are already on the dance floor and a few guys have rolled up their jeans and are sitting on the edge of the pool. One of them throws a beer can in and it lands neatly in the middle of an arrangement of rose petals and candles. There's a burst of laughter. I start looking around for Saad.

'What does Faryal's husband do?' I ask. 'This party is a little insane.'

'Textiles, I think. But you know, he could just as easily be smuggling weapons or something. Who knows.' Zara adjusts her top and plasters on a smile as she sees Faryal. 'Zara, darling, you look gorgeous!' Faryal is one of Zara's friends from college, who—as the legend goes—met her husband on the day she graduated, and was having fittings for a 500,000 rupee wedding outfit six months later. 'And you, Ayesha, so interesting-looking in that jumpsuit!'

'Thanks,' I say, wishing I had a bitchy putdown. 'Interesting-looking' indeed, it's Agha's all over again.

'And try the cupcakes! We brought them in from the Magnolia branch in Dubai!'

She turns away to meet some of the other guests. 'Did you hear what she called me?' I whisper to Zara, but she's staring in the other direction, probably trying to see if she can spot Zain. I make my way to the bar and am toying between ordering a cosmopolitan or a mojito when someone taps me on the shoulder.

It's Saad, looking very tanned and very, very pissed off.

'You are so fucking late. I've just spent the past thirty minutes listening to Faryal and her husband talk about their vacation in Bali.'

'Saad, I walked in and she told me my clothes were "interesting looking"!'

'No one could ever accuse her of looking interesting,' says Saad and I curse fate for not having had him next to me to deliver this line to Faryal two minutes ago.

'Well, you're here now,' he says, hugging me, 'It's so good to see you,' he whispers in my ear. For some reason I feel like I'm going to cry. I haven't seen him in months, and now that he's here I just want to put my head on his shoulder and tell him how miserable I've been.

11

Saad and I have been friends since we met in the fifth grade where he was one of the few boys who enjoyed discussing the merits of the Famous Five series. We went to college together after which I enrolled in business school and Saad flew off to Cambridge. We Skyped every weekend for the four years he was away and have seen each other through death (his father, my mother), divorce (his sister), heartbreak (just me really, though I saw him through a stalker ex-girlfriend), and changing jobs. Saad eventually moved to Dubai, and now lives in a swanky apartment in Jumeirah where, by his own admission, he has dated far more women than he ever would have in a lifetime in Karachi.

'So,' I say, as I take my drink from the bartender and sit down on one of the silk banquettes nearby. 'What's new?'

'Don't ask,' Saad says. 'I'm so glad to be back, even if it's just for a day. I couldn't deal with New Year's in Dubai, and things are a bit weird with this girl I met...'

'You mean, the girl you slept with,' I say.

'It was awful, she was a starfish.'

'A starfish?' I light up a cigarette. 'What the fuck is that?'

'A starfish is a woman who just lies there. Makes you do all the work. Like a starfish.' Saad lies back on the banquette and begins to demonstrate.

'Ugh no, no please. I get it.'

'Zara!' Saad exclaims, waving, as he spots her in a group of people milling by the bar. She walks over and takes a sip of my drink. 'Zain isn't here,' she says to me. 'And hello, Saad.'

'Zara, you look absolutely fantastic. How is it that you're even more gorgeous than the last time I saw you?' Zara rolls her eyes. 'Saad, save the charm for Dubai's burqa babes. Finish your drinks and move. We have a lot of places to get to.'

We put in an appearance at Saad's cousin's house, except his cousin is nineteen and is only serving beer. 'Ah, Justin Bieber,' Saad nods authoritatively as the music changes. We're squashed together on a sofa along with three other girls, who look young enough to be our children. 'Duh. It's One Direction!' one of them squeals.

'Why am I listening to Bieber or whatever this One Direction crap is?' Saad moans in my ear.

'Why am I being offered a joint?' I hiss back, as I pass the joint, which has made its way through everyone sitting on the couch, to Zara. 'I'm twenty-eight years old. Surely a joint is not the height of excitement in my life.'

'Clearly it is to this lot.' Zara takes a drag of the joint and stubs it out in a paper cup. 'Okay, guys,' she calls out loudly. 'The grown-ups are leaving!'

Twenty minutes later we finally end up two streets away from what Zara claimed was the best party this New Year's, except the road to the house has been blocked by a massive container. 'Can't we just move it?' Saad asks. 'No, you're going to have to walk,' the driver informs us. 'In heels?' Zara screeches. 'Jeez, we're going to get mugged.'

We end up walking anyway, Saad holding on to our bags and saying 'Look, it's just like being in London!' A group of guys are trying to manoeuvre their Charade around the container, and then get out to move it a couple of inches so their car goes through. 'Can't we just ask them to drop us?' Zara moans. 'My feet...'

We finally make our way to the house, where the hosts—Zara's second cousin and his wife—direct us to the bar. 'Get a drink, and join us on the dance floor,' her cousin booms. 'We are going to celebrate all bloody night.' Zara hands us tumblers of what I can only hope is whiskey and Coke. 'To 2012!' she says, holding her glass aloft. 'To getting the hell out of Karachi,' I say, taking a large sip, and then spilling half of the rest of it on my jumpsuit when Zara grabs my arm as the DJ plays *The Way You Make Me Feel*. 'We have to dance!'

Saturday, January 1, 2012

Headline of the day: 'Faqir's pet snake stolen'

8 a.m.: Stick arms out to investigate poky thing digging into the small of my back. I can tell it's my hairbrush from having a feel, which is just as well as my eyes are as if glued shut. This is it, I decide. This is going to be a completely different year. I will never spend another New Year's party having arguments about extortion rackets. I will not go to parties where the line for the loo is taken

up by coke addicts pretending that their 50,000 rupee a night habit is 'totally under control, dude'. I will produce an excellent piece of investigative journalism this year, the kind that wins prizes, gets me headhunted to a fantastic job in New York, or at the very least, Dubai. Okay fine, I'll consider an international network in Islamabad. I desperately need to get my act together and this year, I will. Oh, and I will not be single. Is it sad that this is the last thing on my list of priorities? No, I remind myself. I'm being realistic. Where am I ever going to find a guy in the wasteland that is Karachi where it's easier to hire an assassin than meet an attractive, intelligent, normal single man? There are twenty million people in this city, you'd think this would be easier.

Attempt to sit up, which proves tricky in a jumpsuit that appears to have shrunk overnight. Lie there wondering why I'm not in my pyjamas.

8.25 a.m.: A POX ON THE CROWS. WHY ARE THEY SO BLOODY NOISY!?

9 a.m.: Find myself completely unable to get up and go to work. Would much rather lie under the comforter all day. The cat has just come in and looked at me with disgust.

10 a.m.: Still in bed.

10.15 a.m.: Text from Saad: 'Missed my flight. Literally got to the airport just as they closed boarding. Now on standby for the next one. FML.'

Text from Zara: 'Head exploding and I can't feel my neck. Think I might go to the doctor.'

10.30 a.m.: My father, a long-suffering single parent, has just sent me a text message from his office instructing me to feed the cat before I go to work. It's 10.30 a.m., but even he knows that there's a 90 percent chance I'm still in bed trying to find the will to live. Last Monday he found me crying when my alarm went off and asked if I needed psychiatric help. 'NO ABBA, I JUST HATE WORK,' I yelled, before he backed out of the room to feed the cat, who, unlike his daughter, never yowls at him.

Find lucky reporting kurta—a faded red shirt I bought on sale and have worn every time I've landed a good story—and plan to finally leave for work. Today's going to be a good day, I'm going to find a great story, I can feel it.

11 a.m.: Phone buzzes. It's a text from Kamran. 'Blast at train station.' Does this mean I need to go cover it? Which station is it? There are three. I vacillate between texting him to ask which station or just trying to figure it out myself. Kamran can sometimes explode if you ask him a simple question. I make my way to work.

The *Daily News* office is in a decrepit building in the financial district, which would be depressing if it weren't like every other newspaper and TV channel office I'd been to in Karachi. It's as if the media moguls of Pakistan devised their own building code: 'Our offices must be housed in broken down buildings with one functioning light bulb in the lobby and permanently out of service elevators.' It's always amusing to see a visitor gingerly ask in the lobby if they really are in the building of an influential paper, or a fresh-off-the-US-flight Pakistani asking if this is 'midtown'. A stray dog tries to wander in through the metal detector at the same time as I walk through. I head down to the basement, the twilight zone of misery and bad news.

Dial the cafeteria and beg for tea, Diet Coke or any form of caffeine. E-mail from Kamran: 'Can you make a timeline of all bomb blasts at train stations last year?'

Six months ago I offered to do a timeline to accompany a story and that was the end of my reporting career. I am now called, texted, dragged out of bed and forced to sit by myself at restaurants while everyone else enjoys dinner, to make timelines. I am a glorified intern. Can no one else use Google? I am utterly resentful of reporters who write graphic and moving accounts of blood and limbs strewn everywhere, are seconded for junkets to Thailand, and receive writing grants while I trawl through newspaper archives to make a flowchart that will be squeezed onto the bottom of the page.

March 23 – A two-foot section of rail track was damaged when a blast took place on the railway line near the Larkana Press Club.

February 25 – Four improvised explosive devices were detonated in Hyderabad, six in Benazirabad, three near Kotri railway station in Jamshoro, and two in Bin Qasim, Karachi.

July 13 – The bomb disposal squad defused four bombs

17

found by residents on the tracks of the Odero Lal railway station in Hyderabad.

This is thrilling, thrilling stuff, I think to myself.

'Your life sounds like a dreadful Irani film,' Saad once said to me. His favourite film is *Iron Man*, which is what I tell people when they inevitably ask me why I'm not dating my single, straight male friend.

One of the copy-editors asks me what I got up to last night and I'm about to answer when Kamran sticks his head out of his office. 'Why aren't you at the station?' he bellows. 'The other reporter is stuck in traffic. Go. Get out.'

I scrabble about for one of the TV remotes. The television channels are saying the blast happened outside the Central railway station.

Get to the site after spending twenty minutes stuck in traffic begging the cab driver to find a shortcut out of the snarl. He asks me why I'm in such a rush, and when I tell him I'm a journalist, he tells me about his nephew who was shot in broad daylight when a thug from an anti-Pashtun political party heard the Pashto song that was his phone's ringtone.

The Central railway station is a decrepit but elegant colonial building. I'm the first reporter there. There's a pool of blood on the pavement and I can hear the glass from the blown out windows of a nearby building crunch under my shoes. A cop sees me walking around gingerly and tells me to step right up. I realize I am tainting the crime scene but it's hard to tell where the scene is. The police appear to have run out of tape to cordon it off.

'I saw it happen! I did!' a twenty-something guy who runs a mobile phone shop nearby excitedly tells me. 'Basically this guy was on a motorcycle and...'

I'm taking notes and nodding encouragingly at him when Ali strolls in. The sight of Ali, smarmy reporter un-extraordinaire for *News 365*, the country's largest news network, makes me want to hurl. His entire career is built on quid pro quo favours for politicians. According to Zara, who quite possibly hates Ali more than I do, he helped a provincial minister's son get out of a drunk driving charge by pulling strings with his uncle, who was then head of the police. It would be fine if he was just arrogant, but he's also incredibly rude and one of these days I'm going to find a way to crush his soul. The cops wave at him like he's a long lost friend. He slaps one on the shoulder, hugs another. He clocks me and the eyewitness instantly, and the eyewitness unfortunately recognizes him too. My heart sinks. There goes my exclusive. Please make Ali go away, I start praying fervently.

Ali's green-and-yellow mic has the same effect on interviewees that Ryan Gosling has on women. He trains the mic on the witness who subsequently forgets about me and my notebook. Twenty other reporters suddenly descend, cameramen in tow, following Ali like he's the Pied Piper of journalism. Someone steps on my foot. Ali's cameraman shoves me with his tripod. I shove him back with my handbag. The eyewitness is saying something fascinating, I can tell from the look on Ali's face. I try to lean in and listen but Ali's cameraman starts screaming at the eyewitness to step into the sunlight.

'What's this guy's name again?' Ali's cameraman asks me, even as he continues to try to edge me out of the way with the camera. I glare at him. 'Uff ho, attituuuude,' he says, in a singsong tone.

I walk away and see another guy standing there, who with any luck might be another witness. 'Were you here when this happened?'

'No,' the guy replies. 'Wait, don't you write for that blog?' he says, looking at my *Daily News* badge.

My newspaper runs a wildly popular comment section filled with posts such as 'why I hate my hairstylist' or 'I was discriminated against at a job interview because my family is wealthy' and 'I left my air-conditioned room to join the protest for your son's murder case'. It has nothing to do with journalism, but now everyone assumes it's what all of us do.

'No I work for the *paper*,' I say.

'There's a newspaper?'

I hate my life.

I speak to four other people at the site, who all tell me the same story of having seen a van go up in flames. One claims he heard gunshots. Another claims that 'Blackwater did this'. The other two are 10-year-old kids who are collecting pieces of twisted metal and glass. They speak in monosyllables.

Did you see this happen? 'No.'

What are you doing? 'This.'

Why? 'I'll sell it.'

To who? The kid shrugs, and then dances off in a different direction. The other one runs up to me, smacks my butt, and scampers off singing *Munni Badnaam Hui*.

I walk up to the police van on the site and hide behind it to light a cigarette. Ali's cameraman has a penchant for filming footage of women smoking, and showing it to everyone in the *News 365* office. Clearly women smoking passes for pornography these days.

A cop pokes his head out of the van. 'Can I have one too?'

We smoke, and he looks at me again. 'You seem like a nice girl. Why do you smoke?'

Even though I've been smoking for years, the question always sends me into spasms of guilt. I think of my father, who disapproves of the fact that I smoke but is glad I'm not doing drugs instead. I want to tell the cop off for asking me this when every other man on the site is also smoking but I don't want to piss him off. In twenty years, he'll be giving press conferences and I'll still be here, clutching a notebook and scribbling down answers that I can never make sense of afterwards. 'I don't know, I got into the habit and it's so hard to quit you know,' I gabble. 'And we never get any food when reporting or water and you know what I mean, right?'

21

He's already bored of my explanation. In the distance, I see Ali interviewing the head of the Karachi police. I should really go over and listen but the cop is saying something.

'What?'

'Can I have the lighter?'

'Sure. What are you doing here?' I ask. Every other cop on the scene is gathered around the Karachi police head hoping they'll be noticed and fast tracked for a promotion.

'I'm guarding this,' he says, pointing to a bundle of sheets.

'What is that?' I ask, moving towards it hoping to get a look inside.

'It's all we recovered of the bomber', he says. I step back hurriedly. Suddenly, my job doesn't seem so awful.

I trudge into the newsroom and see ten sub-editors watching TV. Ali's exclusive with the eyewitness is on. 'He's such a good reporter,' says Sara, a 24-year-old liberal arts graduate who's under the impression that Imran Khan is going to save the country because she and her friends think he looks good in footage from old cricket matches.

'Seriously. Why can't our reporters be like him? They're all lazy idiots,' says Kamran, who once told me that Ali's refusal to join the paper meant he was a horrible human being and that I was so much better by comparison.

So much for that.

'Hi, I'm back,' I announce. 'Hey,' says Sara waving cheerily at me, 'How was it? Was it fun?'

7 p.m.: Have filed copy, two press releases from political parties condemning the attack, done the timeline, and edited a reporter's story on a dolphin that was found dead near Sukkur barrage. Dead dolphins. Because life couldn't get any worse. I call Zara. 'What happened? Did you go to the doctor?'

'Yeah, it's an infection. She said I should give my liver a rest. Whatever. Are we still on for dinner tonight?'

Oh crap. I'd completely forgotten that I had agreed to go out for dinner with Zara's friends from business school last night in that joyous 'I can totally socialize till 5 a.m. and go to work four hours later' spirit that seems to overtake me when I drink on weekdays. 'Do I have to?'

'Yes. Aliya is bringing along some of her friends, PLEASE don't leave me alone to deal with them.'

I have about an hour to get home, dress and get to the restaurant. What I really want to do is go home, get into my pyjamas and never leave the house again. But no. New Year. New Ayesha. Must socialize and meet new people, preferably of the single male variety. 'Ok, fine.'

I start walking out of the newsroom when Kamran calls me into his office. 'So listen...'

I freeze, petrified at the thought of being sent to cover something worse than body parts wrapped in sheets.

'... can I have your bootlegger's number?'

Ali's editor would never use him as a source for cheap alcohol.

23

8 p.m.: Meeting Zara for dinner at this new seafood restaurant owned by a notoriously sleazy businessman. Zara and I had considered boycotting it on ethical grounds, but the prawns in lemon butter garlic sauce turned out to be too good to abandon on principle. The address is ridiculously vague. House number 34, C-Street. This used to be a residential neighbourhood but now commercial ventures are being run out of several of the houses. Instead of tearing them down to build proper cafés and shop fronts, restaurateurs have just moved into the houses as they were, which makes you feel like you're having dinner in someone's drawing room, however done up it may be. Though I've been a few times, it's impossible to remember where the place is. All of the houses look the same, with fairy lights in the trees and police cars outside, presumably guarding politicians out for dinner. I finally find the restaurant after I wander into someone's driveway and get shooed away by the gardener. 'Next door, next door,' he shrieks.

Walk in and find Zara sitting at a table by herself in the 'courtyard'—the back garden that's been converted into an outdoor seating area. She looks very pale. 'My stomach feels like it's on fire,' she groans when she sees me. 'What the hell did we drink last night?'

None of our friends are on time, which is typical for Karachiites, who start contemplating getting dressed at the time the invitation is for. Zara lights a cigarette while I consider ordering a starter to keep me going.

'I just overheard Kamran book a table at Okra. Okra, for the love of god,' I tell her, referring to the lovely if overpriced Mediterranean restaurant on Zamzama. 'We haven't been paid in a month and a half and he's having dinner at fucking Okra. I just spent an hour on the phone with the WWF rep talking about dead dolphins in Sukkur.'

Our phones start beeping simultaneously. It is our respective offices letting us know we're due to cover Imran Khan's arrival at the airport next week: which means three hours of sitting at the airport, drinking cups of overpriced tea and trying not to get trampled by cameramen.

'Oh for the love of god,' Zara starts off. This rant could go on for a few hours. It has been five years, but Zara—who's had a poster of Imran Khan holding the 1992 World Cup trophy tacked above her bed for most of her life—has never forgiven him first for joining politics and second for everything that's come out of his mouth since.

Before we're able to fully settle into Imran Khan-bashing, her phone beeps again, and her face registers disbelief. 'That was Aliya. She says none of them can bring any booze.'

I call Anil, our bootlegger. 'Do you have vodka?' I ask. 'Yes. Jasmine vodka!' Anil says, with the triumphant air of a sommelier unveiling a 25-year whiskey.

'What the hell is jasmine vodka?' I ask, as Zara shakes her head frantically. 'It's great, it's not from Russia though,' he says.

'I don't care,' I say. 'I'm not drinking something called jasmine vodka.'

'Whatever,' he sniffs. 'You know, all the high-class people are drinking it.'

I confer with Zara and tell him to bring whatever Scotch he has, and maybe throw in a couple of bottles of Murree beer.

'What about your liver thing?' I ask Zara, who's growing paler and paler as the evening progresses. 'Oh, I'll stop drinking tomorrow. If I try to get through tonight sober, my liver will be the least of my problems.'

Our guests Omar and his wife, Aliya, walk in. 'Hi darlings, so sorry we're late, crisis at work,' Omar says, as Aliya sits down, reaches for a cigarette and sighs. 'Whatever, at least you only had to do sales projections for Pampers,' she says, rolling her eyes. 'I've been on the phone all day trying to convince people not to offload all their shares because of the whole Supreme Court verdict thing.' A gold watch glints on her wrist when she flicks her cigarette.

'I love your dress, Aliya,' Zara says, as she butters a bread roll, looks at it longingly and then drops it back into the basket. Aliya's navy Massimo Dutti dress is the only Massimo Dutti dress I've ever considered buying because I saw it in a shop window while visiting Saad in Dubai and he insisted I try it on (only to tell me it made me look fat once I was in it). The price tag sent me into paroxysms of middle-class journalist guilt. 'Saad, do you realize this dress costs as much as most people I interview make in a year? How am I supposed to justify owning a dress this expensive?' Saad rolled his eyes and I walked out sans dress, which I now wish I owned instead of the boring black kurta I was currently wearing with the only pair of my jeans that weren't in the wash.

'Picked it up in New York last summer,' Aliya tells us. Anyway, tell us what's happening these days in the city! Things are so bad, na?'

Omar leans in. 'Wasn't there a bomb blast today? My squash buddy had to cancel our reservation because they'd cordoned off his route.'

An image of a bundle of sheets flashes through my mind and I try to shake it out of my head and tell Omar where the blast took place when Imad, Zara's younger brother, strolls in, plonks himself in a chair and starts rolling a joint. 'IMAD,' Zara says in a warning tone. 'What the fuck are you doing? We're not at home.'

'Chill,' Imad drawls. 'I know the owner.'

Aliya's other banker friends are as impeccably groomed as herself, barring the ubiquitous circles under their eyes from waking up at 6 a.m. every day to get to work on time. The amount of hours they put into their jobs also explains why they have almost nothing to say to either Zara or I and after a very perfunctory exchange they end up discussing which Aman resorts they've been to. People keep dropping by to say hi to them while Zara and I drink our way through the beer. I tune in to overhear Aliya and

Omar arguing bitterly about their kid's music classes. Imad offers me the joint he was nursing. 'Married people. Aren't you glad you don't have to deal with all of this?'

'Right, it's time to go,' I say, trying to count out money for my share of the dinner. 'Forget it, jaan, it's taken care of,' Aliya says, tapping her hand—with a blinding diamond solitaire—on the bill.

Aliya is scandalized when she sees me looking for a cab outside the restaurant and tries to insist that her driver drop us all but I jump into the first taxi I see and almost shout goodbye at them in my haste to get away. As we ride the potholed roads I'm hoping the experience won't make me throw up. The cabbie starts off on a rant against cops who are only interested in collecting bribes from rich kids on Saturday nights. 'They should all be stopped and searched! You know how much alcohol these spoilt kids have?' I pray silently that the cops don't stop us instead; I have a bottle of Murree beer in my handbag.

CHAPTER 2

Sunday, January 2, 2012

Headline of the day: 'Deadly brain-eating amoeba resurfaces in Karachi'

8 a.m.: Wake up coughing manically. Must quit smoking, or at least must quit smoking joints of unknown provenance. Reach out for the Vicks. 'MEOWWWW.' I have reached out for the cat's tail by mistake.

My father comes running in, picks up the cat and hugs her. 'Is Ayesha bothering you? Why are you bothering her, Ayesha?'

'Do you want some kheer?'

I've been awake for about two seconds and I'm already exhausted. My throat hurts and my eyes are sore. Kheer for breakfast is exactly the sort of treat I could do with. Am about to ask for a bowl when I realize the question wasn't meant for me after all. My dad is talking to the cat. I hate my life.

10 a.m.: What is it about a hangover that makes everything seem so gloomy? Even the social pages aren't helping. They are my absolute favourite section of the Sunday papers: where else can one find out which politicians' daughters are decked out in diamonds and carrying Bottega Venetta clutches with no good explanation as to how they can afford them?

Instead of cheering me up, the photos of gleaming socialites make me sad. I have no parties to attend, no mehndi dances to choreograph, no one to brunch with. I remind myself how much I love being single and not having to account for every second of my life to someone, which was the case with my ex, Hasan. It would be nice to share Eggs Benedict with someone though. At least Hasan loved going out for Sunday brunch.

I'd met him one night at dinner with Zara and her brother. I'd reached dinner soaking wet, not because it was raining, but because a group of 20-something boys were throwing water balloons at every girl walking on the road from their car. 'Of course, the fucking icing on the cake was that they had a police escort,' I said, trying to dry myself off with a napkin. 'And everyone on the street was laughing at these poor girls being soaked from head to toe. As if we've committed some sort of crime because we're walking instead of rolling around in an SUV.'

'You're dripping on the menu,' Zara pointed out handing me a hair-tie.

Two very large whiskey drinks and a plate of prawn tempura later, Imad suddenly, all too nonchalantly said, 'Oh, my friend Hasan is joining us for dessert.'

Zara gave me a look. 'You might want to brush your hair.'

'Why?'

Zara shrugged, but it wasn't convincingly nonchalant.

'Wait, what is this?' This smelled like a set-up.

Imad sighed. 'Don't be mad. Hasan's a friend of mine, he's single and we thought you might like to meet him. Seriously, when was the last time you went on a date?'

'Last month, actually,' I said.

'And how did that go?' Zara asked.

I groaned at the memory. I'd tried to engage the guy in conversation but he only responded in monosyllables, then he asked me if I wanted to do a line of coke in the restaurant bathroom.

'Ok, fine. Let me have another drink then.'

Hasan walked in and he was actually kind of... great. He was smart, had a sense of humour, a good job and actually knew that brown shoes didn't go with black pants. He had more than a passing resemblance to Shahid Kapoor, which didn't hurt.

And unlike most guys who think sarcasm is off-putting, he laughed at my bitchy remarks about life in the newsroom. 'You're hilarious,' he said, as he refilled my glass, while Imad and Zara beamed like proud parents. As soon as we were done with dinner, Zara and Imad suddenly 'had to leave', making Hasan promise to see me home safe. 'So, coffee?' he asked.

We ended up at Espresso, my favourite cafe in the city. The server greeted me by name and had my latte ready and placed on the table along with an ashtray, a lighter, and a blueberry muffin before Hasan had even scanned the menu.

'Wow, they really know you here,' Hasan said. 'I'll have... Err, the flat white, I suppose, if you can make a decent one,' he said gruffly to the waiter.

The server looked at me askance. 'Of course they will,' I said, feeling defensive of the shoebox-sized cafe I had spent so many hours in. 'They're really quite good.'

That should have been my first clue.

'Isn't this place amazing?' I said, as I put my feet up on the comfy armchair and stirred my latte.

'It's alright, I suppose,' Hasan sniffed. 'I'm not really a fan of small cramped places that play seventies music. Seriously, I was just in Paris, and the cafés there... this place looks like a dhaba in comparison!'

Hasan got up to go to the bathroom, and I texted Zara.

'He hates Espresso. What kind of person hates Espresso!?'

She replied instantly.

'Listen, sit through this coffee and make a bloody effort. You need to stop spending your evenings eating crisps and watching talk shows.'

The next evening Hasan invited me out for dinner. Having monopolized the conversation the previous evening, I decided not to talk about myself at all. This was easy, since it turned out Hasan loved talking about his job—an analyst for a brokerage house. 'Look,' he whispered as I picked at my crab salad. 'That's Jahangir Ali, one of the richest men in the city.'

The next night I was about to text him to ask if he'd like to go out for coffee when Zara called. 'So I just got done with dinner with Aliya and Omar, and can we come over to your place? We'll bring drinks!'

'Sure,' I said.

Five hours later, my house had turned into the venue for an impromptu dance party. Zara was smashed and insisted on playing 1990s Bollywood hits on repeat. Hasan helped me sequester the cat away to spare it second-hand smoke. I popped in to ask my father if we were being too loud only to have him answer the question by glaring at me while turning the volume of the television all the way up.

Hasan had just asked me if I'd like to go for brunch the next morning when Imad, taking a break from making out with some girl who he had brought along, sniffed at the air and asked if something was burning. It was a floor cushion that Imad had placed a cigarette on. I doused it with a glass of water, snatched away Imad's drink and told everyone it was time to go home. Hasan was the last to leave, and as I stood by the door wondering how I was going to wash what seemed like five hundred glasses and get a few hours of sleep, he leaned down and kissed me. 'I really like you,' he said. And that was it.

We were a couple. Zara ecstatically bragged about how she'd set us up to all of our friends, and for a while, it seemed fairly glorious.

But Hasan's life was kind of like an Excel sheet, where everything neatly added up. Except me.

I had to end conversations because a political party spokesperson was on call waiting, spend dinners filing copy from my BlackBerry while Hasan pushed food around on his plate, and cancelled dates because rallies ran too long. And he never understood why a 6 p.m. event ended at 8, or why I couldn't wait to file a press release or why I couldn't drink a second beer because I had to be up to catch the 7 a.m. bus to Hyderabad. When he wasn't perplexed by my career, he would annoy me to no end by texting to ask if I was 'safe', if I 'really had to be' in a village on the outskirts of Faisalabad.

I think the relationship pretty much died when I had to roll away from him while we were making out on his bed and talk Kamran through the local government bill so he could write an editorial.

But Hasan and I still kept seeing each other. We were a 'couple' and it was just easier to be together. It meant that I always had a dance partner for the countless dholkis and dance practices and mehndis that were part of every friend's, cousin's, and acquaintance's wedding festivities. We were always able to get a table for dinner and could easily leave parties when the conversation got too boring or the booze procured from the bootlegger ran out, both of which usually coincided.

About five months had passed since we'd first met, but there was nothing holding us together other than social obligations. And then came Hasan's birthday dinner, for which I had planned to look stunning—a dress from my favourite boutique, high heels, blow-dried hair.

I was sitting at my desk, looking up the number of a salon to book a hair appointment when my phone began buzzing with texts from Kamran and every emergency service in the city. From what I could piece together, there'd been a dispute between two gangs and one of the leaders had been killed in a gunfight. The neighbourhood had been besieged by his supporters shooting at anyone they could find out on the street. Kamran sent me off to the hospital to interview the families of the victims. 'Find me a story. I want to be able to smell the blood in the paper.'

So I trooped off to the emergency ward at the city's largest hospital in Saddar. As I walked in, I couldn't help but think about what Hasan would say if he knew where I was: for him, and all of my other friends, public hospitals were where the 'public' went. They conjured images of cholera and dysentery, of people being given injections via steel syringes by doctors who should have been disbarred for malpractice.

Instead, I found public hospitals to be far more humane than the sterile private hospitals with their brusque staff, who thought they were doing you a favour by pointing you in the direction of a doctor who routinely misdiagnosed your ailment. The last time I went to the ER at a private hospital with severe stomach cramps, the doctor took one look at me and said, 'Oh, it must be PMS.'

'I think I know what PMS feels like,' I told her, as I wondered how much money I was going to be charged for every minute I spent on the bed with its three hundred-thread count sheets. 'This isn't it.'

'Maybe it's gas then. I'm just going to get a nurse to give you a painkiller injection.'

Even though there was a virtual re-enactment of a Martin Scorsese mafia film going on just ten minutes away, the long walkway to the emergency room was full of children in brightly coloured frocks and corduroy shorts, playing. Ambulance drivers dozed in the garden where a group of Sindhi villagers had spread out a rilli on which to have a picnic. As I walked up the stairs, a teenaged nurse came rushing down with arms full of bandages and syringes. Cats weaved between the patients' beds as I spent the afternoon sitting on bloodstained sheets watching women call their relatives to ask for money to pay for medicines, alternately crying and shouting at their children who were clinging to their legs.

At 9 p.m., I finally walked into Hasan's house, a full two hours late for dinner. Hasan looked at me, then said, 'Wow, so you really weren't lying about having spent the day at work.' My kurta was wrinkled beyond belief and

I could swear the body spray I'd bought at the hospital pharmacy wasn't masking the smell of antiseptic.

He guided me to the dining room, where the house staff was clearing up dinner plates. I said hello to Hasan's friends, before he took me by the hand and introduced me to his mother: a stern looking woman in spite of her absurdly oversized bouffant that had been all the rage twenty years ago.

'And you are?' she asked, refusing to make eye contact with me.

'This is Ayesha, I told you about her,' Hasan said. 'She's…'

I turned to him to see how he would describe us.

'… a good friend of mine, we've spent a lot of time together recently. She's a journalist, which is why she's so late…'

She eyed my kurta and jeans doubtfully. 'Oh. I've never seen you on TV,' she said.

'No, aunty, I actually write for the *Daily News*,' I responded, hoping my stomach wouldn't grumble. I was absolutely starving and the leftovers on the table looked amazing. There was still a kebab left on a serving platter. I was thinking about reaching for it when one of the waitstaff swooped in and took it away.

'So, *Daily News*. Is this that young Kamran's paper?' she said disdainfully. 'We don't subscribe. We've been reading *Morning* for sixty years, you know. It really is the newspaper of record.'

I smiled, unsure of how to respond without telling her that I found the *Morning News* stuffy and old fashioned and that I felt it had to stop using words like 'flay'.

'So Amna...'

'Ayesha,' I corrected her.

'Tell me about yourself, Ayesha...your family?'

'Well I have one sister...' I said.

'What do your parents do?' she asked.

'My father works in advertising. My mother died when I was quite young.'

We both looked at each other expectantly.

'And my grandfather used to have a bit of land near Lahore but he lost that after being jailed for being a Communist Party activist and . . .'

'What is Kamran's paper like?' she asked, cutting me off.

I was about to answer when my phone rang. 'Sorry,' I mumbled, and answered it. 'Yes, Kamran?'

'What's the final death toll today?' he barked. 'A hundred injured, twenty-five dead,' I replied. I could see Hasan's mother looking at me with disgust, as if I'd caused the fatalities.

'I need you to come back into the office,' Kamran said. 'Your story needs some work.'

I apologized to Hasan's mother and then to him and told them I had to dash. Neither of them looked remotely sorry to hear this.

'Oh, of course, work is important!' his mother said,

stirring a spoon in her tea. 'Just ask the guards to help you find your car—they usually park them on the other end of the house.'

'Actually, I took a rickshaw,' I said, 'I don't have a car.'

She shot Hasan a look and turned to speak to another guest.

My kurta smelled of Dettol, my eyes ached and I had no idea what I was doing with my life. I could smell the Chanel No. 5 wafting over from Hasan's mother and I didn't want to be here anymore.

'Yes, well,' I said, more or less to myself.

I stalked out of the party, half-expecting Hasan to follow me out but not entirely surprised when he didn't.

Hasan sent me a text message later that night: 'I think we should take a break.'

I spent the rest of the night on the phone venting to Saad. 'Good riddance,' Saad said, as I took a break from hurling expletives to swig some Diet Coke. 'Never did like the look of him. Imagine a life of having to pretend to be interested in banking or equities or whatever the fuck it is he did. I'm a banker and even I can't stand it.'

The next morning, Hasan texted again. 'Please return my iPod.'

Hasan ultimately moved to Lahore and married a 20-something glamazon who now designs clothes for a living. I haven't dated anyone since.

Which is why I have no one to eat pancakes with at Espresso on a Sunday morning and can't face the thought of eating by myself, sitting on one of the barstools while all around me stick thin women in their oversized sunglasses stare adoringly at their husbands.

My phone buzzes with a message and I pounce on it.

It's a text message from a lawyer I've met twice.

'Assalamualaikum.

You Can't Add more Milk in a Glass Full of Milk

But

You Can Add Sugar in it

This Proves

Sweet People Can Make Their Space in an already Filled Heart.'

I spend the morning eating halwa puri while my father repeats everything from Najam Sethi's TV show. 'Did you know that the PML have threatened to quit the government again?'

I am about to point out that I just wrote a piece called 'Threats to the coalition', but the paper is being used to soak up the grease from the puris. I remind myself that I work as a journalist, and I know that today's news is tomorrow's fish and chip paper but as the grease saturates the newspaper, I can't help but feel that this is a message to me personally.

I can't go out as I'm down to my last five hundred rupee note, having spent the last of my salary paying the bootlegger. I can't wait for the day he starts an instalment plan for journalists. In addition to being a maniac, Kamran hasn't paid us our salaries yet. There hasn't been an explanation or an apology or even a fleetingly guilty look. On the seventh of the month I went to ask Mir in accounts why there had been a delay. He and his colleague exchanged looks and then he took a fake phone call and scuttled out of the room. When I eventually asked Kamran, on the 17th, he said I should be patient and that he'd been shelling out money for an upgrade of our facilities. Then he started telling me that I was irresponsible and should have savings for times like these but then stopped abruptly on seeing the look on my face.

Oh God, I am so broke. I'm replacing actual entertainment with surfing Facebook. My theory about Facebook is that the worse the evening, the more the photos, which is why I have barely any pictures from nights when I have a) looked thin, b) had fun. Instead, I just have lots of photos from nights when I've had to drink myself to the point of alcohol poisoning to get over the pain of having to converse with a 'factory boy'. Factory boys always have the same life story: the father owns a textile mill or sugar mill or cement factory, appoints the son heir apparent to the empire, and the son blows their money on cases of Black Label and a fifteen thousand-rupee a night coke habit. In two years, he's in a rehab facility, four years later, he's married to an 18-year-old who has no idea what her husband does. And they rarely have anything to talk about other than their businesses: conversation with a factory boy usually entails nodding along while they rail against the price of gas and electricity, the 'bloody labour unions' protesting for higher wages or how Bangladesh has 'completely taken over the export market, man, it's insane'. They're like a grown up version of a fraternity, stuck somewhere between being teenagers and elderly gentlemen who go to the club every Sunday. Every Karachi girl I know has dated at least one 'factory boy' and dumped him within the first two weeks, quite possibly because the alternative would have been to slit their wrists.

The phone rings. It's Saad. 'How's Zara? Can you organize drinks for us the next time I'm in town?' As if I haven't heard a million times already how hot he thinks she is and why I am a horrible friend and human being for not setting them up.

I decide to avoid the nightmarish prospect of a) seeing two of my closest friends engage in full-fledged PDA while I drink coffee and complain about my life and b) Zara asking me two weeks later why Saad hasn't called her while I drink coffee and prepare for an extremely awkward conversation. Why do I have such disturbing visions? I tell Saad I'll introduce him to my friend Nadia who's just moved back from New York and doesn't really know a lot of single people. Nadia has changed careers five times in the last five years: she was a consultant for an NGO, helped manage a coffee shop, wrote copy at an advertising agency, worked on a TV show as a researcher, and is now an event manager. She wears heels all the time, can't speak Urdu and parties constantly. 'You'll love her!' I squeal. After all these years, I still don't understand why Saad never really engages with women he can talk to, before growing bored of them and leaving them, generally devastated. 'I've got you for conversation,' he's always said. 'Oh, by the way, can you buy my mother something for her birthday? I'll transfer some money to your account. Take her shopping or something.'

7 p.m.: I call Saad's mother, Riffat aunty, who I perhaps love more than Saad. She is the only person to have not given me that spiel about getting married and 'settling down', as if I'm a cat on heat that needs to stop yowling. 'Where's the fun in that beta? Enjoy yourself. Travel. See the world. Maybe get married. Don't have kids, they're so overrated.'

'Saad wants to buy me a birthday present?' she says. 'Uff, sure, as long as this means I get to see you. Come over next Sunday. We'll have lunch at home.'

8 p.m.: Am flicking cigarette ash off my pyjamas when Kamran calls. 'AYESHAAA. There has been a rape in Defence. We're on it. Just get to the police station and see if you can have a look at the FIR. Go. Now.' I have no idea who has been raped, which police station to get to, and what exactly Kamran needs. I call three cops before one tells me the victim is at his station.

9 p.m.: Arrive at the police station after the rickshaw breaks down midway. 'Baaji, don't worry. No one will mug you. Just sit here,' the driver said as he fiddled with the engine. Wish I could tell him that Kamran won't care about his spluttering rickshaw and will only ask me, wide eyed, 'But why don't you have a car?'

The TV news crews are packing up outside the station,

rolling about eight feet of cables away into their vans and shouting out to each other, 'I've called the office. We're done for tonight. Hey, should we go eat karhai?'

Ali from *News 365* isn't on the scene! Mentally give myself a high five that Ali is not dedicated enough to work on Sundays like I am.

Safdar, who works for CNBC, sidles up to me as I try to plead with the police officer at the gate to let me in. 'Safdar bhai, what happened?'

'Prostitute. She was a prostitute, at some dance party in Defence. What do you think would've happened?'

The officer at the gate chimes in. 'She was wearing jeans when she came, and some man was with her. I heard sahib saying it happened at Seaview at 3 a.m.'

'Exactly,' Safdar says. 'Now what girl from a good home goes to Seaview?' I'm still trying to formulate a comeback when the door opens and a horde of political advisors to the chief minister stomp out. The reporters rush up to interview them. 'The girl seems very disturbed... Her story doesn't really add up,' offers Nadia Baig, who advises the chief minister on human rights. 'I believe she's lying. We have police officers on the road at 3 a.m., how could a girl get raped?'

I ask her how she is so sure. 'I'm a woman, and I talked to her like a woman.' She gives me a once-over, hoists up her quilted Chanel bag and walks away. The doors to the police station are still open so I run inside, and begin asking if anyone knows who brought the girl in.

'They left,' announces a female officer. 'From the back gate. Nadia sahiba asked lots of questions and the girl started crying. You can see them in court tomorrow.'

She holds out the police report, but won't let me make copies. 'Can't you just take notes?'

I copy whatever makes the most sense and walk out. Safdar stops me again. 'So Kamran sent you here because you're a woman, na? This isn't really my beat; I'm just here because it's a Sunday. I don't get why we're making such a big deal of this, thousands of girls are raped every day, and we care about this one girl? And who even knows what her story is. Really, you know Defence has so many of these girls who work out of these big houses where they have these big dance parties, and there's alcohol and drugs.'

As Safdar continues I realize the police report doesn't actually say what the girl does or whether she was at a party. 'How do you know where she was?'

'The station in-charge told us. Defence doesn't really have any "big" crime so they're making a big deal of this because they want some shabashi from the government.'

I used to be offended by crime reporter-speak, which usually featured bits like 'woh larki aise uchal rahi thi jaise uski maa mari ho' (describing a woman at a protest against sectarian killings). But after I got into an argument with a reporter in the smoking area at work who was ranting about how the 'bloody Shias should just cancel their procession for one bloody year if they want to stop being killed' I realized it was easier to keep quiet.

10 p.m.: Arrive at the office to be told that I am too late and the paper will be carrying wire copy instead. Look around for Kamran to ask him why I was sent in the first place but he's nowhere to be found. As I idle outside his office, someone calls out. 'Kamran sahib has gone to Atrium to watch Race 2.'

I call Zara. She cancels my call and sends me a WhatsApp message. 'At Atrium watching Race 2. Kamran's here with his wife. Sana, right? She's wearing green eye shadow in the exact same shade as motifs on her kameez.'

Midnight: Drink last dregs of Murree's latest invention: a copycat version of Bombay Sapphire that's tinted blue since this proved cheaper than manufacturing blue glass.

God, I'm so depressed. I spent the entire evening at work and what do I have to show for it? Absolutely nothing. No story, no byline. I log on to Twitter and all of the journalists I follow are posting links to their exposes and exclusive interviews and long-form pieces. I so desperately want to be one of them that it's actually driving me to tears. Can't I do just one great story that will get me noticed?

I call Saad. He texts back to say he can't talk as he's at the cinema watching Race 2.

2 a.m.: Fall asleep reading comments on the rape story posted online. 'This is vy Karachi needs to be handed over to the ARMY FOR A CLEAN-UP OPERATION and then a caliphate system,' posts Drizzle69. Wish I could reply and tell him that this would probably mean he could never post as 'Drizzle69' again. Flip the laptop shut and roll over.

CHAPTER 3

Friday, February 5, 2012

Headline of the day: 'Books not bombs at Pakistan literature festival'

Oh joy.

The Karachi Literature Festival is Kamran's wet dream. Every year, we basically stop work for two days and Kamran sends the entire newsroom to the festival to report on who wore what and who's writing what. His idea of a treat involves getting me to cover the opening ceremony. At 9 a.m. Saad had flown in for it last year, with his then-girlfriend, a glamazon called Nina who worked with him in Dubai and asked me every half hour if we were 'just friends'. Luckily we'd sat in the row of people who'd all laughed when Karen Armstrong said that we should see the good in the people around us. 'I've had sex with most of the people here,' Saad announced, far too loudly. 'I've already seen the best of them.' Nina whipped her head around. 'What. Do. You. Mean?' The ensuing fight lasted through the festival, with Nina pointing to every girl there—single, married, nine months pregnant—asking if he'd slept with her. He told me later they broke up on the cab ride to the airport, which made for an incredibly awkward two-hour flight.

The literature festival is one of Karachi's biggest cultural events, so everyone turns up. It's free, there's the chance to meet authors, listen to poetry, discuss books and get into long, passionate arguments that aren't fuelled by alcohol. If only it wasn't for the blasted diplomats who turn up in droves: every year, the organizers of the festival schedule at least two—or five—sessions on Afghanistan or Kashmir so it becomes 'newsy'. And the diplomats always put up a chunk of money, which means we have to sit through their unending speeches at the opening ceremony, which usually feature a variation of this quote: 'Reading and books are how we will defy the extremists who want to destroy our way of life.'

The place is buzzing. There are tons of people there, which is rare for 9 a.m. in Karachi unless a clothing sale is somehow involved, in which case all bets are off and you will in all likelihood see women elbowing and clawing at each other.

We're seated beneath bougainvillea boughs in the vast gardens of the Beach Luxury Hotel, which is quite nice really. There's a gorgeous view of the sea and the hotel itself is modernist and retro and has a café called 007. Except there's never a James Bond-esque character there, just a bunch of retirees discussing how bad things are in Pakistan.

A foreign journalist sitting next to two blonde women looks up from his BlackBerry and exclaims: 'This is just like Islamabad. With the sea!'

I hate living in Karachi, but for the city to be compared to Islamabad—one of the dullest, most out of touch places in the country—is ridiculous. I'm about to say something when the last of the ambassadors—Russian? German? French? I'm going to have to get his name from the photographer later—stops talking and people applaud.

'The literature festival is now open!' exclaims the master of ceremonies, who in the past decade, has worked as a PR rep, a journalist, a foreign affairs talk show host, and is now an official 'emcee' at high profile events.

A girl standing next to me makes a sudden dash for the café, where the authors are holding court. One of them is dressed entirely in black even though we are not on the set of a vampire film and more importantly, it is ridiculously hot. He's waxing lyrical to a crowd of society aunties about the bougainvilleas in his old house. 'They were the colour,' he says, with a strategic pause, 'of blood.' Another is chain smoking and looking bemusedly at the bougainvillea author. Another, who specializes in writing fictionalized accounts of major news events, is signing a towering pile of books. His latest, an account of the Osama bin Laden raid in Abbottabad, is being adapted for a film. 'Oh, working on a film is amazing. It's such a privilege. But I'd rather be here with people who really appreciate my work,' he says, smiling at a young teenage girl, who squeals and scurries off.

I figure I have enough material for a 'mood piece', one of those descriptive pieces that are like introductions to a story which never begins. Kamran loves mood pieces. Though there was almost a mini-mutiny in the newsroom last week after he sent out a 2,000-word e-mail insisting reporters should produce more of them as readers enjoyed them so much. 'Haan, log bahut enjoy kar rahe hain "kafir kafir Shia kafir" ke naaray lagate hue,' grumbled Shahrukh, the crime reporter.

I start frantically calling the office driver, hoping he can get me out of here in the next five minutes when the sky, with no warning whatsoever, turns deep grey before erupting in a heavy shower. How is this happening? The speeches were all about the beginning of spring. It isn't supposed to rain. I'm wearing white, and this will soon turn into a one-woman wet t-shirt contest. I look around, trying to figure out an exit strategy. All around me there's the click-clacking of heels as people run to the rooms where the sessions have started. Bougainvillea author is actually standing, arms outstretched, taking in the rain. I think about what his book must be like and shudder.

I end up joining the horde. My choices are attending the fifteenth launch of the same book about Afghanistan,

a session on 'post-9/11 writing', or one on 'the rise of
the left wing' (do we even have such a thing?). I opt for
a discussion on Faiz Ahmed Faiz's poetry instead. At the
door, the photographer is wringing out her shawl. 'This
must be what it feels like to be a flood victim,' she says,
'and Kamran said this would be FUN.' She looks at me
and says, 'Err, I think you may need a shawl. Do you know
your t-shirt is soaking wet?'

Okay, this session was a bad idea. Two old men—so
old that I'm surprised they're not hooked up to oxygen
tanks—are reminiscing about all the times they met Faiz.
'I gave Faiz the idea for that poem,' offers one, wiping
his face with a handkerchief. 'I gave him the page from
my notebook to write it on,' counters the other. I head to
another session, where a self-proclaimed Marxist is reading
a speech against large corporations off his iPad. Someone
sitting behind me squeals, 'Isn't he adorable?' 'Chootiya,'
mutters a young boy sitting next to me. I'm inclined to
agree and head to the session on post-9/11 writing.

The authors are bitterly arguing about US policy in the
region. 'Look, this isn't our war,' says the author who is
touting his account of the Osama bin Laden/Abbottabad
raid at the festival. 'We are liberal, secular people living in
a state that was founded for people of all religions. So this
is really just a spillover of Afghanistan in the 1980s. Look,
we're at a *literature festival*. You don't have literature
festivals in failed states.'

'Oh, of course,' says the moderator, flicking back

auburn highlights with a bejewelled hand. 'I mean, we really were meant to be a pluralistic society.'

'This is really all Zia-ul-Haq's fault,' screeches the feminist poet who has wrested the mic from a volunteer. The audience sighs contently, and some people applaud. If there is ever anything you can count on at Pakistani cultural events, it's that Zia—dead for longer than most people can remember—can still be blamed for everything.

I sidle out as inconspicuously as I can, and am so careful to keep my head down I can't see where I'm going and walk smack into someone on the other side of the door. As I look up to apologize, I see that I've bumped into the most impossibly good looking man I've ever clapped eyes on. Suddenly I am acutely aware of what I must look like: drenched t-shirt, hair all over the place, wearing pants that I'm fairly sure are covered in dust from sitting on the carpet at the session. He must be gay, I think. There is no way someone straight is this put together, at least not in Karachi. He has the most perfect skin. His hair looks like his mother spent hours every day brushing it until it gleamed. His socks and shoes are actually coordinated. 'And you must be Ayesha,' he said.

'Err, yes?'

'I recognize you, from Twitter!'

I have an amazingly glamorous photo of me on Twitter. Or so I thought, given that this man can recognize me in this pitiful state.

'And you are?'

'James Maxwell. Call me Jamie. I'm a new hire at CNN. I follow you on Twitter.'

'Oh. I see. So what do you make of the festival so far?' I ask while rooting around in my bag for a lighter and lifting out something that feels right. It turns out to be a small tub of Vicks. I quickly chuck it back in and continue rooting through the bag. All I can find is a notepad and a half-eaten packet of chocolate digestives. 'Hold on,' I say. I scurry off to a corner, look properly and find it hidden in a side pocket.

When I return, Jamie is staring intently at the schedule. As I light my cigarette, he says abruptly, 'Right then, I'm off to the US ambassador's talk. See you there!' He stalks off, probably disgusted by the contents of my handbag and the fact that I smoke. 'Right then,' I mutter to myself, and walk into the courtyard. The rain has ended as suddenly as it began and the sky looks glorious, a riot of orange and pink. I hate living in Karachi, but it can be so heartbreakingly beautiful when it sets its mind to it.

I find a corner at the ambassador's session with a good view of Jamie, and take out my phone to look him up online. His Facebook profile is virtually locked down—oh, how I hate people like him who make stalking a challenge—but his profile on the CNN page has all kinds of stuff: he's reported from Syria, Lebanon, and Israel. I check his Twitter account. He's 'gearing up for Pakistan' according to his last tweet five days ago. How did I not realize he was following me? He must have gotten lost among my list of followers whose bios are inevitably a variation of 'looking for fraindship' and 'NO MoRe SiSteRz OnLy FrienDz No MoRe ThaN FrienD!!!!!!'. Okay, focus. Jamie. He's studiously taking notes. I notice that the seat next to his has been vacated. I'm about to walk over when someone taps me on the shoulder.

Kamran. Bloody hell. It's like the man has an alert that lets him know when someone around him has a smidgen of hope in their hearts so he can swoop in to destroy it. 'Ayesha! You're here! And great, the driver's here as well so you can get back to work and file now!' Kamran is the reason I will die alone in a newsroom, with the mouse hovering over 'send'.

I trudge miserably to work. The newsroom is empty. Nearly everyone has gone to the festival, except Shahrukh who's smoking in the newsroom despite Kamran's ban.

'You know we're not allowed to smoke, right?' I say, noticing that Shahrukh is using one of the office mugs as an ashtray.

'Whatever,' Shahrukh drawls, and I sit down next to him. I light up a cigarette too and start writing.

Two hours later I've written and filed about 3,000 words of copy, but I don't want to go home. I keep clicking through random things online: Benedict Cumberbatch Tumblrs, handwritten notifications posted on the police website, Facebook albums of people's weddings. My phone beeps with a message. 'Are you free tonight? Hosting some of the litfest crowd. – S'

It's Saad. He's clearly in town and I had no idea. Why didn't he tell me he was coming to Karachi? How has he managed to put together a soiree without me? Why am I being invited at the last minute? I have the urge to say all of this in a text message, but I'm tired and it's Saad so I can't really get upset. There's probably a reason why I'm only just hearing he's in town.

Shahrukh is ranting to someone on the phone about the police commissioner—'the motherfucking asshole thinks he can restrict ME from visiting crime scenes'—so I wave goodbye and walk out.

An hour later, a waiter hands me a chilled glass of white wine at Saad's party and I'm wondering why I agreed to come tonight. I don't feel quite myself. I can't manage small talk about the litfest. I'm far too exhausted from having actually sat through it and filed copy about it. This lot, the writers and their friends, largely came for their own sessions and some green room hobnobbing, and then went home to nap and change it would seem. Even though this is supposed to be the literary crowd and instantly distinguishable from more glamorous celebrities, everyone's dressed to the nines. When did they get the time? It's like a fashion week after party. Are royalty payments so good these days that—holy mother of god, is that a Birkin on the arm of the author who was touting her tell-all marriage saga last year? I am still in my crumpled t-shirt from the festival, the one that got rained on, as did my hair, sporting the remnants of a tube of bronze lipstick I discovered in my bag when I last groped about for a lighter.

Saad is standing in a corner, telling a knot of guests about the year he was vegan, omitting the time he cracked, ate two Zingers and threw up for the rest of the night. I'm about to go over and help the conversation along by imparting this information when a girl swishes by in a pink and green sari, high heels and a cloud of Chanel No. 5 that reminds me of Hasan's mother and makes me want to puke. Her hair is a perfect reflective sheet all the way down her back. Sidling up to Saad, she kisses him hello. He catches me looking and smiles at me. It's a big, warm, Saad smile, but I know him well enough to sense the sheepishness lurking beneath it. He leans into her and tells her something, sending her in the direction of the bar, and comes over.

'So,' I say, eyebrow arched. 'Explain.'

Even to myself, I sound ridiculous. 'Explain'? I'm not his grandmother. I should be happy he's met someone, even if I don't instantly warm to her glossy, airbrushed perfection.

'Oh, we met at a friend's wedding in Islamabad last month. Her name is Samya. With a y. Sam-ya.'

'And your eyes met over the one-dish spread? Did you reach for the qorma at the same time?' I ask, trying to counteract my peevishness with a smile.

'No, it was during *Radha on the Dance Floor*,' Saad replies with that annoying smirk Pakistani men get when they score the Girl of the Mehndi—the good-looking, pushy one who dances better than everyone else, has the best clothes, and usually makes cupcakes for a living. He's still in a state of wonder and can't stop with the stupid, goofy grin. The only reason I put up with it is, well, because I've been putting up with it for too long to stop now. 'Score,' I say, because that's what I normally say when Saad tells me about the latest girl. Except this time it's rather half-hearted. Saad always texts me the minute he's met someone. We sit outside the bootlegger's house to buy bottles of bad whiskey when he's in town and having people over.

'Hey,' he says, reading my thoughts, 'Sorry I didn't tell you about this party. It's not actually my party, really, I'm just providing the venue. Samya's brother is incredibly social and he got talking to the authors at the litfest and Samya thought it would be nice to have them over and here they are. They'll go anywhere there's a steady supply of booze,' Saad says, venturing a smile. 'I had to drop in on my mother and by the time I got here the bartender and caterers had already arrived,' he adds, plaintively. 'By the way, mum was asking about you, something about some clothes exhibition she wants to take you to.'

'I'll call her. And don't worry about the party,' I say, thinking, god, I haven't heard of this girl Samya and she's throwing parties with him? I want to tell him about the Birkin-toting author and today's Cretaceous Era Urdu writers but a group of foreigners wanders in and he goes off to play host. Samya's brother walks past me, then turns around and gestures to someone. 'Drink here, now!'

57

'I'm so sorry,' he drawls. 'The staff are so slow. They're being paid a hundred bucks an hour and they're still shit.' I can tell instantly that he's going to end up as one of those husbands who treats his wife like a slave and ends up running over homeless people in his Land Cruiser. One of the new entrants looks vaguely familiar. Did we talk at the Iftar hosted by the American Consulate over custard with green and white icing? 'It's our way of showing that we're in Pakistan,' enthused a PR rep, as if the layers of security that had divested me of my cell phone, handbag, wallet, cigarettes, and lighter on my way in weren't proof enough.

I'm still trying to figure out who she is when I spy Jamie, looking even more glossy and perfect than he looked this afternoon. What is he doing here? How are he and Saad friends? Why has Saad never mentioned that he knows such an impossibly good looking man before? And why do I always end up meeting men when I am a) depressed b) drunk c) look depressed and drunk? Instantly, I hate everyone: Saad, for telling me about the party so late that I couldn't go home and change; Kamran, for sending me to the litfest in the first place; and myself, for not even looking remotely put together. I realize what I must look like—sitting by myself in a corner of the room, swigging red wine like its water. I feel like Superman in that scene from Superman III, when he gets drunk in a bar and is gawped at by the townspeople for getting shitfaced while the sun's still up. I get up and head to the bar where the vampire author is staring moodily into his glass of whiskey. I can always tell the pakka Karachiites at a party, clutching their drinks with the kind of resignation that comes with living in the city, exchanging stories about the latest mugging in their group of friends. The Islamabad crowd—five foreign journalists, three USAID employees, and one eccentric think tanker—look ecstatic at having met someone they don't see at breakfast, lunch, dinner, and drinks every day, which is typical of life in the capital. They've all crowded around Samya who is holding forth on how entrepreneurial Karachiites are. 'We even have a mobile phone service that sends out alerts when the city goes up in flames!' This is not being entrepreneurial, I think, it's a sign of how things have gone to hell in a hand basket.

'Hey, you're Ayesha Khan, right?' the author says as I fiddle with the bottle. 'Yes,' I respond, hoping that he hasn't somehow had an advance look at my copy from the festival, in which I listed the number of times he talked about the 'power of love'.

'Oh I LOVE your work. That piece you did, about the bloodstained roads and how the gangs were dragging around corpses and playing football with severed heads...' That had been a miserable day and I wasn't dying to be reminded of it. The photographer and I had spent an hour cowering on the roof of someone's house in Lea Market while two gangs shot at each other. By sunset, he'd decided he'd had enough and wanted to get some water, and the minute he stood up the gunmen began firing at us. 'FUCK, FUCK, FUCK,' I'd yelled, while the photographer grabbed my head and forced me to lie on the ground. I can still feel the gravelly, dirty roof pressing into my skin. After about an hour, the noise of the bullets sounded muted and wasn't a scary thing anymore, just some kids playing around with fireworks. I could see a woman hanging up her laundry on the roof of the building, dupattas flapping around in the breeze, a nonchalant look on her face.

When I got back to work and told Kamran what had happened, he muttered something about it not being his idea and offered to order me a cappuccino. I resisted the urge to tell him that polystyrene cups couldn't make up for post-traumatic stress disorder. The next day, I woke up with a pounding earache. I trekked to my ENT who told me I had blood in my eardrum and advised me to sue the paper for putting me at risk. I spent the rest of the week sitting in traffic with my hands over my ears in an attempt to block out the blaring horns of the dozens of trucks, containers, and buses, realizing for the first time just how noisy Karachi is.

'Oh, thank you,' I tell the author. 'That's living in Karachi I guess.' I trail off, ashamed of having been this inane.

'What's living in Karachi?' someone pipes up. It's Jamie. He leans in and kisses my cheek, and says 'hello again' rather close to my ear.

'Oh hello,' I say, far too cheerfully. Is that my voice? What is wrong with me? I'm not even this exuberant when someone brings birthday cake to the office. He scans the bar, downs a whiskey shot and offers up his glass for a refill, which makes me instantly question his age and sanity. The last time I did shots was with my 22-year-old cousin at a wedding. I had to drink about a litre of 7-Up to get rid of the nausea, while my cousin mingled with relatives without any visible sign that she'd been chugging tequila. 'Now now, don't judge,' he says, as my eyebrows involuntarily rise at the shots. 'If there's anything I've learnt in my time as a correspondent, it is that shots are never a bad idea.'

We chug. Mine burns, straight down to my stomach. I realize, belatedly, that I haven't eaten dinner and am going to be terribly sick tomorrow if not later tonight. Jamie pours himself another shot, chugs it down and sets his glass back firmly on the table. 'Now I'm set for the night,' he says. His gleaming hair looks even more perfect than it did that morning.

'So Ms Khan,' Jamie says. 'Shall we circulate?' He offers his arm and I can't stop laughing. 'Are you for real?' I ask. Hamming it up, he pinches himself, 'You know what, I do believe I am. We spies are specially trained to be charming,' he says, with a twinkle. I want to pinch myself instead. This isn't happening to me. Have I actually met someone eligible in Karachi? I haven't had sex in so long that I'm scared I've actually forgotten what one is supposed to do. 'Spy?' I say, arching an eyebrow to go with my tone. 'Well no, not really,' he says, with a grin, 'though I was asked by the immigration officer if I knew Raymond Davis.'

An hour later, Jamie and I have swept the room, going

from group to group. I spot Saad and Samya in a corner; he's smiling at something she's showing him on her phone. Probably her five million selfies.

Jamie has great social skills and seems to have something in common with everyone. And he has the patience of a saint, smiling along to inane chatter, asking questions. That's probably why he's a good reporter. Kamran once told me I was a great actress because I could turn on the charm for interviewees and turn it off the minute I walked into the newsroom. And Jamie seems genuinely happy to be in Pakistan, but without any of that 'save the world' and 'I'm here to do capacity building for xyz issue' bullshit that most foreigners spout.

He's standing next to me nodding at all the right moments while I'm arguing with a think tanker about land mafias, causing said think tanker to splash most of his whiskey-pani on my feet from gesticulating so wildly. My phone beeps. It's a WhatsApp message from Saad. It's probably gossip about someone here.

'So, what's the scene?'

'What scene?'

'You and the goraaaa.'

'Nothing. I met the guy today.'

'Yeah, he doesn't seem your type.'

'What is that supposed to mean?'

'He just seems like a choot. I haven't heard great things about him from the Isloo crowd that's here.'

'What have you heard?'

'That he's not very professional. That he's just a big networker.'

'Do you mean like Samya?'

'E-mail from your editor?' Jamie asks. 'No,' I start. 'Actually, yes. E-mail from my editor, but I've messaged him back to tell him I'm not a bonded labourer and that he'll just have to wait till morning,' I say, enjoying even the illusion of my boss respecting some boundaries. I throw my phone into my handbag in what I hope is an imperious manner and smile at Jamie. Seriously, Saad offering romantic advice? Saad, who once dated a 17-year-old intern at his workplace who didn't know Benazir Bhutto had any siblings, and whose current squeeze's conversational skills seemed to be restricted to prettily flicking her perfect hair off her forehead? A charming, intelligent man has chosen to hang out with me, wrinkled t-shirt and cynicism and all. And he's hot. Smokingly so. Saad can fuck off. 'Could you get me a drink please?' I say, in what I imagine is my sweetest, I-am-adorable tone.

At 2 a.m.—having been responsible for finishing Samya's stock of red wine—I insist to Jamie that I am perfectly sober and call a cab. He's waiting for his ride and we end up waiting in Saad's driveway in completely companionable silence. There's no one about and I still have my wineglass in my hand. The cab honks and we get up together and look towards the gate. 'So,' I say, wondering if I should do the double air kiss or just wave goodbye. But then Jamie kisses me. I can feel my stomach dropping to about my toes. Is this kiss really this amazing, or have I been starved for so long that I can't even tell the difference anymore? I want to stay here forever, kissing this impossibly beautiful stranger whose impossibly soft flaxen hair is tickling my earlobe. I pull away when I hear footsteps. Jamie is smiling at me—one of those pure, genuine, 'I'm really into you' smiles. It's unfortunate that my stomach chooses this moment to growl like a caged panther. I try to save the moment by being enigmatic rather than puking. 'Bye,' I whisper, giving him a last peck on the cheek before heading for the cab.

Sunday, February 6, 2012

Headline of the day: 'India falls in love with Hina Rabbani Khar.'

8 a.m.: Wake up ready to rip my clothes off. Why is it so hot?

The AC is off. Look for the remote. Find it underneath the bed next to my handbag. How did it get there?

My head is pounding. My t-shirt smells of whiskey. I remember insisting to Jamie that I was perfectly sober, calling a cab and then talking to the cabbie the entire way about labour laws.

Oh good god, did I sleep with my contacts on? My measure for how drunk I've gotten is whether I'm able to remove my contacts.

I try and get out of bed and trip over my shoes. Oh god, am I still drunk?

I croak out for coffee. The house is dark and silent. Even my father has abandoned me. I cannot find the will to live anymore. Sit down on the floor.

Bad idea.

Three trips to the bathroom later, having barfed up about two bottles of red wine, I feel marginally better. Wish I had a round-the-clock nurse on weekends who could help me get out of my clothes and bathe me. I cannot do this on my own.

Oh fuck. What time is it?

Try to find my cell phone. It isn't in my handbag, or next to my pillow. Cannot drag myself to the living room to use the landline, which, in a fit of sentimentality, is now connected using my mother's old rotary phone that looks right out of a 1970s Bollywood film, glitzy gold dials and massive earpiece and all. 'I didn't even like it the first time round,' my father had said as I tried to dial the number for KFC, missing the 3 every time.

My cell phone begins beeping from under the bed.

Text from Saad: 'Did you get home okay. My flight's at 4, breakfast before?' I think about texting him back but am so annoyed that of the two days my best friend's spent in the city, he's only managed to carve out the time for one lousy breakfast with me, that I ignore it altogether.

Text from an unknown number: 'Slept well?'

I hope it's Jamie, and feel the beginnings of butterflies

in my stomach (though that could also just be nausea). I ignore it. I have no idea who this person is. The last time I responded to one of these texts, thinking it was Zara on a new number, I got about fifty texts asking for my name.

The phone rings. Same number.

I answer the phone and don't say anything. Ninety-nine per cent of the time, it's usually a random guy who will yell 'Hello' before he realizes his credit is running out.

'Hi,' says a very American voice.

Jamie wants to meet me for brunch but I'm due to cover the second day of the litfest. I think about Samya with a y, Saad's smug face and about how long I've been single and the last time I'd been kissed, let alone had sex (Hasan, two days before we broke up, Kamran rang halfway through). I ask Jamie if he'd like to meet for dinner but he's off to Islamabad that afternoon. He says he'll be back in town soon but I doubt I'll hear from him then, or ever.

CHAPTER 4

Headline of the day: 'Agencies having fun with bugged phone conversations'

11 a.m.: We still haven't been paid, so I am going on strike. I'm not quite prepared to go camp outside the office yet, mostly because my attempts to get other people to go on strike with me have been met with by looks of disbelief and comments such as 'if I stop working, Kamran won't pay me at all and I'll get fired'. So this strike is basically in my head since telling Kamran that perhaps he shouldn't have spent our salaries on bulletproof cars for his family, is a guaranteed way of losing one's job.

'Really, Ayesha?' Kamran said, when I asked him last week about payday. 'You of all people shouldn't complain.

After all, you don't have to pay rent or repay any debts. And how can you not have any money?'

'Because I don't,' I said, trying not to snatch his limited edition Moleskine and hit him on the head with it. 'And it's really not your concern whether I have to pay rent or not—for the record, I do—and I can't afford to come into work any longer.'

'So go home,' Kamran said.

Kamran studiously ignored me and just kept staring at his computer. I walked out of the office and straight to the smoking area. After I'd gulped down a cup of tea and smoked five cigarettes, I hysterically called Saad who told me to calm down and go home. He also mentioned that just like with Nina the year before, he had broken up with Samya in the car on the way to the airport. God bless Saad, he did know how to make me smile. I went back to my PC and searched for jobs on LinkedIn all day.

Kamran called me in the next day to say he had meant 'go home' as a joke.

Not only are we not being paid but Kamran has instructed the IT department to block Facebook in the newsroom except during lunch hour. Instead of decamping to the cafeteria, everyone is in the office between 1 and 2 p.m., skiving off at 3 to eat leftover biryani. I scour through the Jaish-e-Mohammad's newspaper, saving articles in the event that Kamran ever approves my request to go to Bahawalpur to cover the group. I should probably get Zara to go to Bahawalpur and then casually mention it to

Kamran, who will send me on the next flight and book me into whatever Bahawalpur's version of a five star hotel is in order to one-up the *Morning News*.

I walk into the reporters' room, which has the permanent air of mourners at a funeral. Everyone wears white kurtas, and there's the constant remembrance of better times: when we used to get paid on the first of the month, when Kamran genuinely cared about the paper, when political parties actually respected print journalists. The room isn't much bigger than my kitchen, yet somehow it manages to hold seven desks and eight computers, which means there are always two people fighting over the use of one.

The computers are perpetually being shipped off to IT for repairs, except IT's approach to fixing them is to ask us 'have you tried rebooting it?' or hitting the CPU with the back of a shoe. That last tactic has worked twice on my own computer.

'Why don't you ask Kamran when we're getting paid?' says the crime reporter, Shahrukh, who I'm convinced mugs people when he gets off work. 'I had to buy this 7-Up on credit from the cafeteria today.'

I tell him the sob story of last week. 'Why don't we slash Kamran's car tyres?' he remarks. 'I know a guy who can...' I can tell he's about to brag about all the target killers he has on speed dial when his phone rings. He says hello, listens for a minute and then hangs up.

'Finally! The cops have found that guy who killed his mother and chopped off her head.'

Sania, the chief political correspondent, groans. 'Enough Shahrukh. I just ate.'

'Oh, hi Ayesha,' she says, as if she's just noticed me. Sania and I used to be friends, but then Kamran promoted her to chief political correspondent after she scored an interview with President Zardari—the first he'd ever given to the paper—and she refused to cover anything less than briefings with top officials or high profile interviews. She also swapped her kurtas for saris, and now spends her mornings walking around our basement office saying 'yah, but you know, General sahib says the Supreme Court isn't going to crack down this time' and 'no, no, of course I'll have dinner with you and the prime minister, though we really must get him to stop offering me a job!' She's on political talk shows two nights of the week, flipping her hair and laughing coquettishly at the anchors.

Which means that I got stuck covering the pressers and rallies. 'You know I can always talk to the finance minister, he's great friends with Kamran's dad.' Trust her to namedrop. 'And aren't you supposed to be at a presser?'

1 p.m.: Zara and I are crouched in a corner at a press conference, where one of the TPI leaders is answering questions based on how attractive he finds the reporters. At least this was our running theory, because the heavily made up, buxom talk show hosts were the only ones who'd been able to get a word in.

'Welcome to the Pakistan elections!' squeals a reporter as she finishes recording her take.

As the Pakistan Peoples Party has reminded us nearly every day since Benazir was killed, democracy is the best revenge. Kamran has put me on a rotating schedule of covering press conferences. Democracy has so far only given me insomnia, a raging stomach ache, and paranoia. I haven't slept properly in three weeks. The elections are still a full two months away but every morning I wake up gasping for breath, scared the country has been taken over by politicians who find a foreign conspiracy in everything.

I haven't heard from Jamie since he left for Islamabad. I'd followed him on Twitter and added him on Facebook, but beyond a couple of tweets here and there, there was nothing to report. One retweet does not a relationship make.

The only bearable thing about this presser is that it's happening at the politician's house and we are seated in a garden and not inside one of the oppressive rooms in the Karachi Press Club or in a political party office, trying to figure out which chairs might collapse and worrying about rats. Without fail, every press conference in Karachi starts at least an hour late, and is usually taken over by cameramen trying to get reporters to scribble something in their notebooks so they have stock footage to use after. Zara once wrote 'Fuck off' on hers, which only her parents noticed when they saw the broadcast.

I'd asked for a cup of tea before the presser started, only to be told that the political party's policy was to not serve tea before press conferences because reporters tended to leave right after drinking it.

'This would be a great drinking game,' I say, an hour into the politician's repetitive, long-winded speech, which for all the verbiage hadn't yielded any actual information. 'We could do a shot every time he says "tabdeeli", "inquilab", or "change".'

'Or every time he condemns violence, without actually proposing a plan to do anything about it,' Zara says. 'We GET IT.'

'Yaar ab bas bhi karo,' moans Akbar, one of the cameramen. 'I have three more assignments after this and the channel isn't sending a replacement. When is this asshole going to stop talking?'

Zara stays back to try and get an interview. I don't have the heart to sit around and wait for him to deign to respond to questions. The last time I interviewed him he spent twenty minutes complaining about how rude Kamran had been to him at a dinner party in Islamabad.

I try to leave but the entrance is blocked by a troupe of dholwalas and dancing party workers. 'Someone's nomination papers have been accepted,' mutters Akbar. The election is a few months away, and the filing of nomination papers—a ridiculous process involving candidates being questioned on their income statements and the minutiae of Islam—was underway at the court. The dancers have managed to disrupt the rockery in the garden and knock over most of the perfectly glossy potted plants. The politician's wife, drowning in what seems to be an eight-metre kaftan, has just stepped outside to inspect the damage done to her house. She's either not concerned about the cost, or has just had a Botox shot, because her face hasn't registered a reaction.

My phone beeps. Sania.

'Are you done with the presser?'

'Yep.'

'Ok. I'm off to interview the prime minister, so you need to get yourself to the press club. There's a protest at 3 p.m. Sipah-e-Sahaba.'

I'm about to tell Sania that it would take me an hour to get to the press club. It's the 15th and I haven't been paid yet, so am down to three hundred rupees. How am I going to get to work if I don't have money to pay for a rickshaw? Sania has already hung up.

Akbar agrees to take me to the protest and says he'll drop in himself for a bit. I have saved two hundred rupees on rickshaw fare, hurrah, though there is no such thing as a free ride. Akbar decides mid-route that he needs to buy beer, pick up his sister, and drop off his laundry. It's almost 3.30 p.m. when we finally get to the press club, where Akbar double parks in front of the van of a news channel that fired him.

Thank goodness protests, like everything else in Pakistan, don't start on time.

Unlike Akbar and hundreds of other journalists who consider the club their refuge, I find it terribly depressing. It's a gorgeous old colonial building with walls that have been layered with so many posters that if I started peeling them off they'd eventually take me back twenty years. The remnants of Pakistan's history—including a series of posters documenting Nawaz Sharif's hairline—receding, transplant, and back to receding—are found on the press club's walls. Graffiti from 2007 calling on PPP activists to greet Benazir Bhutto on her return from exile, and Jamaat-ud-Dawa posters from 2009 calling for war against India. But to me it's a reminder of where journalism has gone terribly wrong in recent times, with press unions cozying up to politicians for free plots rather than actually doing any advocacy work.

The street outside the press club is permanently full of protestors, sitting in fraying tents, with half torn banners asking for the government to reinstate their jobs or railing against the police for having bumped off a suspect in the middle of the night. I feel for my friend Mikaal who works in the building next door and had to invest in noise-cancelling headphones because of the chanting. Sometimes a TV crew will show up to record their misery, or a government official will stop in on their way home to pay lip service, but otherwise these protestors just stay here—in pouring rain or stifling humidity—until they too, like everyone in Karachi, give up and go home.

Today, there are about a hundred young men neatly lined up in queues, chanting 'death to Shias'. The Sipah-e-Sahaba is one of the vilest groups the country has ever known and specializes in propaganda against Shias, but Kamran decided one day that we would cover every single group ahead of the elections. Because this is a narrow road, the stage is set up in the back of a pick-up van, with a young kid leading the chants on a megaphone. It's a portable rally—they could just as easily drive the van to another destination and set up there—a tactic I feel could work quite well for other things as well, such as weddings. We'd never have to go out, the bride and groom could just go from neighbourhood to neighbourhood. I make a mental note to suggest this to my event manager friends.

The van's driver suddenly decides he'd like to move forward five feet and revs up, and the young kid nearly lurches off the van. The chanting stops as one of the party's leaders takes the mic to start talking. I hoist myself up on one of the concrete barriers nearby to be able to see him properly and transcribe his speech. 'Excuse me,' mutters a protestor standing next to me. 'Bibi, can you get off from there. Your feet are touching one of our posters.' I look down to see the concrete slab has been covered with Sipah-e-Sahaba paraphernalia. Crap. This kind of stuff gets people lynched by mobs screaming blasphemy. I jump off and walk to the other end, where there are a bunch of milkshake, bun kebab and paan stalls, whose workers go about chopping and peeling without batting an eye at the noise. Perhaps they all have hearing loss, or they've just learnt to tune out the noise. I wonder how I can acquire the same skill and learn to ignore Kamran.

I spot the press club's resident spy—who works for the police's intelligence branch—lounging next to the bun kebab stall. When I tell people I have a spy on my speed dial, they conjure images of a James Bond-esque character, authoritatively telling the bartender that he'd like his martini shaken not stirred and jumping out of helicopters. The only thing this spy has ever had shaken is a milkshake, which he's currently sipping noisily. When I first met him, he was hanging around in the anti-terrorism court pretending to be a reporter. He would have gotten away with it, but the court staffers knew all of the reporters who were authorized to be there. I never saw him in court again, but when I found him months later at the press club, he told me that had been his first week in the field and he'd been told he could blend in if he chain-smoked and had a notebook. That was probably the best advice he could get, though I would've added wear a kurta and carry five standard-issue Piano pens to the list. 'How many people do you think there are?' he asks, making space for me to sit on the bench he's managed to appropriate from the bun kebab stall.

'A hundred?'

'I'm going to say about a hundred and fifty,' he says, scribbling in his notebook. 'Our formula is to ask about five people and calculate the average so we know how many people attended. The spokesperson is claiming five hundred—is he blind? How does he think this lane can even fit that many?'

I shrug.

'These people, everyday, the same nonsense. Pakistan

has become a garbage dump. Everyone can throw their trash here. No one in the police even reads these briefings I send. Maybe I should get transferred to another area.' He drains the rest of his milkshake. 'Don't you need to go talk to these people?'

I adjust the dupatta on my head, get off the bench and walk to the Sipah-e-Sahaba spokesperson and introduce myself. He's a potbellied man in his forties, who, if rumours on the religious party circuit are to be believed, has ordered the killings of at least twenty Shias in the past year. Despite the reputation, he refuses to make eye contact with me because I'm a woman, so I'm directing my questions to the ground.

'Ji, my name is Ayesha and I work for the *Daily News*.'

'Oh, yes, Ayesha bibi,' he says, eyes fixed on the ground. 'I know who you are. I keep reading your tweets.'

'Oh.'

'Yes, we have a very active social media team that looks at all of the things being said about us online,' he says.

I cut him off before he starts to analyse my tweets, which as far as I can last recall, were bitching about the literature festival and the state of tea being served at the last presser.

'I believe your group is banned.'

'No.'

'So the list of banned organizations you're on is wrong?'

'Yes.'

'Are you planning on having more protests?'

'Yes.'

'Will you be contesting the elections?'

'Yes. Insha Allah.'

He clearly doesn't want to chat and hands me a press release. 'Oh, wait,' he says, 'What's your number?' I write it out and hand it to him and head back inside the press club. There are about fifty journalists sitting in the courtyard, all crowded around tables in their little cliques. The political reporters for Urdu TV channels are the elite, so they get the best space, the biggest table, and the most food. The Urdu newspaper reporters form huddles based on their beats, the cameramen have occupied three tables for their equipment while the wire photographers sit on the periphery. Even though the wire agency correspondents are fiercely competitive, the photographers always travel in a pack because they feel they work better as a team and get more access. One of them, Karam Ali, once went off the radar for a week and returned with a heartbreaking photo essay on temples being destroyed on the outskirts of Karachi. He was given the cold shoulder for a week. Akbar waves me over to his table and pushes a cup of tea forward. 'Yaar, manhoos gora aya hua hai aur uske saath Lyari jana hai.'

'Why don't you take him to Gizri and tell him it's Lyari?' Karam offers.

'You know being a fixer is kind of like being a baby sitter, right?' I say, still scarred from the time I fixed for a German journalist who needed me to order food around the clock, find him beer, and couldn't go down to the hotel pharmacy to get a Panadol.

'He's a pain. He also wants me to find a Taliban leader, find a fashion show he can attend, and set up an interview with a woman who is married to a Lashkar-e-Taiba member. I think I'll end up dead by the end of this,' Akbar says, before stopping abruptly.

'Hello sir!' he exclaims.

We turn around to see who Akbar is greeting so exuberantly.

It's Jamie. I'm so surprised I almost drop my tea on my kurta. Everyone at the table has turned to stare at him. Akbar gets up and shakes hands with Jamie. 'This is Jamie sir, he's from CNN,' he says. Jamie says hi and turns to look at me. 'These are the wire photographers—AP, Reuters, and AFP—and this is...'

'Hello Ayesha,' Jamie says, smiling. Akbar gives me that look I've seen being exchanged among fixers and photographers since time immemorial. It usually means: 'We're all in this together, don't screw me over.'

'Hi Jamie,' I hear myself say. 'You're lucky to be working with Akbar. He's great.'

'Ready to go?' Jamie asks Akbar. He nods and scurries off. I get up too, realizing I've been sitting here for ages and still have 2,000 words to file.

I find a rickshaw that blessedly agrees to drop me to work for a hundred bucks. My phone beeps a few times but

I've hidden it in a fold of my dupatta so muggers won't be able to spot it when they make off with my handbag. I'm entering the office when I finally take a look at it: Kamran responding to e-mails from pissed off reporters asking when they're getting paid—'please do not discuss this over e-mail, it's inappropriate', twenty press releases from a political party on today's National Assembly session, and one message—from Jamie.

'Free for dinner tonight?'

'Sure. When/Where?'

'Beach Luxury? Casbah? 8 p.m.?'

I haven't seen Jamie since he kissed me outside Saad's flat. Does the fact that he's gotten in touch after almost a month mean that he felt a connection too? Or does he just want to be friends? Or is he bored in Karachi and needs someone to hang out with? Oh fuck it. He's a good looking man who wants to have dinner with ME.

At 8 p.m.—having ignored Kamran's request to stick around at work to celebrate someone's birthday for whom he'd been shamed into buying a cake since no one had any money—I leave for home realizing that I have no money to get my hair done, get waxed or buy anything nice to wear. I leap into the shower hoping to at least give my legs a once over with a razor only to botch it and the next thing I know my knee's spouting a river of blood. Can't wear a dress unless I want to look like my eight-year-old self who had injured herself in the school playground and attempted to hide it with stickers.

9 p.m.: Standing in the Beach Luxury parking lot, looking up at the gorgeous, flaking, greying, modernist façade. Somewhere, up in one of the rooms, Jamie is getting ready to come down for dinner. I look at my clothes: a tank top with two-year old Zara jeans bought at my favourite store in Zainab Market that stocked the excess consignments made for export. 'You paid two thousand rupees for this?!' my cousin Sara shrieked when she looked through my suitcase on a weekend trip to Lahore. 'I paid three hundred dirhams in Dubai and I don't even like the colour I got them in.' I ended up writing a story about the store, which the shopkeeper got framed and hung in what he referred to as a 'changing room'—a closet-sized storeroom with a mirror and a door. I can't find Jamie in the lobby, so I walk into the restaurant.

Spot Jamie peering into the giant boat-shaped freezer with glistening pink prawns and lobster laid out in separate compartments. 'This is priceless,' he says, as I approach. 'This place is worth it for the freezer alone.'

Jamie leads me to our table and tells the server to bring us a couple of beers. 'I wanted to call you yesterday,' he says. 'But Akbar and I were working till about midnight and I didn't want to disturb you.'

We talk about work. I tell him off for picking Lyari as a subject. 'Every journalist in Islamabad has descended upon it, doing the same story comparing Uzair Baloch to a character in the Godfather or the Sopranos, with an accompanying profile on Chaudhry Aslam, who the press corps have anointed the city's bravest cop, except the man is a bloody disaster. Seriously?'

Jamie looks thoughtful. 'You know, no one in Islamabad would say something like that. They're all pretty much throwing out the same ideas. I mean, everyone wants me to go visit Murree Brewery.'

Jamie and I order copious amounts of fried prawns and tempura and we talk. We talk about journalism, reporters' safety and Karachi politics. Jamie tells me stories about reporting from Syria, what his bosses in Atlanta think of the Middle East, and how he's convinced that the person sitting next to him on the flight to Karachi was a military officer. Maybe it's the sea breeze wafting in from the marina, or the food, or the beer but I can't recall having felt so lightheaded, so absolutely free. We order coffee to sober up, and I ask the staff to help find me a cab. Jamie holds me in a hug that lingers on. 'I want you to come upstairs with me,' he whispers in my ear, 'but I can see the spy they've assigned to tail me is still parked in the lobby.' I tell him I'll see him again soon, not especially wanting to be part of the briefing involving Jamie's activities, in spite of the immense desire to press myself up against him.

'Right then,' I say smiling, the kind of involuntary smile you have when you've had far too much to drink. Damn it. I actually wore lacy black underwear tonight. As I get into a cab all I can think about is how much I want to rip Jamie's clothes off.

1 a.m.: That was a pretty fantastic night, I think to myself, as I flip through television channels to see if there's anything worth watching. I am too wired to go to sleep. I wonder if Jamie is sleeping right now. Or thinking about me. Or...ooh, phone ringing. Maybe that's him.

It's the Sipah-e-Sahaba spokesperson. I'm tempted not to pick up, but perhaps it's some sort of breaking news development. Must answer.

'Ji, assalamualaikum,' the guy says, and then clears his throat. 'Actually we didn't get to talk much today, but I was hoping to talk to you now.'

Now? I look at the clock. Its 1 a.m. 'Err, sure.'

'So how long have you been at *Daily News*? And you're a girl, Masha Allah, and you spend all of this time out of the house, how do you do it?'

Oh good god, this is not a breaking news development. The death-mongering spokesperson wants to chat.

'Well, I'm very busy right now,' I say, change the channel to *News 365* and turn up the volume. 'I'm at the office still.'

'Oh, that's sad,' he says. 'Well, please do call me if you ever need anything.'

I cancel the call and wonder if anyone would ever believe me if I told them what had just happened.

CHAPTER 5

Saturday, April 2, 2012

Headline of the day: 'To ward off evil, Zardari kills one black goat every day'

Jolted awake by the sound of the loudest crash ever. Is it an accident? Has someone thrown a rock through the window? There is something digging into my back. No, focus. What was that noise?

Manage to untangle myself from the comforter and turn the light on. The windows are intact. It is still dark outside. Okay, think. We have no guns. I will have to defend the house with an old decoration piece—a wooden fish that conceals a dagger within.

Look around to see the cat sitting on the floor next to a broken glass. She is playing with my lighter. She must have jumped onto the side table and pushed it off along with the glass.

The cat leaps up on the bed. I pull the comforter over my head, hoping she'll get the hint and go. 'What?' I yell, as I feel a paw digging into my side.

'Meow.'

'Its 5 a.m.'

'MEOW.'

I do not understand how and when my father spoiled the cat to the extent that 5 a.m. has become an acceptable hour for her to wake up, then wake him up and demand that she be hand-fed breakfast. Couldn't he just have trained her to find her own food?

I'm not going to give in to this feeding nonsense. I stagger out of bed and put her breakfast—chopped up boiled chicken—on a plate and call her. She looks at me quizzically, trots off to the living room, bounds onto the windowsill and looks at me again. I put the plate there. She glances at me, and then at the plate.

'You can eat it. I know you can.'

'Meow.'

We stare at each other for a minute.

I put a piece of the chicken on my palm.

The cat sniffs at it gingerly. I can instantly tell I have failed her by not cutting it into perfect bite sized pieces.

Fifteen minutes later, after she's been distracted by a crow perched on the electricity wires outside, a cat yowling two lanes away and a car alarm, breakfast is over. She curls up on her chair—a custom built one that is reupholstered every year—and snoozes.

I wish I had her life.

I go back to bed and check what I've missed online in the three hours that I was asleep. There seems to have been an epic fight on Twitter but I can't make head or tail of it. Instagram is full of photos from people's Friday nights in the civilized world: views from a bar, the ensuing 3 a.m. carb-fest, lots of selfies and close-ups of professionally made cocktails.

I feel terribly sad. I want that life. I want to be in those photos, not pressing the 'like' button on autopilot. I recall my last glorious vacation—three years ago, five days in Bangkok with my friend Sam, happily chugging beer in a jazz bar and laughing at the number of women on the streets with fake Louis Vuitton bags and some manner of animal print clothing.

Bangkok reminds me that that was the last time I could wear sleeveless clothes without cringing at the deplorable state of my arms. And that was two years ago. Decide to head to the gym.

An hour later, as I alight from the wretched stationary bike, I realize I may be okay with the way I look. My heart feels like it's permanently lodged in my throat. I wonder, not for the first time, if my gym has an attendant paramedic.

Lie down on a yoga mat and pretend to do crunches. Oh god, I could lie here all afternoon. I wonder what Jamie is doing. Is he thinking about me? Maybe I should Google what flights to Islamabad cost these days. Or would that be too stalkerish?

'Ayesha? Are you planning to work out today or are you just here to lie down??'

My trainer is looming in front of me though I made a point of occupying a mat wedged into a corner of the gym. How did she find me here? Sometimes she reminds me of my Islamiat teacher at college, who had the remarkable ability of calling on students just as they were about to doze off and forcing them to recite the long series of prayers meant to be read at a funeral, which always made the class feel like a perpetual wake.

The trainer points me in the direction of the weights. I would hate her, if I wasn't paying her to get me to lose weight.

After about twenty minutes during which I lose all sensation in my arms and am convinced I've fractured my hand, she releases me to go use the treadmill.

The treadmill area at the gym is a remarkable place. There are about five women obsessively discussing whatever happened in last night's episode of the translated Turkish soap opera that is currently to blame for most of the remote control fights across Pakistan. There are the two teenage sisters who are so super skinny that it makes me sad to see them at the gym at 7 a.m. I want to tell them to go home, eat massive breakfasts and enjoy having flawless skin while it lasts. And then there's my personal hero—the woman who gave birth two months ago and is running on the treadmill like a maniac. She worked out until she was ready to be shipped off to the delivery room—much to the consternation of the rest of the women—and resumed smoking the first day she was back at the gym. I love her and want her branch-like arms.

I walk out to a remarkably beautiful day. The kind of morning that used to make me so happy to be living in Karachi. It's breezy and not humid and the sky is overcast. I sit down on the bench outside the gym and light up. A woman passes by and looks visibly shocked. Smokers may be the new pariahs, but a woman smoking is the worst. The end of humanity. A sign that judgment day is near.

I've taken the day off work, so I head home, take a shower and flop down on the sofa. In the distance, I can hear my father watching *Breaking Bad*. My friends find this terribly amusing given that my father's culinary talents include making killer biryani, not meth, which is what the main protagonist of the show cooks up. I put my feet up on an antique trunk I lugged home from one of the used furniture stalls in Saddar. It looks just like the ones in all those cutesy little apartments in Brooklyn featured on all the home decor websites, usually with a 'vintage, originally found in a Paris flea market' description.

'What is this!?' my father had shrieked when I'd rung the intercom asking if he could come downstairs and help me bring it up.

'It's a trunk!' I said proudly, running my hands over

the pockmarked wood. The lock broke off in my hand.

'Yes, I know, we had one of these when I was five. Seriously, what is this behemoth!?'

It now took pride of place in our lounge, mostly because the cat decided that it doubled as a great scratching post.

I really have no idea what one does in the daytime anymore. On Sundays I end up sleeping till noon, watching TV shows all day, and in the evening develop what I call 'the 7 p.m. itch', a strange restlessness accompanied by the knowledge that it is too late to make a plan and that most organized people have something to do already.

I look up job websites. There are postings for jobs such as 'social media editor' (what is that? Do I get to trawl Twitter and Facebook all day?) and 'ideas editor' (is that just producing pitches? On what?), and I hastily write a cover letter for the social media editor job at a New York-based magazine.

Twenty minutes later I get an auto-generated reply thanking me for my interest in the job, but that I wasn't a 'suitable candidate'.

'I am never going to get out of here, am I?' I say out loud. 'What's that?' my father calls out from his room. 'Nothing,' I sigh and call Zara to ask what she's up to.

Instead of 'hello', Zara opens with, 'So you've heard?'

'Heard what? I've been at the gym, what happened, god, a bomb?'

'No, though you might want to sit down for this. Ali has been hired by NBC.'

A flash of anger courses through my veins. Ali—the smarmy, story-stealing reporter—has been hired by NBC? How did this happen?

'What?'

'Do you want to go have lunch?' Zara bursts out. 'I have the day off work and if I stay home I'll just keep checking Twitter—where he's being congratulated like he won a fucking Nobel prize—and feeling miserable.'

Zara and I end up going to our favourite Thai restaurant. She's twenty minutes late, and walks in lugging her handbag, which I discover is bulging with beer cans. 'Sorry, sorry. To add to how fucking miserable this day is, the wine store guy didn't have change so I had to stand around waiting for him to find two hundred rupees while everyone gawped at me. Anyway. Ali. Please. I cannot get over this.'

'You know Ali is going to get fired the minute they figure out that he actually relies on people like us and his desk for his stories?' I say.

Zara is beyond consoling. 'I don't care. I applied for the same job; except I did it on their stupid job website two months ago and never heard back, while Ali probably made his pitch over drinks in Islamabad and sealed it over those overpriced cappuccinos at Mocca Cafe the next morning. Ugh. Whatever.'

I want to calm Zara down but I know why she's even more upset than I am. Reporting for television is incredibly competitive, with most reporters jumping ship every six months to join another Pakistani television channel, trying to get their hands on the most prestigious beats. The high point for most is to either end up as bureau chief or as the main political correspondent in Islamabad, but being hired by a foreign news channel is joining the major league. It's a way out of covering press briefings and into doing some actual reporting that gets you attention abroad. She's already choked back tears twice while talking about Ali's move: how much it's going to hurt when everyone in the newsroom is discussing it, the kind of stories he'll do while she'll be doing live broadcasts on how much rainwater has gathered on the streets during the monsoon.

I can't understand why Ali has gotten the slot. In a year, he's guaranteed a job offer in D.C. or London. Why am I not the one being offered jobs? I resolve to find a story that will catapult me to some sort of stardom. Just as soon as I've finished this beer.

'Hey, do you think his girlfriend will move to Islamabad with him?' Ali's girlfriend is surprisingly smart—surprising because she's dating Ali—and Zara and I often wonder whether we'd be friends with her if she wasn't sleeping with His Smarminess.

'Probably not,' Zara snorted. 'I bet you anything that he'll be dating one of the capacity building girls (who, as Saad once pointed out, comprise 90 percent of Islamabad's eligible population) in a month, be best friends with the TV anchors in two, and after six months at NBC, he'll quit to join the U.S. embassy.'

'Don't forget the op-eds,' I say, pushing around the last grains of rice on my plate. 'He'll obviously become an expert on American foreign policy after he attends his first embassy reception.'

'Hi, girls,' pipes up a voice from the next table.

I jump and nearly upend my plate. It's Sandra, the spokesperson for the US embassy in Islamabad. Zara's cigarette is dangling from her fingers. I have no idea how much of our conversation Sandra has overheard.

'Um, hi,' Zara eventually finds her voice. 'We're just enjoying our day off.'

Sandra looks at our table, which is a veritable journalists' table of shame: Three cigarette packets, four cans of beer and more food than at a family brunch. Our quick lunch has run until 4 p.m. and Zara looks like she's in no mood to leave. The maître'd has already asked us once if we're ready for the bill.

'Oh my god,' Zara whispers. 'I think we may have single-handedly achieved at least one thing. We're never going to be invited to those "female journalist roundtables" again. I think I nearly passed out at the last one when Sandra said she wanted us to share our hopes and dreams.'

'I don't have hope,' I say, draining the can. 'All I have is gossip. Thank god.'

'Speaking of gossip,' Zara says. 'Anything you'd like to tell me?'

'Not really,' I say, racking my brains for any stories I may have heard about someone sneaking off for a job interview or being spotted at an obscure café to avoid having their date live-tweeted.

'I see. So can you explain why Omar and Aliya saw you looking rather cozy at Casbah with some gora?'

I flush guiltily. I did feel bad about not telling Zara but I'm trying out a new principle whereby I won't discuss any potential men until about eight dates in. After the number of non-starters Zara and I have analysed to pieces I actually thought she would appreciate it.

'Don't worry, I'm not mad. When they first told me I thought you were interviewing for the NBC job but then I knew you would've told me about that. So, explain.'

I give her the short version of the story, how we met, and the great kiss at Saad's party.

'Oooh! So? Do we like him? Like *like* him?'

'We do,' I say, surprising myself at how I don't even have to think about it. 'But there's little I can do about it while I'm stuck in this good for nothing city.'

'What does Saad think?'

'I'm not sure,' I say, keeping my tone neutral.

Things with Saad have been a little odd since he went back to Dubai. We still call each other and chat online, usually for mini-vents, but he hasn't asked me about Jamie and instead of asking him what his problem is, I've also not brought it up. I'll speak to him properly whenever we meet.

The maître'd looks relieved as Zara finally signals for the cheque. 'Look, date a gora all you want, but please don't become a cliché. If I see your photos in *Sunday*

93

Magazine, attending one of those god-awful Islamabad parties where all the foreign correspondents and embassy staff earnestly analyse the country based on what they've read on Twitter—you know, those "Pakistanis take to social media to rail against corruption" stories—I will actually kill you.'

On the way home, I think about what Zara has said. Am I a cliché for liking a foreign reporter? I know that every foreign reporter currently stationed in Islamabad has more notches on their bedpost than even the most legendary partiers in Karachi. But I haven't slept with Jamie yet. 'But you want to,' goes the little voice in my head. I decide to push Zara's objections out of my head. I am single, and even if this whole thing with Jamie ends up with me doing the walk of shame home and never hearing from him again, it'll be worth it to feel like someone finds me desirable. I have a drawer full of lacy lingerie that mocks me every morning. I am reminded of a line in *10 Things I Hate About You*, one of my all-time favourite films, which still makes me want to weep over the dearly departed Heath Ledger. 'You don't buy black underwear unless you want someone to see it.'

The roads seem ridiculously empty. I am worried I have missed out on some great news story breaking somewhere. Then I look at the time. Its 6.15 p.m. The latest episode of *Humsafar* is playing on TV screens across the country as we speak.

Everyone is obsessed with *Humsafar*. I hadn't even

heard of it till Kamran sent me a link to a gossip website and asked me to 'check the story out'.

Apparently a teenage girl was in the hospital for having tried to commit suicide after being inspired by an episode of the show where the femme fatale, trying to steal the lead character away from his goody-two-shoes wife, slashes her wrists to get his attention. I made three calls to hospitals and was rudely reminded of 'doctor-patient confidentiality' and accused of 'tabloid behaviour' by ER personnel before they slammed the phone down.

I started asking around. Why would a girl want to commit suicide based on a TV show? It turns out everyone is hooked to it, and as is the case with Pakistanis, they're fanatical in their devotion: Zara, her family, Saad's mother and khala, my friends from college, my grandmother, and the owners of the convenience store around the corner, who refuse to serve anyone until 8 p.m., when the show ends. 'It's a fantastic show, Ayesha,' Zara's mother told me over dinner one night. Dinner on *Humsafar* nights was served in front of the TV and Zara's parents would only allow us to talk during the ad breaks. 'You know, people don't realize this but it really is a great retelling of what our society is like.'

I resisted the urge to ask her if she identified with the goody-two-shoes wife with the demure 'jees' and 'aaps', or the character of the mother-in-law, who hates the wife and wants her son to marry the femme fatale instead. Zara's brother Imad winked at me. 'So Mummy, does this mean you're going to be like the saas on the show?' His mother opened her mouth to respond but the theme music started playing again.

Perhaps Zara's mother has it right. Surely there is some great aspiration value to the show. Is it that deep down we all desire to be part of a love triangle, replete with a villainous saas? Or does everyone want to be a demure young wife? My tailor has informed me that five of his clients have asked for copies of the flowing white kurta the wife wore in the third episode, and brought in screenshots taken off YouTube of the outfit. There's a wild rumour going around that the local multiplex is going to screen the final episode. Zara's mother has been begging us to use our connections to try and get a ticket for her.

I make it home in time for the first commercial break. Far too many ads seem to feature reporters, usually ones from TV shows, judging contests over which detergent works best. I am about to text Zara to ask why we're being sold detergent by journalists, when Kamran calls.

'Ayesha, when do you get back to work?'

'Kamran, you gave me the day off,' I say hesitantly. I'm wondering if this call means that my day off is effectively over. 'I'll be in at work in the morning.'

'Oh. Ok. Ok. I forgot. Listen, you need to cover Karachi fashion week tomorrow. Everyone from the style desk is a badly dressed imbecile. One of them doesn't know how to spell Hermès. I don't want a 3,000-word fashion review, nobody reads that. Tell me who is wearing what, what the next big trend is going to be, and all the little bitchy things people said.' I assume this little exposition is the influence of his socialite wife or that he's been watching *The Devil Wears Prada*.

'Sure,' I hear myself say. I will probably regret agreeing to this later but I'm actually glad for a change of pace. I'm exhausted from compiling election databases, and it would be nice to get to talk to people for whom political activism means changing their Facebook status.

But Kamran's comment about 'badly dressed imbeciles' reminds me that I probably need to get out of faded khaadi kurtas and into something that will not land me on someone's worst-dressed list. I decide to pull out every single black top I own. Only five are in any condition to be worn. The rest are fraying and/or have cigarette burns. How have I spent the past three years? I seem to have no savings. Where has all my money gone, if not on clothes and vacations? An empty can of Murree beer rolls out of the cupboard. It is a sign from god, reminding me that a quarter of my salary goes to financing the legal and illegal alcohol trade.

CHAPTER 6

Sunday, April 3, 2012

Headline of the day: 'Pakistan's Fashion Week Bares Country's Frothy Side'

6 p.m.: If I hear the word darling one more time I'm going to throw up on the red carpet. We're in the lobby of a posh five-star hotel where fashion week is held every year but there's a press embargo in place on mentioning the location because the organizers fear it'll be bombed to kingdom come. While I understand the need for security, the venue is one of the city's worst-kept secrets. I've had ten staffers at work ask me for passes to fashion week. I got an e-mail in the morning from a PR firm with a list of new cell phone numbers for all their staffers, since their regular phones wouldn't stop ringing with calls from politicians, socialites, and every business executive in

the city, all demanding invites. In any case, anyone could figure out where fashion week is being held, given that the flyover leading to the hotel is completely gridlocked with cars bearing designers and socialites who seem to have coordinated their 'fashionably late' entrance.

There are a couple of burly Russian businessmen in the hotel lobby who look terribly amused at the men and women flitting in. One guy has a pair of antlers on his head. Another is wearing shorts so tight and miniscule that I'm hoping I won't be seated across from him. One woman has a fez on, another has managed to coordinate her orange Birkin with her lipstick and manicure and pedicure.

I've spotted a right-wing columnist, the interior minister, five talk show hosts, and a European woman whom everyone is fawning over. The socialites are incredibly excited, gesturing to a harassed photographer to take yet another group photo. A photographer once told me that he received late night calls from fashion week attendees, all imploring him to airbrush out their wrinkles.

I spot Farah, a model who I interviewed a couple of months ago for the newspaper's weekly magazine, and who has recently taken to spelling her name Farrah. Her face is so thin it actually hurts to air kiss. I compliment her on her dress: a red, backless, full-skirted outfit that looks like it was sewn onto her. 'The choreographer has the gall to tell me not to be "half naked"—so I have a little scarf to go with the dress,' she says, and lights up a cigarette.

The ash falls on the carpet but she doesn't seem bothered that a) this is a hotel, where one isn't allowed to smoke indoors b) there are smoke detectors, and c) she just did an anti-smoking PSA.

There's a loud BOOM.

Everyone ducks.

Of all the places in the world, I really don't want to be held under siege by militants at fashion week. 'It's a light, guys, a light,' shouts an event manager. Everyone turns around to see a blushing assistant standing next to a stepladder.

'Thank goodness,' sighs the photographer. 'We've been saved.'

A designer shrieks, 'I've lost my emerald earring, help!' Her assistant and PR rep get down on their knees and scrabble about for it while trying not to be trampled by the mostly-fake Louboutin wearing crowd. 'HURRY,' she stage whispers. 'I borrowed them from Sam and she's staring at ME.'

The photographer looks rather amused. 'Ayesha, we could have just gone to Abdullah Shah Ghazi's mazaar instead if you wanted malangs.' I realize every single woman here seems to have gotten the memo that faqir chic—aka dressing like a faqir at a shrine, except with patches on outfits placed largely for effect rather than necessity—is the next big trend. I say a silent prayer of thanks for the end of the kaftan trend, which had everyone from 10-year-olds to grandmothers wrapped in about ten metres of fabric, making them all look like they were about to deliver triplets.

One designer is wearing a long green cape and an armful of chunky silver bangles. 'My accessories collection,' she says, jangling the bangles on her wrist. 'They're really affordable too! Only four thousand rupees for a silver bangle!' I wish she would take her arm out of my face. The bangles look exactly like the stuff hawkers outside shrines try to palm off on you—for fifty bucks.

'You know I'm very spiritual. I went to Lal Shahbaz's urs this year...'

'Really?' I remark. 'Wasn't it remarkably hot?'

'Well, yes, but we stayed at this gorgeous guesthouse and had some of the malangs come visit us! I couldn't go inside the shrine, I'm claustrophobic. Anyway, I should never have posted photos on Facebook because now I hear some Lahore designer aunty has stolen my ideas! Thankfully I show before her and so you MUST write about how her collection is just a rip-off of mine.'

After about two hours of posing and hearing every designer describe their line using the beloved mantra of Pakistani designers—'a fusion of eastern sensibilities with western cuts'—and hearing someone referring to trousers as 'lowers', we're shepherded into the hall for the shows. The seating is in a bit of a mess. None of the socialites want to put their Birkins on the floor and have taken up extra seats for them. In my row, one usher whispers to another that there's been a disaster backstage: 'One designer forgot

101

to order shoes. Forgot! How can you forget shoes? None of the models want to walk out barefoot, so someone's gone off to Samia and Azmay Shahzada's warehouse to get every last pair of high heels.'

The lights dim and thumping Arabic music begins to play. A model walks out wearing a cape that looks like it belongs in the Islamic art section of a museum, followed by—'holy mother of...' whispers a journalist sitting next to me—a man dressed as a dervish, who begins whirling around. On a ramp that is possibly just about a foot wide. The model has stopped dead in her tracks because she can't figure out how to get around the whirling man. After about three minutes, he stops and walks back. The sole European woman in the audience gets up and starts clapping enthusiastically. We're treated to what I assume is the onset of the invasion of faqir chic: about ten minutes of velvet capes, tricolored turbans, and the obligatory red bridal outfit, because no Pakistani bride wants to look like a mendicant at her wedding, no matter how fashionable it may be.

The next show is described as a 'garden party'. The first batch of models walk out twirling umbrellas. The DJ is playing an old ABBA song and everyone seems to be getting into it.

And then the last model walks out with—a kitten, a real, live kitten—who understandably looks terrified. As soon as the cameras start clicking, the cat leaps out of the model's arms and climbs up on to her shoulders. The model grimaces, a look I'm all too familiar with—the cat has sunk her claws into her shoulder. To her credit, the model manages to gingerly walk down the runway, turn as well as one can when there's a cat clinging onto one's shoulders for dear life, and walk back to the staging area, where I'm sure she will require several Band-Aids.

I log on to Twitter to find that someone has already posted a photo of the model and the cat and people are tagging PETA in their tweets. Clearly they've never stepped foot in a designer's workshop, where underpaid tailors put in fourteen-hour shifts to make copies of Gucci outfits.

Text from Zara: 'I HATE YOU FOR BEING THERE.'

Text from Zara: 'Ammi wants to know if the *Humsafar* girl is there, and if she is, can you ask her where her black kurta is from?'

Text from Riffat aunty, Saad's mother: 'Beta, what is this nonsense on TV?'

Text from Kamran: 'I just saw a tweet about a cat at fashion week! You're on it, right?'

Text from Jamie: 'Meow. Did you get an exclusive with the cat?'

I actually am a bit curious about whom the cat belongs to. There's a ten-minute interval so I sneak backstage, where as I expected the model is having her shoulder cleaned with antiseptic. I corner an usher. 'Where's the cat?'

She points to a young teenage girl holding a cage, inside which sits the cat, cowering. 'I'm sorry, is she yours?' I ask.

The girl looks tearful. 'This was all mummy's idea,' she wails. 'I told her Pinkie wasn't a prop.'

Her mother sweeps in. 'Shut up, Saira! The driver is outside. Go home.'

'As you can see,' the mother says, turning to me, 'The cat is absolutely fine. The model was clearly unused to pets.'

Pinkie is now meowing pitifully from its cage.

Saira shuffles off, and I look around backstage. Farrah is wiping off her makeup and beckons me over. 'Jaani, here's a tip. Please keep an eye out for the woman who opens the next show.'

I ask her why, and she winks. I have no idea what I'm supposed to infer. Farrah is a little kooky. She quite famously once lit up a joint while walking down the runway and said it was part of the designer's vision.

I hurry back to my seat, which now has a gift bag placed on it. This year's fashion week sponsors, a pharmaceutical company, have decided to fill the bags with anti-aging cream (thoughtful) and condoms (more thoughtful, if there was anyone worth sleeping with on the four-hundred plus guest list).

The lights dim again. The journalist sitting opposite me is swigging from a hip flask.

The emcee announces that the next collection is inspired by 'working women'. I look closely at the first model and nearly fall off my seat. It's Kamran's wife. This explains why he sent me to cover the event. She's in a filmy jumpsuit and teetering on her heels. She blows a kiss at the audience and a woman behind me sniggers, 'Sana's drunk.' I realize that this isn't just a barb. Kamran's wife is actually drunk. She can't seem to walk in a straight line. She reaches the head of the ramp and does some sort of Marilyn Monroe-wind-blowing-up-the-sundress pose that just looks awkward in a jumpsuit. She fluffs her hair and sashays back. Farrah walks out next, looks at me and smiles. I'm digging out my cell phone to text Zara when Sana makes another appearance, this time in an outfit that looks more like a négligée; perhaps I misunderstood what the designer meant by 'working woman'. I wonder how Kamran would react if the newspaper's female staff showed up to work the next day dressed like this.

Sana is still weaving around on the ramp. This is like a car crash that I can't tear my eyes away from. 'OHMYGOD, SHE'S GOING TO FALL,' the usher shrieks. Sana is dangerously close to the edge. No one from the audience makes a move to help her. Farrah swoops in, grabs her by the arm and half-drags her inside.

The audience has stopped looking at the clothes. Everyone is talking excitedly. 'Tsk, you know Kamran should really spend less time at the office. Think of his poor wife sitting at home all evening. Clearly she felt like she had to get his attention,' the woman behind me says. 'Oh please,' responds her companion, who I recognize from a long-forgotten 1990s scandal involving her husband and kickbacks in a shipping company deal.

'If you can't handle it, don't drink. These new money types I tell you.'

I can't help but feel sorry for Kamran. He adores his wife.

The emcee announces that this is the last show of the evening. The lobby is buzzing with post-Sana analyses. One woman in hipster glasses sniffs that it was an 'inspired satire on modelling'—which would be a plausible explanation if Sana had a sense of humour. Sana herself is nowhere to be seen. Farrah bounds out and squeals, 'DIDN'T I TELL YOU!' I smile and offer her a cigarette. 'The woman was drunk out of her mind. I think the poor thing actually had a case of nerves and thought a drink would make it better. And now because of her, we aren't even allowed to have any water backstage! We're going to die of thirst tomorrow. The event managers think we're sneaking in booze in plastic water bottles!'

'Aren't you?' I counter. 'Well, yes, but how else is one supposed to survive fashion week?'

Monday, April 4, 2012

Headline of the day: '10 million Pakistanis drink alcohol'

Wake up to my phone beeping incessantly. Scroll through messages. Most of them are from friends who have read last night's fashion week dispatch and want to know if it 'really happened!?' This is far more enthusiasm than I get from covering press conferences and drive-by shootings. You can barely get Karachiites to raise an eyebrow at disaster any longer. I once went on a date with a guy who had been mugged a dozen times and was still nonchalant about having lost nearly a hundred thousand rupees worth of cell phones. A cat on a model's shoulder on a runway still gets them though. I reply 'YES' to each one of the messages, and promise to tell them the whole story if I ever leave the newsroom.

I log on to Twitter. Some quotes from my piece appear to have gone viral. Normally this would mean a phone call from Kamran as a sign of his appreciation, but I assume he has other things to worry about: such as Sana's presumably epic hangover and how he's going to explain her turn on the runway to his mother.

I check to see if Jamie has retweeted my piece. He hasn't.

I check every other app on my phone: Jamie hasn't gotten in touch with me on WhatsApp or e-mail. There's no post or message on Facebook. I scroll through the texts again to see if I've missed one from him. Nothing.

I rethink the amazing dinner at Casbah again. I was witty and charming and looked if not great then much better than I've looked around him before. What did I do wrong? Was I too forward? Does that even exist? I have never once heard a guy complain about a girl being too forward. Did I say something terrible? Murree Beer has a lot to answer for.

But seriously, how difficult is it to get in touch?

Manage to find a way to untangle myself from the comforter and make a cup of coffee in the microwave, which was something that hugely irritated the ex-boyfriend Hasan, who was a coffee snob and couldn't understand how I could deign to drink instant. 'It would take twenty minutes for me to grind coffee, boil water, put it through a French press, and then savour each sip. I never have twenty minutes,' I snapped at him one day after he had pointed out my coffee drinking habits to his friends at dinner. 'I have ten minutes to shower and change clothes. The last time I thought I had enough time to condition my hair, the MQM decided to call a strike and I barely made it to party headquarters before washing the shampoo out. So yeah, I drink Nescafe that's made in the microwave.' Looking back at my relationship with him, I can't imagine how I conjured up the patience to date him. I vow for the umpteenth time not to engage with fuckwits for fear of ending up alone.

My phone beeps again.

Jamie: 'Are you going to be around at fashion week today? I'm heading into town. Let's do dinner after?'

HE TEXTED! I AM GOOD AT FLIRTING AFTER ALL! HURRAH!

Panic sets in. This is an emergency situation. I need to get waxed, threaded, and find something fabulous to wear. Unfortunately, Kamran will not understand why I can't come in to work just because I'll be working all night, and so I go in deciding to sneak out later to try and get the last available appointment at the salon.

I dump my bag on the desk and check the headlines. Five people have been shot dead so far today. The prime minister is making a speech on the CNG crisis. I rifle through my handbag for cigarettes. Can't find them. Upend handbag.

Contents:
- ATM receipt. Bank balance: Rs 200. Fuck.
- Polo wrapper
- One empty box of cigarettes
- Matches that have escaped the box
- Matchbox
- Red lipstick
- Five Moleskine notebooks
- Press release from Hizb ut-Tahrir warning Pakistan's army to end their crackdown on the group
- Press release from the Jamaat-e-Islami railing against Turkish soap operas. Scribbled note on the back of the press release: 'Call Ali tomorrow.' Who is Ali? I have about fifty Alis in my phone book. Did I ever call him? When was tomorrow?
- Receipt from Espresso
- Jar of Vicks
- Body spray
- Press badge from Jamaat-ud-Dawa rally. 'REPORTER – GO AMERICA GO'
- Crumpled fifty-rupee note

I walk to the stall around the corner, trying to calculate how many loose cigarettes one can buy with fifty rupees...

There is an epic traffic jam outside. There are donkey carts, SUVs, a police van, and every kind of rickshaw ever imported to Pakistan, stretching out for miles. Vendors weave through the vehicles, hawking coconut slices and packs of 'scented tissue paper', which is mostly waxed paper sprinkled with rose water. A passenger in a bus casually leans out of the tinsel festooned window and spits paan on the vendor, who hauls himself into the bus and begins to fight with the guy.

'This much traffic?' I ask the surly stall owner, who is busy rolling a joint. 'CNG,' he replies, without looking up.

The CNG crisis is one of the banes of Karachi's existence. It is a war. The only thing missing is a character from *300* announcing 'THIS IS SPARTAAAA' in booming tones. Or THIS IS CNGPOCALYPSE. It is the only way I can describe the madness surrounding the CNG crisis, which has been fuelled—every pun intended—by years of the government encouraging people to open up gas stations and convert their cars to run on gas. There is nothing more hilarious than seeing a fifty-million rupee car queuing up with rickshaws for cheap gas. Now that the government has finally figured out that Pakistan doesn't have enough gas resources to keep up with the demand, they've mandated that gas stations be shut down three days a week. I suppose the idea was that people would see the light and start walking or convert their cars back to running on petrol. Instead, people just began queuing up at 4 a.m.—this in a city where a 9 a.m. meeting is too early—waiting for the gas stations to reopen, resulting in insane traffic jams by mid-morning. Fights break out every day. People have been mugged repeatedly in the queues. There have been multiple riots and expletive-filled screaming matches that television channels have gleefully covered live. I'm quite convinced in five years I'll meet a kid who was either conceived in one of those queues or whose parents first set eyes on each other while sitting in adjoining cars at a gas station. One of the marketing heads—an abominable man who would gladly drop every bit of reporters' copy for the sake of an ad for a housing scheme in the boonies and once asked 'what exactly is it that all of you do here?'—is also stuck in traffic. It is moments like these that reaffirm my faith in god.

I head back to the office and browse the headlines of the paper.

The opening sentence of a story on the front page makes me want to die. 'The ELL—the Extreme Liberal Left—protested the Supreme Court's rape verdict.'

'Who wrote this?!' I ask. 'And what is the ELL?'

'Ah, I see you finally managed to read the newspaper you work for,' Kamran's voice booms behind me. 'So glad you made the time!'

'Umm, what's the ELL?' I ask.

'You know… liberal lefty types. They all studied under that Marxist professor whom everyone adores, and want to change the world or something,' Kamran replies. 'Anyway,' he says, shoving his BlackBerry towards me. 'Did you see we're trending on Twitter?'

Kamran is obsessed with Facebook likes and tweets, to the point where reporters have taken to begging their friends to please, for the love of god, tweet their story so Kamran might notice them. One reporter on the sports desk told her editor in her resignation letter that she couldn't make men's hockey sexy, and if that's what the paper wanted it should just brand itself as a tabloid. Every time Kamran goes out of town, we gather around and do a dramatic re-enactment of the letter.

At 1 p.m., Shahrukh and the business reporters who spend their days tracking the stock market troop off to have plates of greasy biryani in the cafeteria.

I leave my dupatta on my chair and a half-empty bottle of Diet Coke next to my computer and sidle out of the office to go to the salon where I beg them to let me run a tab. At my old job, my boss would not show up on the days she had salon appointments. 'I'm getting a facial,' she would croon over the phone if I timidly asked who would proofread five pages that needed to go to press in the next thirty minutes. 'You can do it, you're *so good at this*.'

The woman waxing me tries to hold my arm down as I use my other hand to check my e-mails. 'You should really moisturize more,' she says, clicking her tongue in disapproval. 'Your skin is going to look like a 50-year-old's in five years.'

I resist the urge to tell her that I doubt I'll survive the next five years. Waxing done, I dash to the clothing store next door. If I actually like something, maybe I can ask my father for some money to pay for it. The salesperson looks supremely bored. I try on a jumpsuit that looks exactly like a pair of overalls I owned when I was five. The other outfit looks like something from an eighties Pakistani film: black-and-white polka dot kameez with an appliquéd flower that rests on top of my boob. Is this supposed to be some sort of statement on breastfeeding? The last outfit is a dress made from eight yards of fabric. I'm not sure whether it makes me look like I'm carrying twins or could serve as a parachute. I contemplate whether a career designing clothes for women who don't want to wear a tent could pan out.

I go back to the newsroom to find Kamran standing next to my chair. 'We need to talk,' he says.

I follow him into his office, where he's spread out the day's papers on his desk. I sit down, and we stare uncomfortably at each other. 'You didn't mention what happened last night in your copy,' he finally says.

There are a thousand things I want to say, but an image of Sana traipsing down the runway pops into my head.

'Look, I don't want to get into this. The cat thing was the story in any case, and I'd rather avoid your family, honestly,' I say, ignoring the fact that Kamran has made every reporter cover everything associated with his family—a profile of his family's interior decorator, the opening of his father's barber's new shop, his mother's best friend's NGO who's only claim to fame is hosting a fashion show every year. Kamran narrows his eyes and sighs. 'Well, thank you. I'm glad I didn't have to spell it out for you. You've always been smarter than the rest of the morons out there and that's why I sent you.'

This counts as actual praise from Kamran. I could totally put 'NOT A MORON' on my resume.

'You can leave now,' he says, and turns away to examine the front page of *Morning*.

I go back to my computer and check my e-mail. A source has sent over a copy of a sexual harassment investigation that was buried because the government official involved was pals with the prime minister. The report makes me sick. There are direct quotes about the way the officer would refer to his colleague, including him asking her 'why are you getting so upset? I'm just being friendly' and forcing her to accompany him on official trips that she wasn't required to take. I e-mail an excerpt to Kamran who replies with: 'Sick. Good work. File tomorrow. 1,000 words.'

Later that evening, I sit in front of my closet, wondering what to wear. Jamie has posted on Twitter that he's in Karachi, and he *did* text that he wanted to hang out. I read a study once that women spend sixteen minutes on average every day deciding what to wear. Cannot understand why there are phone apps that can measure one's heart rate and calorie intake but none that can provide advice in this area.

I am oddly nervous about seeing Jamie. And I am getting perilously close to breaking my own rule: Never make the first move for sex. Perhaps this is a result of weeks of watching *Humsafar*. All that coyness has reminded me that I really, really need to have sex, to feel someone's body pressing against me other than the cat's. Make a mental note to procure morning after pills at hotel pharmacy. Cannot run the risk of buying them from the convenience store and having the guy tell my father what I've been purchasing.

Of course, the power cuts out the moment I decide to do something to my hair. I think I've used my hair straightener about four times on those rare occasions when the impulse to have better hair coincided with the availability of electricity. Today shan't be one of those days. Still, I remember a neat trick I saw on YouTube involving a sock—you tie your hair up and stuff the sock inside it—gives it a lift, very soignée, if you don't mind a sock on your head, which I at this desperate stage, don't.

8 p.m.: I stride into the hotel in a chiffon sari and high heels, sock in place and hidden within folds of hair pinned over it. I catch sight of my reflection in a mirror in the lobby. Not too bad, if I may say so myself. And not just because everyone else appears to be in a kaftan as per this season's regulations. A designer kisses me hello and whispers, 'So brave, darling, to wear a sari! And you look beautiful!'

Jamie isn't anywhere to be seen in the hotel lobby, even though I spot a couple of the Islamabad types—the foreign correspondents, their faces permanently creased with the disappointment of having to be in Pakistan, with their hapless fixers trailing behind them. One of them, a potbellied court reporter, has the perpetual air of the deeply disinterested. 'Yeh kya bakwaas hai,' he mutters as he nods hello. 'I took her to a court hearing,' he says, gesturing to his charge, a light-haired 20-something woman talking to Farrah. 'And then she drags me here,' he says, looking around at the lobby that has been transformed for fashion week. There's a fake Grecian column that the models are wrapping themselves around in a bizarre fashion, three grubby white sofas that the older socialites have plonked themselves on and a chocolate fountain that no one is touching because who, in their right mind, would drink chocolate when everyone is here for the sole purpose of checking the others out. 'What am I supposed to help translate for her here? At least there'll be hot girls to look at,' he says hopefully.

I head into the hall and try not to trip as I squeeze my way through seats draped in white silk. The programme states that the first show is an 'ode to patriotism'. This is usually a euphemism for a designer having run out of steam and putting together a series of green and white kurtas and Jinnah caps as a 'collection'.

The lights dim amid pleading from ushers for people to take their handbags off empty seats and put out cigarettes.

It's a small miracle we're not all on fire. There is a loud boom from the speakers, followed by what sounds like a shriek—but that could possibly be a model finding a cockroach backstage—and then the lights come back on.

A horde of male models, all dressed in fatigues and combat gear, marches out. No, I swear. They are actually marching, like they're in an army parade. Wait, are there going to be missiles following them like they have during the Republic Day parade? The models' boots clomp on the runway. It feels like I'm watching the 1999 coverage of Pervez Musharraf's coup. One of the models stops at the head of the runway and—get this—salutes. The crowd goes wild. They're clapping. Jeez, one guy is actually standing up on his chair. And then... Oh god, it's getting worse.

The speakers blare an old Noor Jehan song. From 1965. From the WAR, for the love of all that is holy.

The next set of models have bulky jackets, blue backpacks that look exactly like the one sported by Ajmal Kasab in that CCTV shot and what looks like barbed wire wrapped around their legs. What is this supposed to be? OHMYGOD, I AM WATCHING MODELS DRESSED AS SUICIDE BOMBERS.

This isn't happening. This is worse than the clichés associated with fashion. It is actually—oh dear god, the suicide bomber models are now looking at me. Scary.

I'm about to finally exhale when the last set of models appears, wearing kurtas with Imran Khan's image emblazoned on them in a poor imitation of Warhol pop art.

The designer walks out, and I'm sure no one will applaud him. Surely, in a roomful of women whose mothers and aunts were part of democracy movements in the 1980s, there is someone who thinks the Pakistan army isn't a 'look' and that suicide bombers aren't in the best taste.

I am mistaken. Everyone gets up on their feet and applauds. There are calls of 'Bravo' and 'Pakistan Zindabad'. The lights dim again and everyone starts talking. 'Oh my god, that was so moving. I cried!' says a fashion journalist sitting to my left. She isn't kidding, her mascara has actually run. Another points out that it was 'the bravest thing in years' and the show choreographer is hugging people. 'So amazing, so apt! What a brilliant theme! He showed the great, hulking soldiers, those cowardly suicide bombers and then the man who is going to save us from these bloody corrupt jaahil politicians—Imran Khan!'

'Do you realize that that was basically a show of military aggression? Since when is that fashionable?' I ask. A designer, whose father has served in every caretaker cabinet since 1990, sneers at me. 'Our forces have made countless sacrifices, it's only right that we celebrate them.' 'Sure,' I say. 'But they're also responsible for genocide in Bangladesh, hundreds of extrajudicial killings, and for torturing activists and journalists all over the country.'

'Uff, aik to you liberals and your propaganda about war crimes. This is why Imran Khan is so right about you lot.' Had I been at a party, I may have actually considered

slapping the woman. Decide instead to head back to my
seat and vent on Twitter. Stop in my tracks. The seat next
to mine is occupied by Jamie.

'Wow,' he says.

'I know, what the fuck was that show?' I say, wrapping
my sari pallu around my arm so it won't slip off my
shoulder.

'No, I meant you. You look wow. But that show too…
yeah. It'll make for great TV though,' he says, and winks.
'Everyone from Islamabad is going insane over the show.'

I groan. 'Does this mean another year of fashion week
coverage? I don't think I can take it, Jamie.' Over the last
few years, coverage of fashion week in the foreign press has
featured headlines such as, 'Dare to Bare: Pak Fashionistas
Thumb a Nose at Taliban', 'Pakistan's Fashion Week Bares
Country's Frothy Side' and my personal favourite, 'Tattoo
vs. Taliban'.

'Unfortunately, yes. But come on…how often does one
get to see a suicide bomber on a runway?'

'Of course,' I laugh and mentally high five myself for
having worn a sari. When in doubt about whether a sari is
just too over-the-top, I always think about the late Nusrat
Bhutto, who in an interview that only referred to her as
the 'Begum' pointed out that: 'In my country we do not
show our legs. We show a little here,' gesturing toward her
neckline, 'and a little here,' pointing toward her midriff.
'But not our legs. We do not have the miniskirt in Pakistan,
you know.'

We sit back in our chairs and wait for the next collection. Part of me is seething at the army apologists but I'm also excited at being with Jamie again. When the lights finally come on, Jamie holds out a hand to me. 'We're still on for dinner?'

I nod, and gather up my sari. My feet are shredded from the heels they've been encased in for six hours, but I am determined to make it through the night.

CHAPTER 7

Headline of the day: 'Bookies gamble on election candidates'

Mmmmmm.

Last night, after dinner, a bottle of wine and much fluttering of eyelashes (me) and handholding (initiated by him), I kissed Jamie on the cheek and pushed the call button to summon the elevator. Jamie stepped in after me, brushed the hair away from my face and kissed me, a soft, gentle kiss. The elevator stopped abruptly, and I realized Jamie had never pressed the button for the lobby. He ran his fingers through my hair and suddenly stopped and pulled away. I panicked; oh please don't let it be so close and yet so far away! Turns out he'd loosened my chignon, which I'd forgotten was held up by a sock. It tumbled ignominiously to the floor.

'What is this?' Jamie exclaimed, picking it up. 'Are you stuffing your hair with socks? Is this some weird Pakistani sex fetish?' He couldn't stop laughing.

'Don't ask,' I muttered. 'I'll show you one day.'

We were on the third floor of the hotel. Jamie held my hand, drew me out of the elevator and then leant in and whispered, 'I'm dying to see what you look like under that sari.'

The sex was mind-blowingly good. Perhaps it had been too long, or maybe it was the wine, or how absolutely romantic it felt to be unwrapped and laid down on a plush bed, but ohmygod. White men really did do it better. Wondered if I could spin a thesis out of this.

I felt like every single part of me had come alive, like a head rush, an erotic ice cream headache. Was it possible I'd actually spent so many months with this deadened body? Why did I not jump Jamie the first night we met? I turned over to look at him. Hair still perfect. Mouth slightly open, and in spite of the small snorts issuing from it I still wanted to kiss it. Wondered if he'd be weirded out if I made out with him while he slept. Decided not to risk it and stuck to smiling like an idiot instead.

I was still trying to get my breathing to even out when Jamie shifted. An arm rose, and I hoped it would land on me, but instead he turned over and muttered, 'You can stay if you want,' and then promptly fell asleep.

Oh dear. I think I am expected to go home.

I slid out of bed and jabbed my foot with a discarded

heel. Oww. I hobbled across the room and tried to piece my sari back together. Bumped into the side table with a loud báng, but Jamie didn't so much as stir. I admit I was rather hoping he'd spring up and protest my departure but I couldn't really hold his sleep against him. I had no idea where my underwear was, but surely no one would be able to tell with eight metres of fabric wrapped around me.

I called the cab service from the elevator. The operator recognized my voice the minute I said hello. Do no other women call for a cab at 4 a.m.? Hmph. 'All the cabs are at the airport. We've just sent one to your hotel. You can try and intercept it if you're there.'

Most of the lights in the lobby were off. How was this possible? I had always believed that hotels were 24-hour, no-time-zone places akin to airports and train stations. The only benefit was that there was no one in the lobby so I wouldn't be recognized walking out at 4 a.m. in last night's clothes.

The doorman looked at me, and then turned to stare at the floor. I lit a cigarette and leaned against the glass doors. Suddenly, I was overwhelmed with the desire to tell someone about my night. I found my phone and WhatsApped Saad.

'I just had sex with Jamie.'

Saad replied back instantly, even though it was 3 a.m. in Dubai.

'Oh. How was it?'

'Great. Fantastic, actually. You know how long it's been?'

'Yeah, I can imagine. I had no idea you guys were dating btw. Or is this a one-off?'

'I'm not sure, I've only just rolled out of bed.'

'Ugh. TMI.'

I felt a little put out. I've heard about nearly all of Saad's sexcapades in excruciating detail. Why couldn't he hear the same from me?

'Seriously, Saad? TMI is when you tell me how many times you've been to the loo because you ate too much haleem.'

'Acha sorry. Just weird. It's 3 a.m. here and I'm half asleep. Call me in the evening.'

A cab rolled up and I shoved my phone back inside my bag and waved frantically.

Thankfully my father is out of town so I didn't have to explain where I'd been. The cat, on the other hand, looked like she was quivering with rage. She is the judgmental parent I've never had.

'I'm sorry, I'm sorry,' I squealed. I took off the blasted heels, unwrapped my sari and left some food out for the cat.

Headed into the room to finally lie down. The cat had thrown up on the bed. I am scrubbing sheets at 5 a.m. A few hours ago I was having sex with the most gorgeous man I've ever met. How the mighty have fallen.

Oh crap, I forgot to take the morning after pill. Got out

124

of bed. The cat stared at me from the corner as I gulped down two pills. I could sense the judgment in her beady little eyes.

9 a.m.: My phone beeps. I lunge for it. Surely it is Jamie. It is the natural order of things for the man one has slept with the night before to be inquiring gently if one is alive and well and possibly in the mood for a croissant and an Americano.

Check display. It's a text advertising 'herbal Viagra'.

I lie back down. Perhaps Jamie isn't awake yet, though god knows he slept well enough. Wonder if I can call his hotel and ask whether his room still has a 'Do Not Disturb' sign placed outside. Or perhaps I can show up at the hotel under the guise of covering an event for work. Surely there is some seminar on capacity building or disaster management being held. And perhaps I can loiter around in the lobby and pretend this is all just a great coincidence, ha ha, when I bump into Jamie.

Realize that will only make me seem like a crazy stalker. We're grown ups. He doesn't have to call me the moment he wakes up to assuage my insecurity. I'm sure he'll call when he calls. It's not like I don't have a life.

Still, why hasn't he called yet? Was the sex not good for him?

Ohmygod. That's it. I was probably not a patch on the legions of impeccably groomed women in Islamabad who seem to have enough time to get manicures and pedicures and have personal fitness instructors who charge a hundred dollars an hour. I am three—no, let's be honest, Ayesha, five—kilos overweight. Most women bring their A-game; half a dozen tricks gleaned from watching soft-core porn. I brought a sock. A SOCK.

I am going to die alone, living in this flat with sheets the cat has spewed on.

The phone beeps again. It's a text from Jamie. Oh thank god, thank god, thank god.

'Where'd you sneak off to?'

I type out three messages and delete them (too eager, too coy, and too saccharine respectively) and settle for 'Duty calls', hoping to keep the tone mysterious and light. 'I'm heading out of town tomorrow.'

'Oh. So I think I have to do an interview in the afternoon. Let's do coffee?'

'Let's do coffee?' I think. What does this mean? This is what I say to acquaintances I don't know well enough to sit through a dinner or lunch with. Coffee is the most impersonal of dates. I reply, 'Sure, let me know when.' Tempted to throw phone against the wall in dramatic re-enactment of all Bollywood films I have ever seen, but phone is too precious to lose and I don't have the money to replace it. Toss phone on the bed instead and wonder if there's any alcohol in the house to self medicate with.

I keep reliving last night, a minute-by-minute dissection until I feel like my head is about to explode. I call Zara. Her phone is off and then I remember she was flying to Lahore

for a cousin's wedding. I want to scream. Even though I
know that he doesn't want to hear about my back-from-
the-dead sex life, I call Saad. I need to talk.

'I'm coming to town next week,' Saad says before I've
even gotten a word in. I am actually looking forward to
seeing Saad. If Jamie does decide to ignore me after this
coffee, I will need someone to help me drink away the pain
and reassure me that I will not die alone.

'Get here soon!' I yell, and hang up.

Check my phone again. Jamie is posting photos of
fashion week on Twitter. Hmm. So he has enough time to
tweet but not to text. Do not know if it is now appropriate
to comment on his tweets in jokey manner or if this counts
as clingy. It's a miracle everyone isn't in therapy from
constantly guessing whether a like is just a like or means
something more. Try to remind myself that I should stop
acting like a besotted teenager and instead play the cool,
collected woman who does not get into a panicked frenzy
if a man, as gorgeous as he may be, has not called. I am
a hard core reporter, an intelligent, independent woman
who is perfectly happy being single.

Wouldn't hurt to check my phone again though.

Bah. Nothing.

Am listlessly pondering whether I should even go to
work when Kamran calls. 'AYESHA. GET TO SEAVIEW
NOW.'

'Ok. What's happened?'

'There's a lion loose!'

I don't know how to respond. 'You know that's an urban legend right?'

'I know, but can you go check it out please? We'll see.'

I pick up my work handbag and hail a cab. 'Seaview, and can you please hurry?'

'So what do you do?'

'I'm a journalist,' I say, checking my notebook to see how many pages I have left.

'Why are you going to Seaview?' the cab driver asks, as he runs a red light.

'Because there's a lion loose.'

The cab screeches to a halt.

'What?'

'Gari chalao. Bhai, every year someone spreads a rumour that a lion or a tiger has escaped from some rich idiot's private zoo on Seaview, and they have to close the entire stretch down. Except no one has ever seen it.'

'Your job is very strange,' he says, and resumes driving.

At Seaview, the grimy, grey beach lies placidly before a roiling sea. A monkey is napping on the sidewalk with his owner. A few reporters have set up outside the McDonald's branch. One guy is taking a nap on the bench with Ronald McDonald's statue. 'Lion here yet?' I ask.

Everyone shakes their head. I walk up the promenade. A small crowd has gathered outside a house, with a security guard trying unsuccessfully to disperse them. 'What's going on?' I ask, hiding my press badge with my dupatta. Everyone I know wants a press badge, including the owner of the grocery store around the corner from my flat, who believes the badge is a real-life get out of jail free card that will ensure he never gets stopped by the police. In reality, a press badge is a liability, a card that ensures that people shut up instantly when they see you or decide to berate you for something they once read and didn't agree with. 'These people think this is the house the lion escaped from!' the guard says, waving his gun in the air.

'So did it?'

He looks around, and then nods. 'But it's not a lion. It's a baby. It can't have gone very far. Sahib has gone to look for it.'

I edge away nervously from the house. Who knows what a lion cub is capable of? They look adorable on National Geographic, but what if they're really ravenous monsters who will bite off a chunk of your leg? I have not been trained to do this.

There's a screech of tires as a Range Rover careens around the corner and stops in front of the house. A burly man jumps out, holding a cage. In it is the cub, who looks positively terrified. Intense deja vu moment. Didn't this happen at fashion week two days ago?

'It's fine. We caught it. Please leave now,' he says, still holding the cage aloft. I find my voice again. 'Can we at least ask whose house this is? Why do you have a lion on the premises?'

The guy looks at me as if I'm an idiot. 'Read the nameplate.'

I look closely at the nameplate and nearly reel in horror. The house belongs to one of the most notorious gunrunners in the city. Once the guy goes inside, I snap a photo of the nameplate and e-mail it to Kamran. There goes today's feline scoop, unless Kamran suddenly grows a spine in the next hour.

Text from Jamie: 'Coffee at 7 at the hotel?'

The hotel coffee shop?! This is really a brush-off, a caffeinated version of wham, bam, thank you ma'am. I can't even process this. My day is going from bad to worse. I need critical levels of alcohol in my bloodstream.

I get to work and sift through a bunch of press releases and drafts, trying half heartedly to cobble something together to file. Kamran sends me a one-line e-mail about the runaway cub. 'Drop the story.' I don't have to write anything about fashion week either. Kamran's decided he's just going to run lots of photographs with captions.

I can't even be bothered to go home and change. What's the point? Jamie has made it quite evident that this was just a one-night stand. Which I would have probably been alright with, had he not been so damn likeable, had it not been at least six months since I'd had sex, and had he not been a rarity in a city of men who speak only in monosyllables. Or, they're like Hasan, talking incessantly about themselves, their only knowledge of politics coming from reading news stories shared on Facebook.

Hail a rickshaw. Realize five minutes later that I have nothing to tie my hair up with, which means that this ride will turn it into something resembling the bouffant-like styles sported by newscasters in the 1980s. Twist hair up into a bun and find a pen in my bag that can hold it up. Pen falls out and rolls onto the road a second later. Take my dupatta and wrap it around my head.

Idle in the hotel lobby for five minutes before I text Jamie to let him know I'm here. I feel defeated already, that weird kind of feeling you get when you're PMSing or have spent the entire day crying after watching a sad film, and my post-7 p.m. exhaustion has kicked in. I check my reflection in a mirror in the lobby. My hair is passable, and the lipstick I applied in the rickshaw has managed to stay on. Jamie comes bounding out of the elevator, looking possibly more fresh faced and happy than I have ever seen him.

'Hiii,' Jamie says, kissing me on the cheek. We settle down, order coffee and I order one of the cheesecakes in the display case. Since I'm clearly not having sex tonight—or ever again—I really don't care about the calories.

Jamie starts to tell me about his day: the frustrating experience of trying to interview a politician who wouldn't give a straight answer to any of his questions, being stuck in traffic, trying to find a good story. He gets up to use the loo and I check my phone.

Saad has texted me his flight details. He wants to see me as soon as he's in the city. I scroll through the rest of my e-mails. There are a bunch of memos from HR asking employees not to misuse work e-mail to send mass birthday greetings. I'm about to delete the last e-mail—titled 'Hello' and from a sender I don't recognize at first—when I suddenly recall who he is. It's Samir Khan, a guy I met last year on the sidelines of a protest for victims of enforced disappearances. He was the only 20-something guy in the crowd and was smoking. I bummed a box of matches from him and asked him if he'd escaped the office to watch the rally. Wrong move, Ayesha. Samir dryly informed me that he was at the protest because his own father had been detained and shipped off to Guantanamo, where he'd been held without charge for seven years. We ended up exchanging texts every few weeks, and Samir would routinely invite me to other protests and to come to court, where he'd filed a case asking the government to explain why his father had been captured and detained.

'Abbu is back,' Samir's e-mail read. What? How? I sit up and re-read the e-mail. I haven't heard about this at all. Granted, I've been at fashion week for two days but there is no way I would have missed the story of a Guantanamo detainee being released.

I send Samir a quick text message. 'Can I come see him?'

After about ten minutes, I get an e-mail from another address. 'Cannot use phone. You can come, but please don't inform the media. And be careful.'

I'm not sure what that last sentence implies, but I have an idea. Samir has been picked up five times by intelligence agencies for questioning, and if he isn't using his phone it means that it's tapped. This also means his house is probably under surveillance. I am still staring at the phone, filled with a sense of nervous excitement. And if he's told me not to inform the press, then I am the only person who knows.

This is a scoop, and I can't wait to get out of the hotel and figure out what I'm going to do.

Jamie returns to find me staring at my cell phone. 'Is everything alright?'

'Oh,' I say, suddenly remembering why I'm here. 'Yep. Just got a heads-up on a story so a bit distracted.'

'Oh,' he says, disinterestedly, stirring his coffee. 'Anything good?'

I can't resist the urge to brag. 'Oh, just a little story about a Gitmo prisoner being released.'

Jamie stares at me somewhat incredulously before he breaks out into a wide grin. 'That's fantastic, Ayesha,' he says warmly. 'I'm really happy for you! We should get champagne!'

'This is Pakistan,' I reply, pointing to my cup. 'A cappuccino will have to do.'

'No, seriously, this is a big deal! How are you going to do the story? Are you thinking about multimedia options?' Jamie fires off a bunch of questions, and I dig out a notebook and begin jotting ideas down.

'So who's the prisoner?' Jamie asks, as he calls the waiter over for the bill. I tell him. The prisoner's case made headlines when his presence at Guantanamo Bay was first announced, because he was extremely wealthy and well known in Karachi's business circles. No one has heard from him or from his family in the past seven years. If I actually pull off an interview, it could mean a permanent reprieve from researching timelines and sitting through boring press conferences.

Jamie looks thoughtful and puts his hand over mine. 'This is fantastic, fantastic,' he says. 'Let me know if you need any help? I'd love to help edit if you need it.'

I am touched. It's so refreshing to meet a man not turned off by my profession. 'Now,' Jamie says. 'Let's really celebrate.'

He smiles and tugs my hand so I get up. 'Oh,' I say, momentarily disoriented. Did I completely misread this situation?

We head upstairs.

Two hours later, I could kick myself for a) having spent the entire day mooning around b) not looking even somewhat desirable. Jamie is the same wonderful person. I am the crazy person who was over-thinking this to death. And this is SO not a one-night stand.

'Don't leave,' Jamie drawls, as I slide out of bed and call for a cab.

'I have to,' I say. My father is back in town and I do not have a compelling excuse for staying out all night. I also have to get sorted with the interview.'

'Oh, of course. Let me know how it goes?' he says as he reaches for his phone and begins tapping away. 'I'd really like to read it.'

'Sure,' I say, and smile. It feels so different to be with someone who understands what I do for a living, unlike Hasan. With Jamie, it's as if we're on the same wavelength, bound by a connection that I wouldn't be able to replicate with anyone else. Saad always says that if he needs to 'talk' to someone, he calls me—so why would he need a girlfriend? I used to agree with him but looking at Jamie tangled up in bed sheets, smiling at me adorably, I feel like I've managed to strike gold in this barren city.

I kiss him goodbye, which takes another ten minutes because I can't manage to tear myself away. Jamie whispers that he'll miss me. I smile and walk out of the hotel, feeling exhilarated. I look back at the doors, through which I had walked in defeated just a few hours ago. I look up at the sky and smile. Perhaps my luck has finally changed?

I feel water drops on my face. Is it raining? This has to be a sign from god that everything will be okay. I look up and realize it's just the air conditioner above dripping water. Huh. Whatever. I don't need a sign. My luck HAS changed.

CHAPTER 8

Wednesday, April 6, 2012

Headline of the day: 'Pakistan bans condom ad starring controversial actress'

11 p.m.: I'm weaving all kinds of excuses to explain to my father why I'm only just getting home. 'I had to work late and then had to meet someone for dinner,' I say, trailing off. Luckily it's the cat's dinnertime and he's not really paying attention to me.

I open up my laptop to get started on the research for the piece. There are no news updates on him, which is fantastic. I trawl through news archives for the past decades, scribbling down points about when he was first reported missing, a petition filed by his wife and son about his disappearance, a file detailing his initial interrogation at Guantanamo Bay, where he insisted he was just a businessman who had no idea that a client his company had billed was a front man for Al Qaeda. There's another report, from 2008, about him requiring emergency surgery. These are the two things I really want to talk about.

It's a one-line e-mail titled: 'love you'. A jolt goes through me at seeing the word love, before I shake myself. It's Saad. We've always used 'love' as casually as most people say hello or goodbye. I scroll down. He's sent me a bunch of scanned photos of us at school and university. We're in our geeky glasses, drinking Pepsi at the school canteen. There's another one of us on a school trip to Mohenjodaro, goofing around next to a stupa. We're posing at interminable weddings, throwing our mortarboards off gleefully after graduation. But instead of looking older, these photos make us seem younger and happier as the years have gone by.

The last photo makes me laugh hysterically. It's from a late night at home last year, and I'm wrapped in a shawl to go outside to meet the bootlegger. Saad's girlfriends have often told me they find him far too aloof and emotionally detached, but as I stare at this e-mail I realize they only know the urbane, suave Saad with the high-flying job, not the gawky teenager who threw up after his first beer.

Wake up from a nightmare in which Saad is interrogating Jamie regarding his relationship with me. What does this mean? Perhaps I should consult some sort of dream analyser. Do these people even exist? The last time I saw an analysis of dreams was in the back pages of the weekly Urdu magazine *Akhbar-e-Jahan*. Check phone.

Jamie has sent me a bunch of texts, wishing me luck for the interview. I smile. It is kind of heartwarming to have someone care about you.

11 a.m.: Get to work to find Kamran poring over a couple of lunch menus. 'Chairman Mao or Okra?' Kamran asks as I walk into his office. 'Chairman Mao, always,' I reply, hoping Kamran will order me some of their amazing prawn toast and green curry as well.

I run Kamran through the interview.

'This is fantastic,' I urge, as he looks thoughtful. I know that look on his face, it's the same one he gets right before he tells you that you're not being paid on the 1st, or the 5th of the month. Must sell. C'mon, Ayesha, use your business school degree and pitch the hell out of this. 'This is the first exclusive interview with an ex-Guantanamo Bay detainee who no one has heard from in years. He was a businessman—someone everyone who reads our paper knew and socialized with before he was arrested—so we'll get a lot of name recall,' I confidently rattle off, hoping Kamran can't see that my hands are sweaty with tension. 'And it'll be a great interview, y'know? Can you imagine the stories he'll have about his life in jail, the torture, the other inmates, the investigation into his case?'

'Do you want to do this?' Kamran says. 'We can send a guy...'

'Kamran, no,' I retort angrily. 'This is not something

a guy can do better. I've covered everything that most of your male reporters have said no to: Interviewing gangsters—I've interviewed so many that I have more of them on my phone than actual friends, for the love of god—seminaries, rape victims, bootleggers, even the bloody fashion designer lot. I won't be unsafe, I promise.'

'Sure, then,' Kamran says. 'Oh, and can you order a meal from Chairman Mao for me please?'

I exchange a few e-mails with Samir, asking for directions to his house and to set up a time for the interview—3 p.m., which should give me enough time to come back to work and perhaps even file the story—and I'm now sitting around, willing the clock to tick faster so I can head out.

Now that I have a few minutes to absorb this, I realize I'm filled with an odd kind of nervous energy. The cloak-and-dagger way in which the interview has been scheduled makes me a bit wary of what I'm getting myself into. At the back of my mind, I know that there's no real danger. This is not like walking into a training camp for militants or a mosque best known for inciting violence in the Friday sermon. This is just an interview. At the most, I could be followed back to work, but I have a massive dupatta that I plan to wrap firmly around myself, which will help disguise my face. Thank goodness I don't report on television so no one will recognize me.

This is going to be fine, I tell myself.

God, I need a drink.

2 p.m.: I head out and find a rickshaw, promising the driver that I know the address and we won't be driving around in circles. But the house is a nightmare to find. I used to live in the neighbourhood six years ago, but nothing seems familiar. Samir told me the house has a black gate and is near the bakery, but there are about five bakeries in as many lanes. How do these stores run!? Don't flour prices affect them? Must ask someone to come back to this area and investigate the odd rise of bakeries.

I can't recognize anything here. There used to be rows of houses, all designed with the same art deco balconies and low gates—sigh, all built at a time when break-ins were rare—and painted in odd shades of green and beige. Most of them have been torn down and replaced by four-storey apartment buildings. There are about a dozen more mosques than I remember. I look around idly for my old house. The walls used to be routinely defaced by young boys, who thrilled at spray-painting their Internet chat room handles on them. They've been replaced by the Jamaat-ud-Dawa and a bunch of religious parties, all calling for jihad in Kashmir via painted slogans on the walls. I ditch the rickshaw before the driver tacks on another two hundred rupees to my fare for making him drive around. I call Samir. Not unexpectedly, he doesn't answer. Crap. I could be here forever. I start walking through the narrow lane, lifting my dupatta to avoid it touching an overflowing gutter.

'AYESHA! What are you doing here?'

Where did that come from? I look around. Can't see anyone. Am I hearing things now?

'HERE!'

'Where?!' I shriek. A stone lands next to me. I look up and its...

...the Sipah-e-Sahaba spokesperson, waving at me from a balcony.

'This is my house. What are you looking for?' he says. 'House number seventy?' I ask. 'Oh, that's two lanes away. Just go straight and then turn left, and then take a right at the bakery and then another left. Do you want me to walk you?'

'Uh, no,' I mutter, and back away. What are the chances I'd run into him here?

Suddenly, I spot a couple of cops sitting outside a house, which is odd. This is a middle-class neighbourhood and the cops can't be guarding anyone here. I approach it and look at the house numbers as I walk past them. Seventy-two, seventy-one, sixty-nine... hmm. One of the signs is missing. This could be it. I head to the door when a cop looks up at me. 'Why are you going in?' he asks. 'I'm their cousin,' I say nervously. The cop jumps up and knocks on the door. Thankfully, it's opened by Samir, who greets me exuberantly. 'Baji, so good to see you again!'

The house is decorated in the style that was last fashionable in the 1980s: painted deco furniture, room dividers made of shells and beads, and sofas upholstered in floral-print fabric. Samir leads me through the living

room and stops at a door. 'Dad is very weak,' he says.
'Please don't be too harsh.'

He flings the door open, and I freeze in my tracks.
The last photograph taken of the guy was at his eldest
daughter's wedding—he was laughing, dressed in a three-
piece suit, and weighed about 250 pounds. This is a ghost.
There is a ghost lying on the bed. He's frail and weak. I
gingerly step in and sit down. He has a prolonged coughing
fit, then looks at me and croaks, 'Do you want to hear how
I ended up like this?'

As I fill up one notebook, then another, with his story,
I'm convinced that I am going to win more than just a pack
of cigarettes as a sign of Kamran's approval. This could
change my life. Just thinking about that is a strange out
of body experience. I could win an award. I could make
real money. I could never have to make another timeline
again for as long as I live. The guy's story is downright
chilling: living in shackles, being force-fed when he went
on hunger strike, the detainees whispering in their cells.
But it's his account of how he ended up being mistaken
for a 'terrorist'—the client he never thought could be a
front for Al Qaeda—that is fascinating and the names he
throws out could potentially embroil scores of Karachi's
top businessmen in embezzlement scandals. After a couple
of hours, he sighs and says he can't talk anymore.

I say my goodbyes and head out the door with Samir,
who is thanking me profusely for visiting. 'This will get
published, right?' he asks, as he opens the gate.

'Yes,' I say, and step out to be confronted by the cop, who ignores me and looks at Samir. 'We need this person's contact information,' he says. Samir looks scared. 'Of course,' I say confidently and rattle off my sister's number—one of the few cell phone numbers I know by heart—which has been disconnected for the past two years.

They note it down, and I walk off to find a rickshaw. After about thirty minutes, I finally find one, promise the driver five hundred rupees if he can get me back to civilization, and run into the office.

Kamran is sitting at his desk, and as I walk by he calls out. 'AYESHA. IN HERE. NOW.'

'Listen, sit down,' Kamran says, gesturing to the only other chair in the office, which has a pile of old newspapers on it. I put them on the floor and sit on the edge of the seat. 'Look, Ayesha, we got a call from intelligence. They seem to know you were interviewing that guy today.'

'What?' I stammer. 'How is that possible? I didn't have a press badge on; they couldn't have followed me from work...'

'We don't know. Believe me, I didn't want to ask. They probably have a trace on your phone and your laptop or on the guy you interviewed. It's possible he's under surveillance, and not you. But I think it would be best if you take a few days off, keep a low profile and don't file your story right now. We're already in a bit of a mess because of a court case and we'll take a look at the story next week.'

I can feel my award, my promotion, and my new work wardrobe slip away.

Kamran and I end up arguing for the next hour, during which time his secretary pops in with two cups of tea. I eat a pack of chocolate biscuits in my rage. 'Why is the newspaper so spineless,' I scream. 'How can you give up on a story that could—no, fuck it, I know for sure that it will—MAKE HEADLINES WORLDWIDE.' Kamran shrugs. 'This is a corporation. I'm running a business here. This is not a place where you live out your fantasy of doing some expose that the world will love. I have to put my interests first. How am I going to pay your salary if the government cracks down on us because of this story!?'

I am desperately trying to hold back tears. I will not be one of those girls who sobs in the office and is then looked upon with pity and derision. 'Look, the story isn't going anywhere,' Kamran eventually says. 'Tell your source it'll be okay. And also—don't come in to work for a few days.'

Crap. I had completely forgotten that the spooks could have me under surveillance. 'What am I supposed to do?' I ask. 'I don't know!' Kamran exclaims, shoving a bunch of papers off his desk. 'You told me you'd be safe. Now leave the office before they come back looking for you or some crap.'

What being under surveillance really means doesn't sink in until I get out of the office. Every stranger seems a potential spy, including the office accountant, the guards, and the rickshaw driver taking me home who can't make out a word I'm saying since I've covered my face, niqab style, with a dupatta to avoid being recognized.

I consider not going directly home in case I'm being followed. Perhaps I can just pace the streets, going from place to place, cut my hair maybe, go by another name for a while. As the rickshaw reaches my flat, it occurs to me that I'm not Jason Bourne and that he too probably wouldn't get very far on the run in Karachi. I take a long look up and down my street. It looks the same but is it really? My heart stops racing as I lock the apartment door behind me. But am I safe here? I take out my phone but it seems like an object of betrayal right now. I can't trust the phone, or my e-mail. In a fit of inspiration, I remember that I have an extra SIM card that I bought to use in rural Sindh, which isn't registered in my name. I plug it into my phone and check my e-mail. Jamie wants to meet up tonight, but I don't see how I can leave the house. Or should I just act as if everything is normal and run the risk of ending up in a detention centre in some godforsaken military base? I e-mail Jamie back. 'I'm a bit caught up with something.' Damn the intelligence for screwing over my love life. Jamie sweetly offers to send a car to fetch me. I'm sorely tempted, there's nothing quite like the fear of being dragged off by intelligence agencies to make one really, really want a warm hug, but I need to be smart about this.

The landline rings. For a moment I wonder where the sound is coming from. Nobody's called on this number since the nineties. Ask not for whom the bells toll, Ayesha.

I am staring at it as if it's going to explode, until my father hurries irritably out of his room, asking why I can't, for once, do a single thing around the house. He barks hello into it and I wait, holding my breath. 'Oh hello beta,' he says, smiling warmly. Beta? Has the cat learnt how to use the phone? He hands it to me. 'It's Saad.'

I gratefully snatch the receiver, exhaling for what must be the first time in about ten minutes. 'Hi Saad.'

'WHY are you not answering your phone? You always answer your phone. You answer it if you're in the shower or on the treadmill.'

I drag the phone into my room, nearly tripping over the wire. 'Saad, I can't get into it over the phone, can you text me? I'm texting you a number.'

'Are you alright?' Saad says, sounding concerned. I resist the urge to start bawling. 'No, but I'll just tell you.'

Five minutes later, I am babbling my entire story in a series of texts, studded with frowny faces.

'Fuck,' Saad replies, succinct as always. 'I'm booking you on a flight to Dubai. I'll reschedule my trip.'

I am about to reply 'no fucking way' as I always do when trips to Dubai are proposed but then I realize Saad's right and this is just what I need. It would be nice to not spend the week expecting the landline to explode. I can't live like this let alone try to write this story. 'You're crazy, but sure. Yes. Thank you!' I hurriedly tell my father that I need to be in Dubai this weekend, thank my stars that

I actually have a valid visa, which Saad forced me to get last year 'because, Ayesha, what if you want a drunken weekend?' and start packing haphazardly.

Thursday, April 7, 2012

9 a.m.: I'm packed, have given my father a version of what happened and implored him to be very cautious the entire weekend, just in case the spooks decide to follow him around.

I'm about to call a cab to take me to the airport when Saad's 15-year-old cousin Ali shows up. He hands me a copy of my ticket. 'Saad bhai asked me to drop you to the airport, and I've brought my Pajero and my guard, so you don't have to worry.'

I kiss the cat goodbye, remind my father again not to answer any calls from unknown phone numbers or tell anyone in the neighbourhood where I've gone, and hurriedly write Jamie a text telling him I'll be out of town this weekend. 'That sucks,' he replies. 'Hope your story worked out okay! Call me when you're back in town.'

'It didn't,' I reply. 'But more on that later. Speak soon!'

Saad's cousin Ali bundles me into the car and I sit sandwiched between him and his steely-gazed guard. This seems a bit extreme to me, god knows what kind of trouble

Saad told him I was in. Ali makes a couple of phone calls on the way, then puts the phone down and says, 'Can I ask you something?'

'Sure,' I say, hoping he's not going to ask me why I'm making such a quick trip or why he's been deputed to take me to the airport.

'Did you ever date Saad bhai?'

'NO!' I almost shout. Am I imagining this or is the guard also straining to hear my answer? 'No, we're just friends. We've been friends for longer than you've been born, silly,' I say, remembering how Saad and I snuck out of the hospital to find a place to smoke while Ali's mother was in labour.

'Why not?' Ali persists. I'm about to answer but stop. This kid is fifteen. I don't have to justify my platonic friendship to him. I'd smack him if it weren't for his armed guard. I start to formulate an answer, but I just don't have one for this question—one either understands or one doesn't.

'Just because. Your cousin isn't my type,' I say, and begin looking in my handbag for something to serve as a distraction. I pull out a grotty tissue and blow my nose. This seems to serve as a full stop.

Why didn't Saad and I date? I haven't been asked this question since our first year of college. As teenagers, we were far too involved with our own convoluted love lives. But increasingly, more of our friends gave up on the dating scene and ended up marrying each other, prompting Saad to sardonically remark that weddings now seemed like a game of musical chairs. 'Honestly, isn't it just a bit desperate?' he said, attacking a plate of kulfi as his ex-girlfriend said her qabool hais to my ex-crush five feet away at a wedding last year. 'It's as if they ran out of people to date, landed up on Facebook and clicked on the first profile photo that came up and thought "ha, this could be the one, he's been here all along".'

Three hours later the claustrophobic heat smacks me in the face as I step out of the airport, making me want to rip my clothes off and throw myself into the shower. I am tugging my shrug off when Saad bounds up, gives me a hug—one arm out of the shrug and the other at an awkward angle and all—and pats my head. 'You're alive. I was not looking forward to having to organize your funeral.'

'Of course I'm alive, you idiot,' I say. Saad offers me a cigarette and we light up. I grin happily and watch people streaming out of the airport.

I feel relieved, like I've been running a marathon and now that Saad's here everything is okay. I don't have to be anyone else—the perfectly witty and charming woman to Jamie, the perfectly capable reporter to Kamran—around him. I can just be myself. 'Should we go?' Saad asks, lifting my bag. 'Jeez, that's light. Didn't you bring anything?'

'No, I was terribly panicked when I packed and had no idea what I was throwing in.'

'Don't worry. We're going shopping tomorrow. And to the beach. No scratch that. The beach is for people who didn't grow up in Karachi. Dinner. We'll have falafel and shawarma so good it'll make you cry. And then I'm taking you to this bar that has a view of the entire city—and get this, the cheapest cocktail is about four hundred dirhams and is served with gold paper shavings—and we are going to get drunk.'

'Don't you have to work?' I ask Saad as he speeds down the highway. It feels amazing to be in a city where I'm not concerned that we're going to get stopped by a gun-toting teenager demanding our cell phones. The highway stretches out, a bunch of Porsches zip by, the air-conditioner is on full blast, and my favourite song of all time—Khaled's *Didi*—is on the radio. I feel... oh good god, is this happiness? Peace of mind?

'Nope. It's the weekend, remember? And I'd already taken time off until Tuesday because I was planning to be in Karachi so...'

'Sorry about that,' I say.

'Are you kidding me?' Saad says. 'I was coming to see you anyway.'

At his apartment, there's a photo of us—one of the pictures he sent me earlier this week—in a silver frame. 'Ha, look at us,' I say. 'Don't your dates ever wonder why you have a random girl's photo in your apartment?'

'I tell them it's my sister,' he says, and winks. Saad digs out a bottle of wine, plonks it in front of me and uncorks the bottle. 'Talk.'

150

'Really? It's pretty late.'

'Yeah and neither of us have to be at work tomorrow. So, first things first, tell me the work issue.'

I run through the entire story. 'You know, there are a lot of editors right here in Dubai. My friend Ali is a freelancer here too. Screw the paper and Kamran. Why don't you pitch this to them?'

Maybe it's the two glasses of wine I've already had, but this actually sounds like a good idea. 'That could work! And I could tell Kamran that he can just excerpt it from them. That way he doesn't get into trouble and this story still gets told.'

Saad smiles. 'See, that's a problem solved. Now what else is up?'

'Jamie,' I say, and sigh.

'Oh right,' Saad says, smiling a little too brightly. 'How is that going?'

'Really good, actually,' I say. 'I thought it was a one-night stand thing, it turns out it isn't. I mean, he's still really thoughtful and the sex is actually better than it was the first time, which I did not think was possible...'

Saad grimaces. 'I love you Ayesha, but do we really have to do the sex talk? I'm glad you're having good sex. Now move on.'

'Ok fine,' I say, pouring more wine. 'It's good with Jamie. But I don't know where this is going, and now I've just kind of upped and disappeared. It'll probably work out?'

I sigh and down my glass of wine.

'You were drinking wine that night when you met Jamie. Is wine your fall-in-love drink?'

'What?!' I shriek. My voice seems to boom when I've had more than two glasses of wine. 'You know,' Saad says with a shrug. 'Everyone has a drink that makes them feel a certain way. Vodka makes me violent—don't laugh, you're exactly the same on tequila—I get chatty after a lot of scotch, and you clearly fall in love with goras when you have too much red wine.'

'Not with desi men then,' I say, laughing. Saad suddenly clams up. 'Clearly not,' he says, and abruptly gets up from the sofa and yawns loudly. 'I'm going to crash. Wake me up whenever you're up, and we'll get some breakfast. Night.'

I'm wondering why he was so abrupt till I see the clock. Its 5.30 a.m. He must just be tired. It's enough that he bailed me out, he doesn't have to love my—what the hell, I'm just going to say it—my boyfriend. Though I'm sure he'll adore him when they spend more time together. I turn off the lights and stagger into my room feeling the giddiness that comes from using the word boyfriend, and also from seeing Saad's wonderfully familiar things in his flat. It's hard to get the blues around Saad.

The next day, Saad and I go shopping at the Mall of Emirates. After about an hour of looking at dresses and sighing at the price tags, Saad exasperatedly snatches a black dress from me and pushes me towards a changing room. 'Go. Please, I can't take this anymore. I'm buying this for you. Birthday present. Or something.'

The dress looks really, really good on me, except I can't imagine where I would wear this. 'Clubbing, silly,' Saad says, as he steers me out of the store and to the food court. 'We're going dancing tonight. Oh, and check your e-mail.'

I look at my phone. There's no message from Jamie, which bums me out. But there is one from Saad's freelancer friend. He has already spoken about me to the editor of one of the UK's most well known news websites. I hastily write a pitch to the editor, pray silently that I'll get to do this story and beam happily at Saad. 'You are the best,' I say.

'Of course I am. Now, let's load up on carbs before we get smashed tonight.'

The club is great fun. The theme for the night is the nineties, which I am secretly glad for since that's the only decade I seem to know songs from. My dress looks amazing, but Saad has really upped his game since we last partied together. He's in head-to-toe black but without the air of someone who's trying too hard to be cool. And everyone at the club seems to know Saad. As we wait at the bar, two super-thin girls in mini-dresses walk up to him and kiss him hello. One strokes his arm and asks him to join them at their table. 'Nope, hanging out with a friend tonight,' Saad says, turning away. I raise an eyebrow. 'Friends of a friend,' he says, gulping down his whiskey sour. I smile, and look around the club, which looks like the set for a vodka ad campaign. There's a row of flaming shots on the bar, the women all seem to be dressed in head-to-toe couture and the men look like they spent the entire day getting gorgeous, golden tans.

Two days later, I find myself standing outside Saad's apartment, waiting for a cab. He would have dropped me, but we'd spent the last two nights staying out at bars, then eating ridiculous amounts of fried chicken and talking till 6 a.m. about everything: our childhoods, old crushes, random gossip, and how guilty Saad feels about having left his mother in Karachi to move to Dubai. I knew he'd be a train wreck driving. 'I love you, you know,' I say. 'Even if this pitch doesn't work out and I'm going to be hunted by spies forever, I'm really thankful for this...'

'Oh shut up,' Saad says, and gives me a hug. 'I love you too. Call me when you get in.'

I'm idling around the airport wondering if I should actually make my way to the smoking room—or what I like to think of as a preview of hell given the number of people that are stuffed in there, smoking their lungs out like it is their last cigarette—when my phone rings. It's a UK number.

'This is fantastic,' the gravelly-voiced editor says, after I run him through the story. 'I'd be really glad to publish this, and we can e-mail the military for their response to the allegations, so you won't be in harm's way.'

Five minutes later, I'm standing in that smoking room. But I'm the only one who doesn't have the air of the condemned. I am writing this story for one of the most reputable news websites in the UK. Suck on that, spies.

CHAPTER 9

Monday, April 11, 2012

Headline of the day: '23% of Pakistanis say white is their favorite colour: poll'

9 a.m.: After a short but agonizing internal battle ending with me deciding not to take this opportunity to knock back many tiny bottles of free drinks, I dig out my laptop and start writing the story. The seat next to mine is empty and I spread out my notebooks and start typing manically. I plug in my headphones and start listening to my favourite song, trying to recall exactly how I felt during the interview. It's a trick I do to be able to write from memory.

I run out of places to spread my notebooks, and prop one up in the window. The flight attendant walks by and starts yelling. 'Please remove that, NOW.' Hmph.

I don't even notice that the plane is circling Karachi until the cell phone ringtones begin. 'Yes, so you'll be at the gate, right?' the man behind me says loudly. 'I have five bags, two TVs, and a food processor.'

I close my laptop. I've reread it five times by now and for the first time, I'm not racked with self-doubt about the story or how it'll be received. It really is kind of fantastic. Kamran still hasn't replied to the e-mail I sent him about having someone else publish the story first, but I can bulldoze him into agreeing I suppose.

I check my phone as I wait for my luggage at the carousel. Still nothing from Jamie, but then I suppose he did ask me to let him know when I was back. Attempt to compose short flirty text. Cannot think of flirtatious things to say. Settle for uplifting: 'Back in town after a great weekend away. Hope all is well.'

I move closer to the carousel to see if I can find my bag. It's covered with what I can only hope is water. One woman is examining the back of her suitcase. 'Oh God, I hope the Chantilly lace isn't ruined!'

'What happened?' I ask a porter. 'Someone had Zam Zam in their bag. The thing's exploded.'

God is laughing at us, I know.

I head home, where my father has just woken up to feed the cat. He tells me there have been no strange phone calls or anyone lurking outside.

I take my notebooks out again and go through the story and the notes. I read it for the sixth and then the seventh time and finally attach it to an e-mail to the gravelly-voiced editor at the website. My hand is shaking when I press send. Is this really happening? Am I actually going to get a story published abroad? This is the first time I've ever written for someone outside of Pakistan.

Oh god, I really hope the story is good enough.

I keep staring at the screen, hoping the editor will reply right away.

It's only 4 a.m. in London. Right. What do I do now? I suppose I should go to work, even though I'm yawning my head off and can feel the tiredness finally sinking in. I should probably take the day off, but I have discovered that the trick to being sent home after one has already been absent the entire weekend is to show up, fall asleep at the desk, attempt to write and then be told to leave after filing illegible copy.

1 p.m.: Kamran is in his office. I run to the kitchen and procure two cups of tea as a peace offering. 'Oh, you're still alive,' Kamran says, as I balance the tea, my phone, cigarettes and lighter. 'Ha ha,' I say, setting the tea down on his desk. 'I got your e-mail,' he says, sipping his tea. 'Look, its fine if you want to take this elsewhere. I don't think we'll be able to publish it, which is sad. You did a good job getting the story.'

I'm speechless. I had a whole emotional blackmail spiel ready, which included the past five years of slavery for the greater cause of Kamran's paper. 'Thanks,' I say.

I yawn loudly and gulp my tea.

'So where'd you go this weekend? I heard through the office grapevine that you went to Dubai.'

'I did,' I say. 'Like every political leader in this country, I sought temporary relief in the malls and boulevards of the city.'

Kamran laughs. 'Well, you look exhausted. Might as well go home,' he says absently, staring at his computer screen.

I resist the urge to high five myself.

I go home and attempt to take a nap. Wake up twenty minutes later and lunge for my phone. There's still no reply from the editor.

And there's no reply from Jamie either. I double-check the Internet connection. It's still working. Why isn't anyone replying to my e-mails?! Did some major news story break in the time that I took a nap?

Nada.

I check Jamie's Facebook and Twitter. He hasn't updated either since we last spoke. I have no way of finding out if he's still in Karachi, other than calling his hotel. Or him. But no, that would be too desperate since it's only been six hours since I texted. Maybe I should give it half a day before I start to panic.

Now that the stress of the past few days is over, I can't stop thinking about Jamie. Why hasn't he called? Why can I never have a functional relationship with a non-troll like human being? Did leaving for the weekend make him forget about me?

And why did I not think about him in the last four days? Am I incapable of multi-tasking my emotions? Do stories matter more than sex? Or was I too busy having a good time with Saad and chugging bottles of wine to even think about Jamie?

Am I happier with Saad than I am with Jamie? Thinking of Saad—his retorts, his commentary about everyone walking by, the framed photo of us in his apartment—makes me smile.

My head is going to explode if I think about this any longer. I can't compare the two. Saad is my oldest friend, someone who I'm going to love unconditionally until the day I die. But the past few days have made me realize that while I love Saad, he won't always be around. He was hit on left, right and centre when we went out drinking, and I know he isn't starved for friends in Dubai. One of these days, he is going to get married or find a girl he really likes and then there won't be any more long weekends in Dubai eating buckets of fried chicken and wondering if there's any wine left.

Ooh, e-mails.

Crap. They're not from Jamie. I have five e-mails from Kamran.

E-mail 1: 'Your salary has been transferred.'

E-mail 2: 'Where are the stories I asked for?' Attached to the e-mail is a set of pitches I wrote six months ago that Kamran never replied to.

E-mail 3: 'We need someone in Larkana.'

E-mail 4: 'When are you going to Larkana?'

E-mail 5: 'Call me when you get these, I have your itinerary for Larkana.'

I call Kamran, and try to reason that I can't possibly be expected to leave tonight. I wish I could tell him the real reason: that I desperately need to figure out what's going to happen with Jamie. Kamran isn't buying my excuses. 'Ayesha, a few months ago you were begging me to send you anywhere. Now I need someone in Larkana to report on the election campaign there—I needed someone there yesterday—and if you don't want to go, there are five other reporters who can write just as well as you. Sania is producing a fantastic series of exclusive interviews, Shahrukh has the crime angle covered, and we've hired a new girl, Alina, who is going to report from Punjab. I don't pay you just so you can report on cupcake shop openings and fly off to Dubai whenever the fuck you want.'

The Golden Age of Kamran being kind and almost respectful has turned out to be a brief if wondrous thing. 'But Kamran, I don't even know who the candidates are! I'd really like to spend some time doing research and maybe line up a few interviews.' I manage to convince him that I can't leave before the next morning in any case as it's a seven hour drive and that's the only reasonable time to set out. 'And I still need to get a bus ticket, find a hotel to stay in, and arrange for a car or something.'

Miraculously, Kamran sees sense. I ask him what my budget will be for the hotel, hoping to stay somewhere nice and peaceful where I can get a comfortable night's sleep.

'It's ten thousand rupees. And non-negotiable. Make it work,' he says, as if I'm a contestant on *Project Runway* being forced to make a prom dress from bubble wrap.

Tuesday, April 12, 2012

Headline of the day:

5:30 a.m.: I've just set foot in the Geo Larkana bus and any excitement I felt at getting to cover the election is swiftly draining away. The seats are tiny, the windows are bolted shut, and I can already sense that the bus will not have a working fan or AC. I put my bag on my seat and jump off. 'When are we leaving?' I ask the conductor, who is counting out tickets.

'6 a.m.,' he says. 'We're not going to stop for food so you should get some tea or something.'

The bus depot is on a corner of a street in Saddar, in an old house bearing a sign that says 'Krishna Mahal—1922'. The occupants must have fled anticipating the bloody carnage that followed the partition of the subcontinent, like so many others did, abandoning their pristine havelis, which are now bus stands and low-budget motels. I sit down on one of the plastic chairs in the waiting area and the conductor walks in and shouts out, 'Basheer! Tea for baji here.'

A young boy careens in, holding a tray of cups. There's so much milk in the tea that it has already formed a skin on the surface, but I gulp it down anyway. 'Can you get me a newspaper?' I ask him, handing him a fifty-rupee note.

'Which one?' he says, tucking the note into his pocket. 'Oh, and don't put your feet on the ground, there's a rat behind you.'

I jump up and run to the gate. 'Baji, which newspaper?' the kid calls out. 'C'mon, I don't have all day.'

'A Sindhi paper,' I say, hoping the rat hasn't followed me outside.

8 a.m.: It takes me hours to read the paper, but by the end I'm rather proud of myself for remembering enough of the language from ninth grade to be able to do so. The bus drive isn't so bad. The driver's blaring some really catchy Sindhi music, and there's no one sitting next to me so I have more space, except the arm rest won't move so I'm going to have to rest my legs on that.

I recheck the notes Kamran has sent: I'm supposed to interview residents about who they'll be voting for, try to attend a rally or two and visit the Bhutto family mausoleum to see if I can dig up any stories on how it's being managed. Larkana is the Bhutto dynasty's home district, where they lived and worked, protested and rallied, faced house arrest and were mourned. There are four generations of the family buried in the nearby village of Garhi Khuda Bux. The last time I travelled to Larkana was for the funeral rites for Nusrat Bhutto, Benazir Bhutto's mother. The sight of her grave being dug next to those of her late husband and daughter and son had the entire press corps walking around with reddened eyes. That is, until a government minister fell into the open grave in a bid to be photographed 'at the scene'.

9 a.m.: Trying to nap. The volume of the stereo is a bit annoying though.

Noon: I need to get off this bus. Maybe I can just lie down in this rice field we're passing by.

2 p.m.: LARKANA!

2.10 p.m.: My legs won't move. Isn't it supposed to be bad for one's blood circulation to be sitting in one place for more than five hours? Try to walk and promptly fall over.

2.30 p.m.: This is my third trip to Larkana city in two years, and each time it seems filthier than before. The rickshaw driver is giving me a tour of the city as we make our way to the hotel. 'This is THE rice canal,' he says, gesturing grandly.

'What, this?' It's a murky stream with about twenty buffaloes in it, all looking rather askance at the lack of water.

All I want in life is to find this hotel and crash. I forgot how bad the traffic in Larkana is. Everyone drives like a maniac on speed. There are motorcycle drivers careening on and off the pavements with no one yelling after them to stick to the road. After about twenty minutes, I finally come face to face with the pink façade of the hotel, next door to a kebab roll establishment called 'Lick a Chick' with a couple of mournful looking chickens in a cage outside.

I trudge into the hotel lobby, which looks like it was designed with the Shish Mahal in mind. There are mirrors everywhere. Even the chairs are inlaid with mirrors. The bellboy and I walk up the stairs and he opens the door of the room.

It looks like a storeroom. Cobwebs hang from the fan. The bedspread is a lurid green, with a yellow blanket thrown on top and rose petals sprinkled across the pillows. I can hear the clucking of the chickens next door. 'If you use the AC, that's another thousand rupees per night,' the bellboy informs me. I can just imagine Kamran's face when I show him the hotel bill, so I open the windows and crank up the fan, shuddering as the cobwebs scatter over the yellow blanket.

The bathroom is surprisingly clean, but there's no cold water so after about five seconds, my skin feels like it's going to peel off from the boiling hot water. I look around for a TV. There isn't one. I open the cupboard. It looks like it was last used to store Miss Havisham's dress.

Oh well. There's nothing to do but sleep I suppose.

I haul myself out of bed at 7 a.m. and order a cup of tea. The waiter brings it in and looks disapprovingly at the overflowing ashtray.

After a scalding shower, I head downstairs and ask the manager how long it would take to get to Garhi Khuda Bux in a rickshaw. He laughs at first, and then goes to confer with someone. 'Oh, an hour,' he says. 'You really don't have a car?' I want to tell him that if I can't afford to pay for an air conditioned room, I definitely can't afford to be chauffeured around. My entire budget for this trip is less than the amount Kamran spends on a dinner for two on a weekend. I'm going to Garhi Khuda Bux to check on a widely criticized plan to close off access to the graves, and a rumour that the old caretaker who looked after the graves for years has been sacked.

I hail a Qingqi rickshaw—the ridiculous Chinese-made rickshaws that seat eight people but have barely any railings to hold on to. The teenaged driver is convinced he knows the way to Garhi Khuda Bux. I open up Google Maps on my phone, thankful that the scourge of cell phone robberies hasn't reached Larkana yet and one can still use one's phone as is done in the rest of the civilized world. The water in the rice canal looks even murkier. The buffaloes are looking especially despondent. I make a mental note to tell Kamran this when he grills me about the trip.

Twenty minutes later, we stop at a gas station. The only person there apart from the attendant is a biker. When we leave, Google Maps reassures me that we're on the right path, though I'm a tad concerned that we're driving through what looks like wilderness. Although the surrounding countryside is beautiful—acres and acres of rice fields that look incredibly glossy. There's the odd patch of sunflowers—real sunflowers!—and I ask the rickshaw driver to stop so I can take photos. I want to remind myself that there is beauty in this world. It feels bizarre to be on a road where there's no other vehicle in sight. Why can't Karachi be like this?

After a while, I finally see someone else on the deserted road. It's the biker from the gas station. If this were Karachi, I'd have tossed my cell phone to him in anticipation of a mugging. The rickshaw driver looks a little worried. 'Baji, he's following us.'

'Then can you speed up?' I say, hopefully.

He tries, but it turns out Qingqis don't go very fast. The biker follows us for about thirty minutes, as we drive on dirt roads through fields that I can't even focus on because I'm so scared. I wrap my dupatta tightly around myself and run through curse words in my head. Does this man have nothing else to do but follow me to Garhi Khuda Bux? I am convinced this is how I'm going to die. He's going to rape me and leave me for dead here, where the landowners' legendary dogs will consume my remains. Or this is the spy I'd been waiting for. He found out I've done the story and is here to haul me off to some detention centre from where I'll never be heard from again. 'Oh God,' I whisper, and begin reciting every half-forgotten Quranic verse I know. After what seems like years, we near the turnoff for Garhi Khuda Bux where there are a few more cars. CIVILIZATION! The motorcyclist suddenly turns back.

The rickshaw driver halts by the side of the road, gets off and kneels in relief. 'Baji, I thought we were dead, for sure. I didn't want to scare you before, but that man belongs to one of the dacoit gangs from a nearby village.'

I realize my clothes are drenched in sweat, even though it isn't even hot. I light up a cigarette and offer him one.

My legs still feel a bit clammy when I get off the rickshaw at the tomb gates. I open my wallet to pay the driver but he frantically shakes his head. 'No no, I could never take this. What if something had happened to you?' He drives off, leaving me standing there with a five hundred-rupee note in my hand.

I turn to look at the mausoleum, an imposing white structure which a Pakistani author once wrote is like the Disney version of the Taj Mahal. She's a total ditz and I cannot believe I actually agree with her on something, but the mausoleum is a bit Taj Mahal-esque in its design. And with its high ceilings and whirring fans, I could see myself getting a better night's sleep here than in my terrible hotel room. People walk in and out, clutching bags of flower petals to scatter on the graves. A few men kneel at Benazir's grave and start weeping.

After about two hours of interviews, I hitch a ride back with a bunch of women traveling to Larkana in a Qingqi rickshaw. At least there's some safety in numbers.

6 p.m.: I've just filed my story and am wondering what I'm going to do with the rest of the evening. I'm mentally preparing myself to brave a meal at Lick a Chick and eat one of those mournful chickens when there's a knock at the door. I open it expecting the bellboy bringing the ashtray I asked for.

It's not the bellboy. It's smarmy Ali from *News 365*.

What the hell is he doing here, and why is he at my door? God, I hope he's not here to deliver some bad news in the manner of the kindly army officer deputed to tell someone's parents that their son has died on the frontlines. Except, why would anyone depute Ali? I shake myself awake. 'Oh, hi. What are you doing here?'

'Oh, I'm here on assignment with NBC,' Ali says, fingering the ID badge around his neck. 'The hotel staff just told me another journalist from Karachi had checked in and I thought I'd come say hello, though I had no idea it was you.'

Ali is being surprisingly polite. This is weird.

'Well, yeah, I'm here for a few days. Good to see you.'

I'm about to close the door when Ali nervously coughs. 'So we've managed to bring in a fair bit of booze from Karachi,' he says. 'Do you want to have a drink with us?'

'We?' I ask. The look on my face must be one of frozen horror. 'Oh, sorry, I should have been clear. I'm here with my bureau chief from NBC, Andrea Altman. We're pretty much done for the day and I thought you might like a drink or at least a cup of coffee, if they can rustle one up in this hell hole.'

I'm about to say no, but then I contemplate a night spent trying to catch a breeze from the creaky, dusty ceiling fan while checking my phone to see if Jamie's called or the editor's gotten back to me about my story. This way I might at least get some gossip out of the evening and will have some gems to share with Zara. 'Sure,' I say.

I follow Ali up the corridor, which is even grimmer than my room. The walls are lined with cracked mirrors. It's borderline Dickensian. We walk into Ali's room. His bureau chief is angrily tapping away on her iPhone. 'Fuckers,' she mutters. 'Hi, I'm Andrea. It's so nice to see there's another woman here.'

The room is thrice the size of mine, and they haven't scrimped on the air conditioning. I plant myself on a chair.

'Beer?' Ali asks and I nod. 'I told Andrea that working in Sindh is intolerable without booze,' he says. I know what he means. It hasn't even been an hour since I returned to the hotel and I'm already quite prepared to drug myself to sleep with a bottle of cough syrup rather than face an evening of clucking chickens and the insane noise from the traffic.

A few hours and two beers later, I'm laughing hysterically at Andrea's stories. She's a really warm person, and is sarcastically commenting about life in Islamabad. 'And then the army chief turned to his brother—you know, the one who's a talk show host—and said "you're a fucking sell-out",' she says, recalling a dinner party she'd been to last weekend. 'Can you imagine? The entire room fell silent as the two bickered like schoolboys. And this is the head of the army!'

She asks me lots of questions about what it's like to work as a woman in a Pakistani newsroom, and what I think about political developments and the elections. Even Ali seems to have lost much of his smarminess in her company. 'So have you ever written abroad?' she asks. 'I just wrote my first piece, actually,' I say. 'It should be out soon. And I really want to freelance more, it's just that I haven't had much luck with pitching stories.'

'Well, keep at it,' Andrea says. 'The first piece is the most important, that should hopefully open more doors for you.'

I smile, and suddenly feel the exhaustion of the day wash over me. 'I should leave. Thank you so much for the really entertaining evening!'

'Anytime,' Andrea says. I politely excuse myself and head to my room to write to Zara about my evening. Halt in my tracks. There is a cockroach in the room. A flying cockroach. I can hear its wings flapping, oh fuck, it's making its way towards me. I slam the door shut and race down the stairs to ask one of the staff to help kill it. The hotel guard reluctantly follows me upstairs, stamps it with his slipper and gives me a pitying look.

CHAPTER 10

Thursday, April 15, 2012

Headline of the day: 'National assets can't be handed over to capitalists: Chief Justice'

8 a.m.: Walk into the house after three days in Larkana and want to set fire to all of my clothes. They're covered in dust. My shawl has been used as a face towel, a pillow, and a makeshift bed sheet to avoid catching lice from the hotel's linen. The cat is refusing to let me pet her. I clearly smell of desperation and despair. My phone ran out of battery before I even got on the bus for the cramped and bumpy seven-hour trip back and I have no idea what's going on in the world.

My father is running after the cat with two bowls of bite-sized chicken and sausages. 'Beta, please eat something. Just one bite.' Sometimes I wonder if my father really wanted another child and is living out his dream of being a typical Pakistani parent by stuffing the cat with food and being overly protective. The cat is not even allowed to go outside. Frankly, I have a feeling that she doesn't want to. My father can accurately tell when the cat is happy or depressed, yet has rarely noticed when his own daughter sneaks away with the entire icebox to drink away her problems.

I plug the phone in to the charger and about twenty minutes later, it comes back to life and starts beeping. I have a few missed calls, from Kamran and Zara, and one from Akbar, the cameraman who Jamie uses as a fixer. That's odd. Maybe he needs a favour or something.

I call him back. 'Oh, Ayesha, sorry, I was calling because I needed the number for this fashion designer Jamie wants to interview. I got it from the office anyway.'

'Wait, what? Are you still fixing for Jamie?'

'Yep, he's been in Karachi for the past two weeks, since fashion week. I'm so tired of this fixing crap, I swear I can't wait for him to leave. Is everything okay with you?'

'Yeah it is,' I say dazedly. 'Bye.'

Jamie is in Karachi. He never left. Which means that he has ignored my texts. Why? Should I call him? No, that'll make me seem like a jilted wife. I start dialing Saad's number but stop midway. What can Saad do? He doesn't even like Jamie. It's not like he can fly in from Dubai and force Jamie to reply to my messages.

I call Kamran back.

'Hi, I just got in,' I say. 'I'm not sure if I can come in today, I'm exhausted. I can file from home though...'

'That's not why I was calling. I thought you were doing this story on the Gitmo detainee for some website abroad.'

'Yeah, I did send it to them.'

'Ayesha, it's on the CNN website. Anyway, someone sent us an op-ed on this and I wanted to read the original so I looked it up. It sounds just like your story. Did you sell it to CNN?'

'CNN? What?' There's a strange, hot panic setting into my stomach.

'Yeah, Google it.'

I cut the call and run for my laptop.

I do a search for the detainee's name. About five hundred news stories pop up, all with variations of the headline 'Ex-Gitmo detainee speaks about torture'. One of them links back to CNN. I am going to call Jamie right now and ask him which chootiya did this story and how.

The byline makes me stop halfway through dialing. The CNN story is bylined 'James Maxwell, reporting from Karachi, Pakistan.'

I start to read. Two minutes later I feel physically ill.

The motherfucker stole my story. The interview isn't as good as mine—some of the quotes were lost in translation—but it's what the guy said. His entire life story—the one he told me, coughing and whispering, is here.

I check Twitter. The first twenty tweets on my timeline

are calling Jamie one of the best foreign correspondents to have worked in Pakistan. One NYT editor has tweeted that Jamie has a shot at a Pulitzer.

I sit on the floor. This isn't happening to me.

Check my e-mail. Surely Jamie has an explanation for this. There's just one e-mail, from the British editor. 'Sorry Ayesha, looks like you've been scooped by CNN. We won't be able to run this story after all. Quite unfortunate.'

I reach for a cigarette. There are none left in the box. And then I start to cry.

11 a.m.: My phone keeps ringing but I don't want to answer. There are only a handful of people who knew about the story, and I can't bear being pitied and the all-too-obvious attempts to make me feel better about my missed chance. Check my phone. Ten missed calls. Kamran. Kamran. Kamran. Oh shut the hell up. Kamran. Zara. Saad. Zara. Saad. A number I don't recognize.

What am I going to do? How am I going to explain this to Kamran? And why would Jamie do this to me? I need to know exactly how this happened. There is no way in hell he managed to steal my story. How did he even get in touch with the family?

I can't work up the strength to dial his number. I feel so…humiliated. And used. I try Saad, but he doesn't answer and sends me a text instead: 'In a meeting. Call you when I get out of here.' I sigh and call Zara, the only person I can fathom talking to right now.

I rant and rave, sobbing between gulps of Diet Coke.

I can't even afford to drown my sorrows in a grown-up drink.

'I am such a cliché: white man comes to Pakistan, befriends local, steals her due right. It's like the bloody East India Company all over again.'

'Ayesha, it'll be fine,' Zara says. 'Look, I know we say this all the time, but it is just a story, and there'll be more. We're in Pakistan, for the love of God, there's always someone blowing themselves up. And look, he's just another guy. It's not as if you'll never meet anyone again.'

'Do you think I should call him?' I ask, wiping my nose with my shirt. I've even run out of tissues. 'NO,' Zara yells. 'But if you really want to find out, why don't you ask the guy's son how this happened?'

That's an idea. I hang up and start scrolling through my phone book when I spot Akbar's number. If Akbar did the interview with Jamie, he would know how it was set up, and it'll spare me the awkwardness of having to ask the detainee's son the details.

I clear my throat and call. 'Akbar bhai, hiiii,' I say, trying to sound relaxed, like nothing has happened. I don't know if he'll end up repeating my conversation to Jamie. 'I just wanted to say congratulations on the story! How'd you pull it off?'

'Oh, thanks,' Akbar replies, sounding a bit surprised. I imagine no one has called to congratulate him, since the attention must be on Jamie. 'It was Jamie's idea. He has really good sources. He heard the guy was living in Karachi.

So I tried a few people, but no one would confirm. Then I called a few intelligence wallahs and finally someone told me where he was living.'

'Acha, how nice,' I say.

'Why are you asking?' Akbar says. 'Do you want to do the same story?'

'Sorry Akbar bhai, I have to go, the office is calling me,' I hurriedly say, and disconnect the call before he puts two and two together.

So that's how Jamie did it. How could I have been so stupid as to give Jamie a heads up on such a fantastic story? And how could I HAVE SLEPT WITH HIM?!?

I finally answer one of Kamran's calls. He doesn't bother with saying hello. 'What happened, Ayesha? I thought you were publishing this story, and then we'd carry it later. What is going on?'

'I don't know,' I tell Kamran. A fresh wave of tears is bubbling up inside me. 'Do you mind if I take a couple of days off?'

'What? Why?'

'I'm a bit unwell,' I say. Actually, no, I'm not going to make up excuses anymore. 'I'd like some time off to think.'

'No.'

'Kamran, I've never asked you for more than a day off at a time. Please.'

'Okay, then,' Kamran says. How has he caved in so quickly? 'E-mail me a leave application.'

I call Zara back to continue my rant but she cancels the

call and then texts that she's out on a work assignment. Of course, the entire world is out and about and doing productive things. I'm still sitting on the floor, unable to process what just happened. Why did Jamie even flirt with me in the first place, if he was planning to screw me over afterwards? Or could he not believe his luck that a naïve girl would drop her sari and a gem of a story at the same time?

The British editor's 'quite unfortunate' e-mail keeps circling in my head. No one will ever commission me to do a story again. The editor probably thinks I am an idiot. This was my one shot at getting ahead in life, of landing more commissions, of maybe even securing a fellowship or a job abroad. Instead, I am still here, stuck in Karachi. And I never want to date again. This is it. I will be single forever, the drunk old auntie who kids hate at parties because they keep making them refill their drinks and fetch ice. I'll be that girl who everyone invites to dinners out of pity because I am unloved and broke.

I try to seek refuge online. Bad idea. The bloody story is everywhere. It's on Facebook—even my great-aunt in South Africa has just posted a link to it—my Twitter feed is a nauseating love fest for Jamie, and at least five friends have e-mailed me the story. I turn on the TV to find a news anchor discussing the article in excruciating detail.

I cannot help but remember a story I read about a man who believed he was allergic to wireless devices and the Internet and decided to go live in a forest in the UK. I wonder if I could go join him in his tree, because there is no escape from Jamie and how betrayed I feel.

10 p.m.: Doorbell. It's Zara, clutching a brown paper bag.

'I got paid and went straight to the wine shop,' she says, as she gingerly steps around the ashtray and Diet Coke bottles strewn around the room, and my bag of laundry from Larkana, which I haven't even bothered to toss into the hamper yet. 'Get some glasses, let's open this up.'

She unveils a bottle of Murree Brewery's blue-tinted gin. 'That stuff tastes like nail varnish,' I point out. 'Whatever, it's booze,' Zara says as she pours out two measures. 'Now tell me why you're so upset over a story.'

'It's not just a story,' I say, and take a huge gulp of the gin. It burns my throat and whatever's left of my stomach given my diet of chilli chips, Diet Coke, and whiskey. 'I thought Jamie and I were in a relationship. I feel so betrayed.'

'Ayesha, do you hear yourself? You sound like one of those women on a morning talk show, sobbing their hearts out because they gained twenty kilos and their husbands went and married their teenage neighbour. I have never seen you like this. You're the one who actually has more common sense than everyone else. You're usually my voice of reason. For the love of god, it's just a guy who clearly is a grade-A chootiya. You're better off not being with someone who doesn't give a fuck about you or your career. Does he realize how he's really screwed you over?'

'How would I know?' I say. 'I haven't called him. Should I call him?'

'I'll tell you,' she growls, and grabs my laptop. Five minutes later, I'm staring at Jamie's tweets—about a hundred of them thanking everyone individually for their praise. I scroll down. There's even a mention of Akbar, and how he's the best fixer Jamie has ever worked with, but nothing about me, the person who gave him the story that is going to turn his career around and put him in the running for a dozen awards.

'See,' Zara takes the laptop back from me and slams the lid down. 'He is such a lying asshole.'

'Now forget about this, and let me tell you what happened at today's presser.' Zara launches into a long story about a politician's ex-wife who turned up at the press club to reveal a list of all of his secret bank accounts and how much money he'd siphoned away in twenty years. I can't stop thinking about Jamie and the story and how it could have changed my career. The gin is making me feel queasy and Zara's upbeat tone is giving me a headache. 'Zara, would you mind terribly if I asked you to leave?' I start. 'I should probably get some sleep, I just got back from Larkana this morning and then this entire drama began.'

'Oh, sure,' she says, looking a bit put out. 'I'm sorry,' I say, trying to mollify her. 'It's just that I'm exhausted and I shouldn't have had the gin.'

Zara's gathering up her handbag when her phone rings. She looks puzzled by the phone display. 'Oh, hi Saad,' she says, and hands it to me. 'He wants to talk to you.'

I take the phone from her and say hello. 'I've been trying to call you but clearly you've turned your phone on silent. Can you talk now?'

'Sure,' I say resignedly. I don't really feel like discussing Jamie with Saad. He will remind me that he had warned me against Jamie and thought he was a chootiya. But then again, Saad is my best friend. Surely he'll understand how heartbroken I am. 'Just call me back in five.'

Zara takes the phone back from me. 'You know, Saad really cares about you. He wrote me an e-mail this morning too.'

'Really?' I say, suddenly remembering that Saad thinks Zara is hot and wanted me to set them up. Clearly he's decided to take a shot at it himself.

'He wanted to know if you were okay, and actually asked me to come over and check on you. I know he's your friend, but the guy's such a sweetheart even though he acts like he's completely together and with it. That's the kind of guy you should be with.'

'What?' The thought of Saad and me together is... hmm. I inject the same tone of outrage in my voice that I normally do when someone hints at this. 'No, not Saad, OF COURSE NOT!'

'Calm down,' she says. 'I didn't mean the two of you, just someone like him. Or him, you know?'

'NO!' I say, and she holds her hands up. 'Fine, fine, I'm leaving now anyway. We'll talk tomorrow, just message me when you feel up to human company and I'll be around.'

I look for my phone. Where is it? Has it decided to desert me as well? Suddenly I see a flash of light under the cat. She is asleep on top of my phone. Whoever said cats had amazing reflexes and could detect earthquakes and what not needs to meet my cat, who can't tell that there's a phone ringing underneath her belly.

Nudge the cat. She growls and moves about an inch away. I slide the phone out from under her. Thankfully Saad hasn't given up dialling my number, so I don't have to call him back and hit my phone limit in five minutes.

'Hey,' Saad says. His voice is so low and hushed that I'm concerned he's sick. 'Do you have the flu?' What's wrong with his voice? Why does he sound like this? This is the kind of voice I last remember Saad using when we were in college and he would call me up in the middle of the night, dialling from under the covers so his mother wouldn't hear him talking on the phone when he was supposed to be studying. There's a long pause.

'Hello?'

'No, just a bit tired,' Saad eventually says. 'It's been a long day, but Jesus, Ayesha. I got an e-mail from my friend about the story, asking if this was the same one that you wanted to pitch and he was really confused about what happened. I got called into a meeting and I only got to my laptop two hours later. Then I read Jamie's story. What happened? Did you end up giving it to him to use?

I repeat my tale of how I told Jamie about the story,

how helpful and kind and encouraging he had been and then Akbar and the tweets and that no, he had not been in touch. 'I knew the asshole wasn't good news the minute I saw him at that party,' Saad says. I can imagine him sitting in his apartment, staring out the window at the gorgeous Dubai skyline, his jaw set with anger. Saad rarely shouts. 'I wish I had kicked him out of the party that night.'

'It's not your fault,' I say. 'I should've been smarter.'

'How are you?' I love Saad for not asking me if I was 'okay'.

'I've been crying all day.'

'I can imagine. Did Jamie call you to explain? Do you know what happened?'

'No. And then what's worse, the editor from the UK told me he couldn't use the story anymore. I am such a failure, Saad. You went to all of this effort for me, introducing me to your friend, and now I've completely lost my chance. All because I thought this amazing guy was into me and there was nothing wrong with telling him about a story.'

'You shouldn't think this way,' Saad says. 'I mean, you told him because you thought he was your boyfriend, someone you could trust.'

'I suppose you can't trust anyone.'

'No, just not assholes. Look, I wish I could be there but I can't leave work just now. I'll call you tomorrow, but listen, don't sit there and feel miserable all day. I mean, sure, it's you and you'll do that for a couple of hours but just don't cry all day. I don't want to think of you being alone.'

'Thanks,' I say. 'Do you realize you've made the "don't cry all day" call to me about once every year since we've met? Don't cry about your exam results, don't cry about your job, don't cry about some boy.'

'I love you.'

'Me too,' I say, and cancel the call. How is it that this conversation is making the sinking feeling in my stomach worse?

Friday, April 16, 2012

Headline of the day: 'MQM sends haleem and nihari to the prime minister'

8 a.m.: Wake up from a horrible night of tossing and turning. Every time I fell asleep I'd be jolted awake by a booming voice in my head reminding me JAMIE STOLE YOUR STORY, YOUR LIFE IS OVER, AND YOU THOUGHT YOU WERE IN LOVE, HA HA.

I can't take it anymore. Decide to go lie down in the cat's room. She smacks me for trying to put my feet up next to her.

Check my e-mail. There's nothing but a few memos from work, reminding people that they can't use the stairs between 2 and 8 p.m. because they're being retiled again. The last time the stairs were redone Kamran insisted on

Italian marble because he wanted to impress visitors, but then one of the office staffers slipped and dropped about twenty cups of hot tea.

I have given up on ever checking Twitter or Facebook again. The story is still being posted incessantly.

Dad walks in, looking slightly abashed. 'Ayesha, are you home today? Can you go to the mall? I broke the French press.'

I grudgingly change clothes and head out. The mall is so peaceful on a weekday. It's almost wondrous. Everything looks new and gleaming, screaming out 'try me', 'touch me', 'buy me'.

It's a wonderful thing to have your father's debit card.

Armed with bags, I settle down at the mall's only open-air café to have a cigarette. Someone is playing the soundtrack of my favourite film, *Jab We Met*.

Someone taps me on the shoulder and I jump up. 'What?'

It's Andrea, Ali's boss. I met her three days ago but it already feels like a lifetime ago. 'Oh hello, sorry about that, I'm just a bit jumpy these days.'

'No problem,' she says. 'Would you like to join me for coffee?'

'Of course,' I drag all of my bags to her table. She looks bemused. 'My father sent me out to buy a French press and I got a bit carried away.'

'Ah,' she says, and sips her coffee.

We sit in silence for a bit. I'm not quite sure why we're

hanging out given she doesn't seem to have anything to say to me. I pray to god she's not using me as a character in a story about how Karachiites are obsessed with consumerism or some such. 'So did you read this story James Maxwell did on CNN?'

'Yeah,' I say, stirring the coffee a bit manically. It's sloshing out of the cup and onto the saucer now. I don't quite trust myself to not start crying again.

'What did you think of it?'

'It would have been great had it been his own story,' I retort. Fuck. Why did I say that? She's probably best friends with Jamie. She probably thinks I am a bitter Pakistani hating on foreigners.

To my surprise, she starts laughing. 'Of course it wasn't,' she says. 'You know I worked with him once? Guy had a reputation for stealing stuff from others. My editor found out and fired him. He has a really bad reputation with fixers in Lebanon too.'

'Really?' Jamie had come across as this hard core correspondent who was completely committed to his work. I should have listened to Saad, damn it.

'So who did he steal this one from?' Andrea asks.

'Err, me,' I say. She sits up. 'How?'

'I told him that I was interviewing the detainee, but he never let on that he was interested in the story. Then I went to Larkana and came back to discover he'd dug out a contact for the guy and had interviewed him.'

'I see,' she says, looking thoughtful. 'That is terrible. It was clearly a great scoop. Didn't your editor do anything?'

An image of Kamran perusing the Chairman Mao menu with steely-eyed intensity pops into my head. 'No. And I pitched it to someone else in the UK but the commission didn't work out because CNN ran it first.'

'That is quite sad. Tell me again, what kind of stories do you usually focus on? I remember in Larkana you were talking about gangs and their political wings.'

'Yep,' I say. 'I do pretty much everything, you know what it's like in a newspaper, but I'm really interested in reporting more deeply on gang violence, as well as religious movements.'

We end up discussing our own experiences with covering religious parties in Pakistan. She's a bit surprised to hear that I've spent a lot of time hanging out at rallies. 'And they're fine with you? I mean, you're a young girl.'

I don't know how to explain to her how long it took for me to gain anyone's trust, the days I spent at protests covering stories and writing copy that never made it into the paper, the mad guy on the bike chasing me to Garhi Khuda Bux or the Sipah-e-Sahaba spokesperson who wouldn't look me in the eye but called me at midnight to 'chat'. I've never really considered any of these things to be the worst part of my job.

'I suppose. They're still a bit suspicious, but that's to be expected because they clearly know that I don't adhere to any of their ideologies.'

'You know, I may have some work for you,' Andrea

says, and reaches for her iPhone. 'I just got this e-mail from a former colleague of mine, who now works at *Al Jazeera* in New York. They're looking for someone to contribute to their website from Pakistan and they wanted me to recommend someone.'

'Oh, thanks. You really don't have to.'

Andrea waves her phone in the air. 'Of course I do. It's such a pity about James stealing your story and honestly, I have long found the man to be a parasite. I'm really glad you told me about this.'

I give Andrea my e-mail address and phone number, and she dashes off an e-mail introducing me to the editor. 'A piece of advice,' she says, as she calls for the check. 'Use this opportunity wisely. It could potentially lead to something bigger. And never tell James about a story ever again!'

She walks off. The last twenty-four hours of my life have been the most bizarre experience. How did I go from joy to crushing sadness to optimism in just a day?

I spend the evening exchanging e-mails with the *Al Jazeera* editor, who appears to be really excited about me contributing. We decide on four stories and when she tells me how much she'll be paying me for each, I nearly keel over. Why have I never considered freelancing before?

6 p.m.: Call from Zara's brother Imad. I answer it, wondering why he's calling me. Maybe he wants to throw a surprise party for her or something.

It's not Imad. It's just someone crying hysterically. I'm going to cancel the call when I hear, 'Ayeshaaaa.'

'Zara? Is that you? What's wrong?'

'What's wrong? Well, I bloody well got mugged, that's what's wrong.'

'Shit. Okay. I'll be right over.'

I get to her house to find Imad pacing the foyer. 'She's in the lounge,' he says, 'She's really shaken up.'

Zara has stopped crying, but I can see where her tears have cut tracks through her make-up. Her cropped hair is all mussed up.

'I'm so sorry Zara, what happened?'

'Oh Ayesha, you know how we always tell people that muggings are just part of life in Karachi and they should either move on or move out?' Zara is twisting a tissue and shredding it into bits.

'Err, yeah,' I say, trying to figure out whether she's in shock or just upset.

'Yeah, I'm never saying that again. It's so horrible when it happens to you.'

'So what happened? Where were you? They didn't hit you or anything, right?' Memories of friends telling me that they'd been smacked across the face with a gun are flashing through my head.

'No, no, they were just really frantic. I'd gone to the market to buy some fresh juice and was at the signal to turn towards the house when two teenage boys—you know, really young, they were barely 18—came out of nowhere and started tapping on the window with their guns. So I rolled the window down, and they just started

SCREAMING. "Give us your phone, give us your phone". So I obviously handed it over…and then they wanted money, so I took out my wallet—hai, Ayesha, I'd only just bought it from Charles & Keith—but they kept screaming "more, more".'

'So then?'

'Well, then I gave them my handbag but they still kept screaming! That fucking signal wouldn't turn green, it's like I was frozen in time with these two boys just asking me for things.'

'Oh you poor thing,' I say, handing her a glass of water. 'What did you do?'

'Well, I had picked up booze from Anil this morning but I never got around to taking it out of the car so it was in the glove compartment. I took the bottle of whiskey out and gave it to them.'

I'm trying not to laugh. Zara got mugged, this is horrible, but who has ever handed over alcohol during a mugging?

'But they kept saying "give us everything", and the only thing I could see in front of me was the falsa juice I'd just bought from the market, so I just shoved the bag at them and then the signal turned green and they ran away, clutching my bright pink bag, the whiskey I spent three thousand rupees on, and falsa juice.'

I can't hold the laughter in anymore. I giggle and Zara looks at me like I'm crazy. 'So, you basically gave them a new wallet with money, booze, and mixers?'

Zara starts laughing too. 'Yeah, it is kind of funny isn't it?'

'Those boys must be having such a party tonight,' I say, and that sets Zara off. She's laughing hysterically and then eventually flops back on the sofa. 'God, I really needed to laugh. I just couldn't believe what was happening to me. And then Imad wants me to go to the cops—what am I going to tell them, that I basically handed over booze?'

Saturday, April 18, 2012

Headline of the day: 'Taliban gift car to militant who shot at a drone'

Woken up by a call from a woman who describes herself as Kamran's PA. Kamran has an assistant now? What happened to him using the first staffer he could find in the office to order his lunch, track down his missing notebooks, and write his e-mails? 'This is Meher,' the woman informs me. 'Kamran sahib would like to see you in the office today for your appraisal.'

We have appraisals?!?

There's a crowd of people gathered outside Kamran's office. One reporter is clutching printouts of all his stories from the past year. 'What is this?' I ask. 'Who knows,' one of the sub-editors pipes up. 'This has been going on for two days. The receptionist said she overheard the HR

191

manager's driver telling Kamran's guard that they would lay off 10 percent of the staff. How am I going to pay for my trip to Thailand if Kamran fires me?'

When my turn comes, Kamran first asks me to explain what happened with the story. I am so tired of repeating the gory details, but I go ahead anyway. 'Right,' he says. 'Well, that was no reason to take time off work but whatever.

'So, the last year... what do you think you've achieved in the last six months?'

I am so unprepared for this. I can't think of a single story I've done. 'I've helped contribute significantly to our coverage of events,' I say. 'And I've spent a lot of time researching timelines etc., you know, the kind of stuff you wanted to enhance our coverage.' What is wrong with me? Surely I can think of something better to say.

'Exclusives?' Kamran says, writing something down. I rack my brains. 'I did do the story on sexual harassment involving the government official, and I also had a few exclusive interviews from the winter round of rallies. We were the only English paper to interview Hafiz Saeed. We had exceptionally good coverage of last month's rape case.'

'Acha,' Kamran says. 'Look Ayesha, I personally admire you a great deal...'

Oh no. This sounds ominous.

'...but I can't really make a case for you getting a raise this year. And I think you need to evaluate your own contribution to the paper. You seem more interested in doing stories on religion but you know we're an English language paper, and most of our readers think anyone with a beard is a militant. It doesn't sell. You insist on doing stories that will get us into trouble with the establishment. Do you know how many times I've had calls from the ISI after your work has been published?'

'I'm not quite sure what you mean by doing anti-establishment stories. Really. Explain this to me.'

'There's no need to be so defensive,' Kamran says. 'I just said evaluate your own work. And I can get a sub-editor to make timelines too.'

'But this is what you assigned me to do,' I say. 'You were the one who made me do this. I'd be ready to go cover something and you'd tell me to stay back and research the back story. And I did bring you an exclusive that you shot down and is now making headlines worldwide.'

'If you're so unhappy, why don't you leave? Make my life easier.'

I can't believe this. I gave five years of my life to Kamran. I once sorted through the debris of a cinema that had been bombed to find documents that might have survived the flames. I had cockroaches running over my hands when I finally found a sheaf of documents listing all the celebrities who had supported the cinema. Six lean months and he's letting me go? I have ten thousand rupees in the bank. What am I going to do?

'Sure,' I say. 'I'll have my resignation to you in an hour.

It really was quite a pleasure working with you.'

'No, no, Ayesha, that's not what I meant,' Kamran says. 'I don't want you to leave.'

'Why? I'm sure someone else will order your cappuccino. Best of luck teaching them how to spell the word.'

I storm out. The group of people outside his office seems frozen. 'What happened?'

'I'm leaving,' I say. 'Best of luck.' I head to my computer, and thank god that I had the foresight to back up my work on to my e-mail the last time I had to come in to work on a Sunday, when I knew the IT department wouldn't be there and tracking my every move. I send Kamran a terse e-mail, copy HR and in a fit of spite, write that I will not be serving notice in lieu of vacation time. There's nothing of any value on my desk. I run up the stairs and wave to the receptionist as I open the doors. 'Leaving so soon?' he asks.

'Not soon enough,' I retort.

It's raining outside—how bizarre for this time of the year—and I stop for a second to think about what I've just done. At the back of my mind, I know that my behaviour is entirely irresponsible and completely out of character for me. You're in shock, Ayesha, you've had a bad week and you've just thrown away your one chance at a stable income. I'm about to turn back when I remember the cockroaches and the condescension in Kamran's voice, and the number of holidays and Eids and Saturday nights I spent at work. Fuck Kamran and fuck this job. I have a potential Al Jazeera story, a bunch of great ideas, and hundreds of contacts, including a guy who claims to know an entire gang of contract killers. I'll be fine.

CHAPTER 11

Headline of the day: 'City wears anti-dengue look'

3 p.m.: The rain accompanying my defiant stomp out of the office gives the whole event the effect of an emo video. Within a minute and a half the street, with its rubbish clogged drains, has started to fill up with rainwater, which is now lapping at the pavement. Attempt to flag down a rickshaw as it speeds past me without the driver so much as looking in my direction. One rickshaw stops. 'Can you take me to...' I start. 'No, can't go there,' the driver says before I even get to the end of the sentence. Manage to flag down a cab, which stalls just as it nears the curb. The driver gets out, kicks the cab and starts pushing it to the side. 'MOVE, MOTHERFUCKER!' shrieks a tanker driver leaning out of his window. 'DON'T YOU KNOW HOW TO MOVE A FUCKING CAR?'

As always, everyone's left their offices before the first

drop of rain even hit the ground, turning the streets into a nightmarish, apocalyptic scene with buses, rickshaws, and cars caught up in a snarl, the sound of motorcycles backfiring booming like a hundred little bomb blasts.

In spite of this, the rain always brings on the romantic 'oh such beautiful weather, want to dance in the rain' Facebook statuses. I'm going to hit the next person who says they love the rain. I expect it's pleasurable if you're rich and can enjoy it from the comfort of your four-wheel behemoth while singing along to *November Rain* on the radio, played by all the stations even if it is raining in bloody April.

3.30 p.m.: Finally spot a rickshaw that's empty. Hurl self inside and beg the driver to take me home.

'That will be three hundred rupees,' he says, adding, 'it's raining,' in case I hadn't noticed, or in case I missed it as I sat back against the rickshaw's wet plastic seats.

5.30 p.m.: After two hours in traffic and a near crash with a motorcyclist and a bewildered cow, we finally get to my neighbourhood. The rickshaw driver takes one look at the flooded lane and refuses to go any further. I get off and stand on the muddy pavement. A kindly old man is setting up a mini obstacle course that involves gingerly stepping on tyres, concrete blocks, and what appears to be an old billboard instead of wading through the ankle-deep water that is surely infested with snakes. Kindly Old Man for office, I say.

An hour later, I'm dry and sitting in the dark staring

out of the window. The utility company shuts down the power the minute it starts raining, hoping to avoid fatalities caused by electrocution, so now one just has to worry about things like falling down the stairs in the dark and breaking one's neck instead.

It occurs to me that I have absolutely nothing to do—no stories to file, no timelines to research, no violent religious extremists to interview. The excitement of having finally told Kamran to shove it is slowly being replaced by severe trepidation. Make that out and out terror. My stomach somersaults every time I think of my 'savings', i.e. the contents of my current account.

Oh my god, I'm going to be the 28-year-old who needs to ask her father for money to pay her phone bill. I have become the culmination of the disappointed look he gave me when I didn't pursue a corporate job. Speaking of which, how does one go about getting another job anyway? The thought of having to work for fourteen hours a day and grovel before some new Kamran-like editor is horrifying. The thought of sitting at home eating daal roti and not being able to afford coffee at Espresso is equally dreadful.

A photo of me on the dresser, taken when I was eighteen and still had some hope in life, is staring at me. Eighteen-year-old me, who hadn't started smoking yet and still thought she had years to lose weight is telling me, 'You're a failure. You've done nothing in the past—jeez—ten years.' Am I now going to turn into a crazy person who talks to a portrait? Perhaps I have taken after my distant aunt who, according to family lore, 'fell in love with the sun' when she was sixty and spent the rest of her days lying on a charpoy in the courtyard talking to a fiery blob in the sky.

Must not panic. I'm a great reporter. I can make this work. I was born to do this. This isn't a setback, this is an opportunity.

The rain's stopped and there's suddenly total silence. The cat, who was trying to chase raindrops on the wrong side of the window, is taking a nap. Why is it so quiet? Is my phone not on? Check phone and realize why. My work e-mail account has been suspended and so my phone hasn't beeped incessantly with the six dozen e-mails that would have arrived in my inbox by this point.

The electricity suddenly comes back on. But for the first time in years, I don't have to leap at the laptop to check what I missed. I may never have to check the news ever again. My life lies ahead of me, suddenly feeling like a really, really tediously long time.

Ooh, phone. It's Zara. 'Hey, did you call? Was stuck in bloody traffic for an hour and my phone ran out of battery.'

'Yep. So listen, I resigned.'

'You what? Jeez, I think there's some water in my phone. Fucking rain.'

'No, I RESIGNED.'

'What. The. Hell.'

The next hour is spent rehashing the entire saga with Zara on the phone. She curses, I sigh. We plot revenge against Kamran. 'I mean, Ayesha, what are you going to do now?'

'No idea,' I say, aimlessly switching television channels. An earnest young cleric is demonstrating how to make a pumpkin milkshake on a religious programming channel. There's a repeat of *Humsafar*. Instead of turning into sun-obsessed aunt, will I spend my days watching TV and lying on the sofa while everyone else goes out and makes money? There's an ad for a gated community in Dubai and I suddenly sit up. I need to tell Saad. After Zara promises to drop in with an aid package made up of Anil's finest wares I start dialling Saad, but I feel exhausted.

I don't have the energy to sit through another phone conversation about what I'm going to do with my life. I write him a short e-mail instead, promising that I'll send more details when I feel up to it.

My father comes home and is surprised at seeing me home before 7 p.m. 'Did you get off early?' he asks, between wringing out water from his jacket and trying not to trip over the cat who is winding herself around his legs.

Consider lying about why I'm home rather than telling my father that I am an enormous failure and furthermore now unemployed and planning to live off him for the unforeseeable future. Take a deep breath, my stomach full of the same nerves I had when I had to tell him years ago that I was failing Calculus. 'I actually quit my job today,' I say, stammering slightly.

'Oh, well that's okay beta.'

'You're fine with this?' How is this possible? My father has never advocated quitting. If he had, I would've left business school after the first semester.

'Of course I am. In fact, I have been worried about you for quite a while. You were clearly very unhappy,' my father says, as the cat yowls, hoping to get his attention. 'You were always tired, you didn't eat well, and I don't say anything because you don't listen, but you were drinking too much.'

I can feel my eyes welling up. 'Are you disappointed in me?'

He gets up and hugs me. 'In my brave, hardworking daughter? Of course not, beta. Your happiness is the most important thing to me.' I'm so moved, I can't even look at him. I look down.

'This means that I won't be getting paid for a while...' I don't quite know how to say that I have absolutely no savings and will need to ask him for money to pay the bootlegger and buy cigarettes.

'Beta, money doesn't matter. Just tell me how much you'll need every month, and don't worry about anything.'

'I don't know why you fret, you've always been my favourite daughter,' my father says. I feel an enormous lump in my throat and turn to him with watery eyes. He's talking to the cat who is gazing up at him adoringly.

8 p.m.: My father's reassurances aside, my stomach is still twisted into knots. I'd always imagined striking out on my own, but not after having a messy fight with my

boss and walking out with no backup options. Spend the rest of the evening in and out of a cold sweat wondering why I didn't have anything at all lined up before flouncing out of the *Daily News*. My heart feels heavy, and my breath keeps catching in my throat. I know I need to cry and get this out of my system. It feels like I've failed at everything. For years, I've focused all of my energy and time on my career because trying to work at relationships with douchebags like Hasan just didn't seem to make sense. But now, nothing seems right. I couldn't stop myself from liking Jamie, who unlike Hasan, actually seemed to understand the kind of life I led. But I couldn't do anything when the fucker stole my story and ruined my life. I try to envision scenarios where I somehow exact a delicious revenge.

Yeah, right, Ayesha. You're going to bring down a beloved CNN correspondent. Even if he is a chootiya.

Text. Perhaps it's Zara coming over with some booze? Or Kamran begging me to come back to work with the lure of a massive pay rise?

'Married or Getting Married Soon?

Introducing Men-Taur, Ultra Men Power!

Complete Herbal Cure for treating Erectile Dysfunction, Enhance stamina & timing for sexual satisfaction with zero side-effects.'

Fuck my life.

11 p.m.: As I'm going to sleep, I get an e-mail from Saad. It's a photo of us at a club in Dubai, taken late at

night after we had just downed a couple of tequila shots. The lighting must have been really good, I think, looking at how my skin is glowing and how happy I seem. Saad looks more relaxed than I've seen him in years. We look really good together, I think. No. I'm just letting Zara's comment from the other day get to me. Must sleep before I start obsessing about this.

Sunday, April 19, 2012

Headline of the day: 'Tomato goes out of reach'

The next morning, I wake up feeling better. How is this possible? Realize it is the first time in years I haven't set an alarm and my phone hasn't beeped all night long with incoming work e-mails. I've slept through the night. I haven't woken up with a feeling of dread at the prospect of another day at work, chasing someone down for an interview and competing with a dozen reporters for the same story.

I suppose I can always ask Zara to get me an interview at *Morning*. Surely there's some job at a TV channel that won't involve me having to interview people to find out how they feel about the price of tomatoes.

Or I could always get a job at one of the dozens of magazines that specialize in publishing photos of parties and socialites. I did put in a few weeks interning for a lifestyle magazine when I was twenty-one. Sure, it was mind numbing but would it be so bad to get paid for writing captions such as 'Pinky and Pepsi take in a lawn exhibition'? Am looking through my e-mail to see if I still have the contact information for the magazine editor when I come across the press release she sent me to edit that almost put me off journalism altogether.

'Ali Ansari (Intoxicated)

One of the busy famous fashion personalities, Ali is getting fame day by day both at national level and at international level.

He is a very intelligent and hard working fashion designer. His fashion collection really clicks someone aesthetic sense, especially those who have good fashion sense. Ali always try to give some unique and classic touch to his work, Although he is already admired and appreciated by many fashion personalities, especially on his latest 'intoxicated' collection but still Saim want to design something extravaganza.

He gets lots of inspiration from his mother and wants her to be with him forever, his mother was also a fashion designer.

Ali is a man who loves challenges and he is on the view that we have to survive in all type of circumstances.'

Surely if Ali can have survived his circumstances, so can I.

5 p.m.: I'm in a park in Lyari, having tea with Zafar Baloch after finishing my interview for the *Al Jazeera* story.

'We're just social workers, political workers, you know?' he says, as the sunlight flashes off his iPhone and massive gold ring. I hope my face isn't registering my amusement at this. Zafar's rap sheet is a thing of legend— he's accused of about a hundred murders.

In the years since I was first introduced to him at a rally, he's grown from being a figure on the sidelines to the second-in-command of a criminal syndicate.

Zafar is now regaling me and a coterie of his guards—a bunch of skinny boys in their teens with guns draped around them—with a story about the latest politician who showed up at his office asking for a favour.

The government has just announced a ten million rupee reward for his capture and every week without fail, a foreign correspondent flies in to Karachi to do an 'exclusive' interview with him. Zafar now has a press team, and the spokesperson laughs while telling us about the latest guy who came looking for a story. 'He wanted us to show him where we keep our weapons!' he says, and everyone sniggers.

'I told him we don't have guns here, only for our own protection,' Zafar adds, patting his pocket. There's a sniper on the roof of the building next door, two guys are keeping guard near the park gate and for all I know, there are guns buried underneath the table.

'You know this latest gora reporter who showed up, he said, "Have you ever shot someone?" I mean we get some real idiots, but this guy was really bad,' the spokesperson chimes in. 'Honestly, I felt bad for poor Akbar who was translating.'

'Akbar?' I suddenly sit up. 'Who was the guy?'

'Some CNN guy,' the spokesperson says, and hands me a plate of biscuits. 'Eat.'

So Jamie has been here, which means he is *still* in Karachi and *still* hasn't bothered to tweet, call, WhatsApp, text, or e-mail any kind of explanation or apology. My state of calm—induced by seven hours of sleep and the post-deluge overcast sky—is slowly dissipating. I don't want to feel so much rage at Jamie, but the urge to get one of Zafar's boys to rough him up is overpowering. Or perhaps I can ask Zafar to call Jamie here so I can scream my lungs out and finally be able to tell him to his face that he is an asshole who doesn't even deserve to work as a delivery boy, let alone a correspondent.

Reminded of a yoga instructor who would always say that one should 'breathe through the spine and envision something calm'. Close my eyes for a second and the first image that pops into my head is the photo Saad sent of the two of us at that club in Dubai.

No, cannot think about boys right now. Though Saad doesn't count because he's a friend. Focus, Ayesha, Focus. 'So what else is going on?' We end up talking about betting on cricket matches, and Zafar promises he'll show me around the next time there's a Pakistan-India match so I can witness the fortunes being made at about a hundred times the speed of stock exchange transactions. Between him, my hairstylist, the bumbling spy at the press club, and a server at Espresso who often lets slip who was at the coffee shop, I could quite possibly keep track of 95 percent of the city. Even though I've lived in Karachi my entire life, these are the only relationships I've actually invested time and effort in. This should make me sad, except I'm oddly comforted by the fact that inasmuch as I don't like this city, this is a fantastic place to be a journalist.

7 p.m.: Head back home, changing rickshaws twice en route because the drivers don't want to cross from one gang-controlled area into another. Check online to see if Jamie has written anything new. Nope. Check his Twitter feed. The last tweet is from two days ago: 'Dinner at Okra—fabulous!' I wish he had choked on a mussel.

Zara texts to ask if I'd like to go out for coffee or have a boozy dinner. But now that I know Jamie's in the city, I'm filled with a weird sense of dread. If I do run into him, I can't count on myself to react in a civil manner. If I don't see him, I'll be wondering where he's eating overpriced pasta instead. Even though I'm dying to analyse the post-job situation with Zara, my mind is still racing with ideas from my interview with Zafar and I want to get started on my story. I make plans with her for the next day and get writing.

10 p.m.: My father knocks on the door. 'Are you not answering your phone again? Saad's just called on the landline.'

I call Saad back but his phone's switched off. That's

odd, wasn't he just calling me? Write him an e-mail asking if he was calling. No reply.

11 p.m.: Decide to call it a day. Have written about a thousand words already and have a surprisingly good feeling about this, the kind of optimism I last felt when I was banging out the detainee interview on that flight back from Dubai.

11:15 p.m.: Dad knocks on the door again. Only when I get up to open it, it's not Dad, it's Saad.

'What are you doing here?!' I yell, before hugging him and knocking over a bottle of Diet Coke in my enthusiasm. 'Had some time off,' he says, sitting down and lighting a cigarette. 'Haven't been to town in a while, it's Mum's birthday and I got your e-mail literally when I was packing, so it all worked out. Now go get me something to drink, and jeez, what are you wearing?'

Look at myself. Am in ratty pyjamas and thick-framed, for-home-only glasses. My hair has escaped its clip, so I look like I'm sporting a Mohawk and a mullet at the same time. 'Oh shut up Saad, it's not like all of us have a fancy job that pays for our bills at Armani.

'I don't have anything,' I say, rummaging around in the closet compartment where I keep liquor, hidden behind bags full of empty beer cans, a pair of old sneakers, and, oh look, a shawl I've been looking for for a year now. 'Maybe there's a shot or two left in one of these old bottles.'

'Oh, please,' Saad says, 'I brought booze from Dubai for you.'

He hands me a bottle of Glenfiddich and I could swoon right then and there. I pour out two drinks and settle on the couch with him. 'So, how is life without the job... and Jamie? Have you spoken to him at all?'

'No,' I say with a snort, and add Diet Coke to my whiskey after the first swig. I am still too much of a philistine to appreciate expensive booze.

'Well, you know what I told you. You're better off without that choot. But your job, Ayesha. You hated the place but you love being a reporter.'

'Well, things might not be so bad,' I say, and tell him about running into Andrea and the *Al Jazeera* stories. 'That's great,' Saad says. 'We're always going to land on our feet.'

'Well, speak for yourself. I might have to move to Dubai and work as your maid if this doesn't pan out.'

'Ha, that's not a possibility anymore. I'm quitting my job and moving back home.'

'What?' I start. 'Is everything ok? Did you have an accident? Are you insane? I know you get nostalgic after eating kebab rolls, but seriously, why?'

'Believe me,' Saad says, staring into his drink, 'I never imagined I'd be doing this so soon. But I kind of have to. Ammi's been getting really lonely. She was perfectly fine with me being in Dubai and didn't want to guilt me into staying in Karachi, but I knew she missed me. And honestly, I don't mind,' he says with a shrug.

'You don't mind?' I shriek. 'It's Karachi. It's where life and love come to die. It has nothing.'

'Oh c'mon. You're here. I won't be worried sick about mom all the time. And I don't even need to look for another job. Work will transfer me here, and I'll actually make better money. And there's great food, cheap beer, and I won't have to go to god awful bars anymore.'

'Wow,' I say. But Saad's jaw is still set and he's staring into his drink. I can tell he's not entirely happy with this decision. I decide not to be a Grinch about Karachi—at least for now. There'll be plenty of time for us to bitch about the city when he's actually here and the honeymoon period ends and he's complaining with the rest of us about extortionists and muggings and sectarian groups calling for carnage. I put on my best fake excited tone, which I usually use around people who insist on showing one endless photos of their babies/nephews/nieces on their phones. 'Do you realize we haven't lived in the same city in years? This is going to be fantastic. And Anil is going to make SO much more money off you.' Saad puts his glass aside and suddenly reaches out to hug me. It feels a bit strange. I really can't figure out why. Maybe I'm just surprised, since I'm holding a lit cigarette and am scared it will burn his shirt, but also because Saad has never really hugged me spontaneously since our respective parents' funerals. I awkwardly stroke his hair and he eventually lets go. I can't place the look on his face, which is odd, since I've known him for so long that I can quite accurately tell what he's thinking at any given moment, including when he's so bored at a dinner that he would rather hang out in the car park than eat Carpaccio. 'Your hair is nicer than mine,' I mumble, for lack of anything better to say. Saad bursts out laughing. 'Thanks Ayesha. I wouldn't have agreed to come home if you weren't here.'

'When are you moving back?' I get up to fix another drink. I am still a bit startled by the hug and feel like I need to put some physical distance between us, even though there's no reason for me to feel this way. 'In a couple of weeks,' Saad says.

Saad leaves a little while later because he doesn't want to drink more and get completely smashed for the drive home. I open my laptop and try to work on the interview some more but I can't quite focus and I keep thinking about Saad's decision to move back. Part of me really feels bad for Saad, but on the other hand, I am desperately excited that he'll be back in the city. I won't be alone again.

'But for how long?' a voice in my head pipes up. Saad will be lonely for a bit at first and will want to hang out but then he'll meet someone and will be occupied being starry-eyed all over town. Oh well. Given Saad's track record, that will fizzle out pretty soon and he'll be back to haranguing me to join him in a quest to find the city's best bun kebabs.

Wednesday, April 22, 2012

Headline of the day: 'Cannibals had disturbed childhood'

8.30 p.m.: Saad and I have spent the past few days hanging out, usually at Espresso where he would keep up a running commentary on everyone around. He asked me to come over for dinner to his house this evening since his cook has rustled up some amazing haleem. I've never been able to say no to haleem, and I realize I haven't hung out with Saad's mother in a few months. After Saad is dispatched to buy naans, his mother, who has been idly chatting about sales at Khaadi and lawn prices, furtively looks around and draws her chair closer to mine. She relaxes when she hears Saad's car leave the driveway. 'Beta,' she says urgently, in a tone that suggests that she's just murdered someone and needs my help to roll the victim up in a carpet and dump it in the plot next door. 'Ji Riffat aunty,' I say cautiously.

'Ayesha, can you talk some sense into Saad? I don't want him to move back.'

Oh no. Cannot land myself in the middle of a family drama. She might be offended if I tell her that Saad was driven by a sense of obligation and guilt because he thought she was 'terribly lonely' living in Karachi.

'Aunty, isn't it a good thing? I think Saad wants to spend time with you, to be with you. You've been an incredible rock since uncle passed away, but I'm sure it isn't easy living in this huge house alone...'

'Do you seriously believe that?' she says impatiently, gesturing towards the small army of cooks in the kitchen, the cleaners mopping around them as they cook and her housekeeper setting the table for dinner. 'There are so many people in this house, I barely get a moment to myself. I'm out all morning anyway because I'm teaching English part time at your old school, and then one of my friends comes over for lunch or tea. In the evenings, I go for a walk in the park with my neighbour. When I'm bored, I go shopping. I don't need a 28-year-old boy to be here having dinner with me every night! When I miss my child I can fly to Dubai and have dinner with him there.'

I ask her if instead of venting to me, she's had a chance to talk about this with Saad. 'Beta, of course I have,' she says and sighs. 'But each time it's the same response: "I want to be here with you, I'll be happier in Karachi, Ayesha is here".'

I can't believe Saad is telling his mother that I'm one of the reasons why he wants to move back. I am going to rip his head off. 'This is why I'm asking you beta, please tell him how unsafe it is here. You're a journalist. You know how terrible things really are. Also tell him that I'm really independent and I don't need him to look after me all the time.'

The door opens and Saad walks in with a bag of naans, munching on one. 'What are you two talking about so intently?' he asks, and I instantly feel guilty. 'Aunty has just been telling me how she wants to get you married off,' I say. When in doubt in Pakistan, always use marriage as

213

a way to take the conversation completely off track. Saad rolls his eyes and I keep up a stream of chatter over dinner about everyone I know who's been mugged, and Saad's mother pitches in enthusiastically with a story about her 70-year-old friend who told her mugger off. In our zeal though, our stories end up sounding a tad ludicrous and exaggerated. At least, that's what I think, because instead of being horrified by the tales, Saad laughed hysterically throughout dinner. I suppose I could have toned down my retelling of Zara's mugging a bit—surely I didn't have to mention the falsa juice that Zara handed over to the mugger—but Saad's mother actually put on accents when describing what happened to her friend, like a crime scene reconstruction. Saad offers to drop me off, and the minute we get into his car he suggests we get juice from a roadside stand near my house. Just as I've taken my first sip of the pomegranate-apple mix, Saad asks, 'So what were you and my mother talking about? She's not really thinking about getting me married, is she?'

'Oh, of course,' I say. 'You should really rethink this moving back idea; before you know it she'll stage a jhatt-mangni-patt-viyah type scene.'

'I know for a fact she isn't, so what were you talking about?'

'Oh nothing,' I say. 'I was asking her how she manages to fill up her days and she sounds like she's really busy. I thought you said she was quite lonely but her social life sounds better than mine.'

'Oh whatever,' Saad says, rolling his eyes. 'I see what you're doing here. You don't think she needs me and I shouldn't move back.'

'No, of course not...' I start, but Saad holds his hand up. 'I mean, seriously, I thought you'd be happy I was coming back. You're always saying that you miss having me around.'

'I do,' I say, trying to figure out a sensitive way to frame his mother's point. 'But you know I'm perpetually worried and tense living in Karachi and I just don't want to have to worry about you as well. I know you laugh off the muggings and kidnappings and bombs, but just take a look around. Look in front of you. The juice guy has a security guard, for the love of god, because he's scared someone will make off with his day's earnings and the canned pineapples.'

Saad doesn't reply and he drops me off after we've finished our juice.

Midnight

I'm transcribing an exchange from my notebook when the phone beeps. WhatsApp message from Saad.

'What's up?' I type back, while squinting at the notebook, trying to decipher whether I've written 'achanak' or 'ailaan' in my illegible Urdu handwriting.

Saad: 'I'm outside. Can I come in?'

'Is everything okay?' I ask, opening the door.

'Yeah, I just wanted to talk.'

He walks around my room, idly picking things up off my dresser and putting them back. 'So I'm not really moving back for my mother,' he says, and flops down on the bed.

'Okay.' I close the lid of the laptop. I wish I was a more nurturing, caring person and could offer something more sage than 'okay'. What does one give to people who appear to be in the midst of a crisis? A Xanax or a cup of hot milk? Or perhaps I have it all wrong and Saad is the one who needs help with disposing of a body. 'So, what is it?'

'I really need to get out of Dubai. You know that night we went clubbing when you were there? I looked at the photos later. Even though I knew so many people there that night...'

'Including the skanky girls,' I interject, remembering the flock of incredibly gorgeous girls who thronged around him at the club.

'Yeah, them too,' Saad says. 'Anyway. Well since then I've been thinking about how I don't really have any friends in the city and how I had fun that night because you were there. It would be so much easier to be here, where I actually have friends who care about me rather than about how much booze I have in the cabinet on any given night.'

'I didn't realize you felt this way,' I say.

'Well, so I just came to tell you that,' Saad says abruptly and gets up. 'I'm flying out tomorrow morning, but I'll see you in a couple of weeks?'

'Sure,' I say, and lock the door behind him. There is something really bizarre going on with Saad but I can't put my finger on it yet. Why did he look so upset when he was telling me he was moving back because of his mother? Why did I not guess that he was so unhappy in Dubai? He's never mentioned any of this to me before. All I've ever heard about is the fantastic concerts and the great bars. Weird.

Friday, April 24, 2012

9 a.m.: E-mail my story to *Al Jazeera*—all three thousand words of gritty interviews—and stare at the laptop. Refresh e-mail. Nothing. Maybe the Internet connection isn't working. Reboot the router. Still no reply. Perhaps a watched laptop doesn't beep. Check time zone for editor. Unless she's an insomniac, there's no way she's seen my story yet. Am about to turn the laptop off in exasperation when yes! New e-mail!

Hmph. Turns out it's just a BuzzFeed forward from Zara. '50 reasons you know it's time to quit your job.'

10 a.m.: Maybe I'll just go to the gym instead.

11 a.m.: Gym is actually buzzing. Its 11 a.m. Find this incredibly bizarre. When I was employed, I lived under the delusional cloud that like me, everyone else was also working and so I should not feel bad about the hours ticking away while I was stuck in editorial meetings or

covering legislative assembly proceedings. Nearly all of the treadmills are occupied. I peek into the men's gym. It's even busier. Clearly there are a lot of trust fund kids running around the city.

There's a yellow Corvette in the gym's parking lot with the licence plate number 'CIA-111'. It's being guarded by a carload of policemen. I have never understood why Karachiites buy ridiculously expensive cars that scream 'I'm rich!' only to then have to get cops to save them from the inevitability of being mugged. Snap photo and am posting it to Twitter when a cop comes running up. 'What are you doing?' 'Nothing,' I casually say, and put my phone away. 'I'm checking my phone.'

3 p.m.: The photo has already been retweeted half a dozen times. Still no e-mail from *Al Jazeera* though. I am an abject failure.

I drink the dregs of the whiskey Saad brought over. Now that I am unemployed, I feel no shame in drinking in the daytime. Saad. I really don't understand what is going on with him. Why does he want to move back to Karachi? Surely the appeal of cheap bun kebabs and the comfort of always having someone to call up and have drinks with on a Saturday night isn't much when compared to being able to live in a city where one can actually have a life. I don't know how to tell Saad how often I long for any kind of nightlife beyond listening to the neighbourhood boys angrily debating the umpire's decision in a street cricket match or blaring the latest weepy Bollywood song. But we're twenty-eight, not fourteen anymore. I can no longer dissuade Saad from doing things the way I could when we were kids. The only possibility I can bank on is that Saad will move to Karachi, have a miserable time, and then eventually realize he needs to leave.

E-mail! From the editor! 'This is really fantastic—just what I was looking for! We should have this online in an hour. You should get started on the next story too. And send me your bank details asap.'

I AM NOT AN ABJECT FAILURE! I AM A BRILLIANT REPORTER AND I AM GOING TO BE RICH AND FAMOUS AND WIN A PULITZER.

Five minutes later: Wonder if the story is up yet. Click refresh on the page. Not yet.

20 minutes later: No story yet.

25 minutes later: Still no story.

27 minutes later: Dammit, have closed the browser with a streamed episode of Sherlock.

50 minutes later: Click refresh...oh bloody hell, the electricity has gone.

Am finishing the rest of my drink and wondering if I can make the fan start working with sheer willpower. Maybe I'll just lie down for a bit.

4.30 p.m.: Am about to doze off when the phone rings. Zara. 'Ayesha! I just saw the story you did. It's fantastic! When did you do this, you sneaky cow?'

'What, it's out?'

'Yep, haven't you checked Twitter? At least a dozen

people on my timeline posted it, including Sara, or one of those girls from your newsroom. They all look the same.'

'Omygod, omygod, thanks—gotta go look!'

I log on using the neighbour's WiFi, hooked up to their UPS, and hurriedly get on to Twitter. Zara was right. Even my timeline is full of people tweeting the story and quotes from it. Check the article. It looks beautiful online. Ooh, someone else has just tweeted it. This would have never happened to me when I was writing for the *Daily News*. I would perpetually plug stories on Twitter, Facebook, my Google Talk status and even LinkedIn, until someone would finally take pity on me and share them. Is this really happening to me? For once, I feel proud of the work I've done. I feel... happy, I realize with a shock, given that I seem to have spent the past few weeks in a rage-filled haze. It's finally happening. I am actually doing the kind of stories I've wanted to do for so long.

Should probably calm down a bit. Oh, another retweet! No, must look away from the screen.

Hmm. Maybe I'll read the article just one more time.

CHAPTER 12

Saturday, May 2, 2012

Headline of the day: 'Man sues Al-Khan Tonight Restaurant for Rs 1 million for mental torture and humiliation'

7 p.m.: My father has just walked in to my room to find me in the exact same position I've been in for the past few days: in pyjamas, hunched over a laptop, and eating chili chips by the fistful.

'Don't you think you should change your clothes?' He sniffs the air and picks up an empty bottle of Diet Coke from the floor. 'And how many cigarettes have you smoked?'

I look at the overflowing ashtray and try to kick an empty can of Murree beer under the bed. 'The usual,' I mutter and get back to my laptop. I'm five hundred words into an article about the police investigating threats to journalists.

'And can you stop eating those chips? I read online they give you ulcers.'

I look at him in horror. Chili chips are part of a Karachiite's DNA. They're tangy, made from some amazing combination of potatoes, oil, copious amounts of salt, and enough red chilli to burn the lining of your stomach. I was hooked, like all of my friends, when I was first introduced to them by the school canteen, because no parent would ever bring them into the home. As soon as the lunch bell rang, students would make a beeline for the canteen to buy the sticky white packets of chips, which would inevitably run out in the first ten minutes. And despite dire warnings like those my father—or any out-of-towner who couldn't fathom why anyone would eat them—routinely issued, no one had managed to overcome the addiction even decades after leaving school. Zara sprinkled them on biryani and promptly drank a glass of Eno after, Saad ate them whenever he was feeling homesick, and there was a khao suey delivery joint in the neighbourhood that featured them prominently on the menu.

I'm about to repeat all of this for the fiftieth time when the phone rings. Zara.

'I don't care what you're doing tonight,' she says, before I've even said hello. 'I am getting you out of this social hibernation. Put on your best white kurta, we're going to hear Rahat Fateh Ali Khan perform.'

'I don't know,' I start. I've just opened a pack of chili chips and a new episode of *Masterchef* is about to start. 'No, you're coming. Get moving. I'll pick you up in thirty.'

I race around trying to find a white kurta and straighten my hair—a fruitless exercise, since it just keeps frizzing up again thanks to the humidity. The first kurta has a large cigarette burn. The other isn't ironed and the third, while clean and mercifully free of rips and cigarette burns, is too long. That's the one, I suppose. I realize the event will probably be in some garden somewhere, so there really is no point in doing anything to my hair. Twist hair up, and look for the cut up sock I use to hold it together and make a faux chignon. Oh. The last time I saw that sock was when I slept with Jamie, that glorious evening in the hotel. It feels like a lifetime ago, even though it's barely been a few weeks. Why does it still hurt so much? Why am I still so enraged? Tempted to text Zara and tell her to blow off the concert and bring a bottle of wine over so we can dissect this in detail. No. Cannot become a cliché, sobbing over a man. I kick my pyjamas away—sigh, they do look terribly comfy—and find my stash of bobby pins and start savagely pinning up my hair.

An hour later, Zara and I, cocktails in hand, are walking around the venue where Rahat Fateh Ali Khan is set to perform. The performance is part of a three-day classical music conference that Zara's paper is sponsoring and she's managed to sweet talk the advertising department into giving her free passes. The venue is an empty plot where the neighbourhood dumps garbage on weekdays, which has been transformed by a chic tent and all-white décor that is surely going to be splattered with food and spilled drinks by the end of the night. The crowd is made up largely of corporate types, men sporting an air of discomfort at having shed their uniform-like suits for shalwars. There's a smattering of politicians, all knocking back their drinks and laughing raucously with legislators from rival parties whom they're going to skewer in parliament on Monday. 'Isn't that Jackie?' Zara whispers, pointing to a skinny man in his fifties whose claim to fame is not his property development empire, but the fact that he did time in jail for running a ring of assassins. In court, he told the judge, 'Even if I have killed someone, and I'm not saying I have, isn't it better to have organized crime instead of handing a gun to every Tom, Dick, and Harry?' He's smoking a cigar and looking on as two ministers bicker.

'Isn't that bartender cute,' Zara says as she stares at a kid, who is barely twenty, if that, and is deftly using a cocktail shaker. I spot Farrah, the model, reclining on a cushion and smoking a cigarette. She waves and gestures at me to sit down next to her. Zara goes off to chat up the bartender and I go talk to Farrah. 'Darling, haven't seen you in ages,' she says. 'How's that horrible boss of yours?'

'I quit, actually,' I say, sneaking a cigarette from her pack.

'Good for you. By the way, his wife's just had another Botox shot, her eyebrows are so far up her forehead they look like they were drawn on. And I swear I heard her saying that she wants a second nose job, even though she now snores thanks to the first one she got because she wanted to look like Nicole Kidman.'

I really don't want to bitch out Kamran and his wife to Farrah given her propensity for gossip and the likelihood that she could be best friends with Kamran next week. 'And how are you? How's life after fashion week?'

'Amazing!' she says, 'Doing some great campaigns. And there's some gora reporter in town who's following me around for a week to do a story on how models live in Pakistan. Totally clichéd bullshit stuff, but hey, it's CNN!'

'CNN?' I repeat slowly. Oh no. Please let it be someone else, please don't let this be who I think it is...

'Yeah, oh look, there's the guy.' She points to someone standing nearby and even though I can only see his profile, I instantly recognize him. It's Jamie, drink in hand, and the only man here in a suit.

I stomp out my cigarette and tell Farrah I have to run. Where the hell is Zara?! I do a quick scan of the venue but damn the white kurta code, everyone looks the same. Oh thank goodness, she's still standing near the bar trying to catch the 20-year-old's attention. I rush up and drag her to a corner.

'Jamie's here!'

'What? Where?'

'Err, two o' clock.'

Zara starts looking the other way.

'Jeez, Zara, TWO O' CLOCK. Do you not know how to tell time?!'

Zara quickly glances at him and then stares at me. 'Ok. We're ignoring him. He doesn't exist. We're going to have a great time. Here, drink this,' she says, pushing her martini at me. 'Liquid courage.'

'Don't you think I should confront him?' I say. The urge to ask Jamie what the hell happened is overwhelming. He's confidently chatting away with someone, and I feel a distant longing for the time when he turned all that charm on me. Is it possible that he's gotten even better looking in the past few weeks?

'Are you out of your mind?' Zara hisses. 'Do you really want to have this discussion here, in front of all these people? And no, you are not talking to him. If anything, he should be here on his knees apologizing to you for ruining your life. Now let's go find someplace to sit.'

We start walking around, trying to find an empty space that isn't next to the speakers or any of the men who are already wavering slightly. Clearly the bartender has some skills. I'm trying to angle the cushion behind me when I hear a voice. 'Ayesha?'

I turn around slowly. It's Jamie, drink in hand, his skin glowing as if he's just returned from a spa weekend. I so desperately want to say something but I feel like I've lost the ability to form words other than youmotherfuckingassholewhathehellareyoudoinghere. I say hello and start staring at my phone, a part of me wishing that he would just disappear into thin air. Jamie stands there for a minute before Zara loudly interjects. 'Excuse me?'

'Yes?' Jamie says.

'You're standing on my dupatta.'

Jamie looks at me again and then walks off, a wounded expression on his face. How can he be the wounded party here?! Zara looks at me angrily. 'You were about to talk to him. Seriously, what the fuck is wrong with you?'

'I just want to know what happened, okay,' I say. 'But see, I didn't talk to him.'

'Whatever,' Zara says. 'Just remember how hurt and upset you were, and if you don't recall, just go online and search for his fucking exclusive and tell me if it doesn't make you want to kill him.'

'I know, I know,' I say, but I don't sound convincing even to myself. What is wrong with me?

Sunday, May 3, 2012

Headline of the day: 'Dissident cleric rushed to hospital after eating toxic halwa'

9 a.m.: There's no time to process what happened last night. I'm woken up by the sound of my phone ringing, which after one has only gone to bed at 4 a.m. after about a dozen drinks, sounds like the trumpets I anticipate hearing on judgment day. Check the display. Saad's mother. 'Beta, I'm just leaving the house, are you ready?' Fuck. I'd

forgotten Saad is moving back to Karachi today, and his mother had asked me to accompany her to the airport. I'm so hungover that even the thought of getting out of bed is making me want to hurl. Somehow manage to throw on a t-shirt and harem pants—the closest thing to pyjamas that is considered acceptable to wear in public.

Saad's mother sighs as she stares out of the window. 'Never did I think I would be so worried at the idea of him being back,' she says, fiddling with the bracelet on her arm that she hasn't taken off since her husband died. 'Look around us. Everyone is driving like a maniac because they don't want to risk stopping at a traffic light and being mugged.'

'There's nothing we can do,' I say, hoping my oversized sunglasses are shielding just how hungover I am. 'I know, beta,' she says, before she starts flipping through a lawn catalogue she has in the car. 'Do you think I can pull off floral prints at my age?'

Saad is possibly the only person smiling in the arrivals area. Everyone else looks like they've just been handed a death sentence. One girl walks out, peeling off layers of cardigans and shawls, much to the amusement of Saad's mother. 'Where did she think she was coming back to, Siberia?'

Saad bounds up and hugs his mother, and then me. His mother starts sniffling right away. 'Uff, Ammi, are these tears of joy?' She looks at him despairingly and I grab one of Saad's suitcases. 'Let's get out of here.'

Five hours, two plates of biryani, and three cups of tea later, I'm sitting in a corner of Saad's room as he unpacks. 'Hey, I bought you something,' he says, tossing a bag at me. Inside is a gorgeous tan leather satchel.

'Thanks!' I say, 'But you really shouldn't have, silly.'

'Oh, I also bought something for Zara,' Saad says.

'Zara? Did she ask you to get something for her?' I ask. Zara has a never-ending list of requests for people coming to Pakistan, featuring shampoo, make-up, and about twenty skincare products, as well as dark rum and red wine. 'No, it's just a gift. I was thinking now that I'm back, maybe we can hang out or something. Did you see the photos she posted on Facebook the other day? So. Much. Hotness.'

'Oh,' I say. I'd forgotten about Saad's Zara thing, even though she's never done more than flirt back when she's had too much to drink. The thought of the two of them together still irks me. Why can't Saad pick someone I don't know, someone following the same identikit pattern of a 20-something, incredibly well-dressed girl whose knowledge of politics is gleaned from the five links she sees on her Facebook feed, and who he'll inevitably get bored with in three weeks?

'Let's have coffee tonight,' Saad suggests. 'Invite Zara too?'

'Sure,' I say, and take out my phone to text and ask her if she's free, praying that she is stuck at work, has a prior engagement, anything. Am sorely tempted to not message her at all, but cannot risk running into her in the evening, given that Zara and I only frequent three cafés, having blacklisted the rest for not having a smoking section, being too popular with families, and serving instant coffee and charging us for gourmet cappuccinos. Zara replies immediately. 'Yeah, I'm free. Let me know when.'

Saad smiles when I tell him we'll see Zara tonight, and suddenly I feel terribly exhausted. Is Saad's cheeriness getting to me or last night's cocktails and Jamie-induced drama? 'I'll meet you in the evening. I'm going home to nap and change.'

'Sure,' he says, lifting up a mountain of shirts to stuff into his cupboard. His mother is going to sneak into his room when he goes out and get her maid to clean the closet anyway, so this is a fairly fruitless exercise.

9 p.m.: Waiting for Saad and Zara to show up. I've actually dressed up for coffee, I've even applied some make-up and worn dangly earrings. Saad and Zara enter within a minute of each other, and I stir my coffee as they catch up and Zara squeals over her gift (a really beautiful patterned silk scarf). Saad hasn't even noticed that I am not in clothes that resemble pyjamas. I get the uncomfortable feeling of being the third wheel on a date, which is ridiculous. This is just friends having coffee.

'I'm so glad you're back,' Zara says, 'Now you can knock some sense into Ayesha too.'

'What's that?' I ask, just as Saad looks at me questioningly. 'Why?'

'Oh, she didn't tell you? After all that's happened, Ayesha wanted to talk to Jamie last night!' In that moment, I could actually reach across the table and stab Zara. I know she's not saying this to be spiteful, but she has no idea how much Saad hates Jamie and how annoyed he's going to be with me.

Saad looks at me incredulously. 'You were what? Where? Did you call him?'

'No, of course not,' I say, trying not to be defensive. 'We ran into him at a concert last night and he came up to say hi, and I did ignore him before Zara chased him off.'

'And you would have talked to him, Ayesha, I saw the look on your face.' I shoot her an annoyed look that's supposed to communicate 'shut up', but she doesn't seem to get it.

'I cannot believe you,' Saad says, shaking his head. 'Ayesha, seriously? I mean, the man screwed you over in every possible way—you were a mess. Why would you even want to talk to him?'

I really don't know what to say. 'Because I'd still like an explanation...' This sets Saad and Zara off who begin ranting about how I am turning into a weak person full of self pity. I listen to this for about five minutes before I snap. 'Fine. I get it. Can we move on now?'

Zara begins telling the story of her mugging. Even though Saad has just heard the same—albeit dramatized—account over dinner, he laughs hysterically, and I force myself to smile.

After a couple of hours of stilted conversation—at least, I feel its stilted, Saad and Zara look like they're having the time of their lives—Zara realizes she has to be up at 7 a.m. tomorrow. 'Saad, can you drop me home?' I ask. I really want to explain to him properly what happened with Jamie and how I feel.

But the minute we get into the car, Saad starts off again. 'I'm really disappointed in you.'

'Yeah, I got it the first five times you said it,' I shoot back. 'There really was no need to gang up on me like that. I wasn't planning to grovel or whatever. I'd just really like to tell him to his face what an asshole he was.'

Saad looks at me like I am speaking a foreign language. 'Why are you overreacting?' I ask, wishing he would drive faster so I can exit his car and escape this discussion. 'I'm not,' he says, 'you are. I just don't want you to inflict more misery on yourself.'

'Don't worry, I don't plan to,' I retort.

'Sure,' Saad says exasperatedly, and then lapses into silence. I stare out of the window until we stop outside my building. 'Bye,' I say, and he half-heartedly waves back.

Wednesday, May 6, 2012

Headline of the day: 'Prayers of general's pir did not help'

I don't hear from Saad for the next few days. We've had these passive-aggressive arguments before but not over something this silly. I keep typing messages to him and deleting them. Saad's not going anywhere, I think, so I'm not driven by the same sense of urgency I usually have to patch things up before he leaves town again. He'll come around.

5 p.m.: Check my e-mail. The *Al Jazeera* editor has recommended me to a colleague at an academic journal, who wants me to write a two thousand-word essay for... eight hundred dollars. That's enough money to keep me afloat for another month. I'm just about to reply saying I'd love to do the essay when my phone rings. Kamran.

Why is he calling me? Pick phone up hesitantly, convinced he's calling to tell me that the paper is suing me or some such thing. 'Hi?'

'Ayesha! How are you?' Kamran's voice is oozing the warmth he usually reserves for old-moneyed folk who hold the key to his membership being approved at the private colonial-era club that he's been angling to get into for years. 'I'm fine, Kamran. How are you?'

'Excellent, but listen, we all miss you around here. Someone sent me a link to your *Al Jazeera* work, I'm glad you're doing so well, but come on, you need to get back to the world of beat reporting. So come back into the office tomorrow, and we'll talk?'

It's too early for Kamran to be drinking so this is actually a serious call. 'Kamran, I'm very happy freelancing,' I say. 'I don't think I want to come back.'

'You're happy? I mean, sure, the freelancing is fun for now but it's not a stable income. I mean, what are you going to do about money?'

'Kamran, we never got paid on time, surely I'll learn to live.'

'We're changing all that!' Kamran exclaims. 'I mean, we can't hire you back at a higher salary because you weren't eligible for a raise, but you'll definitely get paid on time. Look, all of your friends are here; this is what you're meant to do. This is your paper as much as it's mine. This is where you learnt everything.'

'I'm sorry, Kamran,' I say resolutely. 'I'm going to have to decline.'

'Oh,' Kamran's tone changes. 'Well, I hope there's someone ready to hire you when the freelancing work runs out.' I can just picture his condescending smile. 'We might not be able to later.'

'I'm sure I'll be fine. Good speaking to you, bye now!'

Check Twitter to find that Kamran has posted a series of snarky tweets about ungrateful reporters. Reach for my phone to text Zara but we haven't spoken since we had coffee with Saad. But there's no reason for her to be pissed at me. And I really need to gloat about Kamran's call and turning down his offer. Send her the link to Kamran's tweet on WhatsApp.

'Ha, that's hilarious. GTG, am at Atrium to watch movie with Saad.'

Saad and Zara are hanging out without me. Clearly he moved fast. I feel an inexplicable sense of hurt at the idea of them having fun while I'm at home replying to e-mails.

7 p.m.: Wonder what film they went to watch.

7.30 p.m.: Will just check online to see what's playing at the cinema. Did they go to watch the cutesy animated film for kids? The Bollywood romcom? The big-budget action thriller? Why is Saad hanging out with Zara and not me, or any of the dozens of friends he has in the city?

7.40 p.m.: Why am I at home alone? Why have my two best friends deserted me? Why am I still single? I invested so much time and effort and flirting only to be screwed over by Jamie. I am never chasing after a guy again.

8 p.m.: Maybe Jamie is still in town and will want to hang out. No. Cannot call him and make a fool of myself. Or worse, risk another fight with Saad.

8.30 p.m.: Watch television to distract myself. There are screaming politicians on every channel. One has just accused another of 'questionable morals'. On another channel, a legislator is shouting at politicians who want to negotiate with militants. Imran Khan is telling an interviewer he sees 'nothing wrong' in being on the same stage as right-wing extremists. One talk show host is hurling abuse at the president. I can feel the onset of a headache, but the problem with talk shows is that they can be terribly compelling in the manner of the *Jerry Springer Show*. I'm expecting the shrill host to intercept a thrown chair at any minute.

9 p.m.: Surely Zara is free by now. Text her again asking if she's free later. 'Can't do, am just grabbing a meal with Saad and then I have to be home.'

11 p.m.: My mind is exhausted with the arguments going on in my head. Wish I had a sleeping pill so I could doze off and not have to think about this. Don't have any booze either. The only other option is Benadryl, but surely I have not reached such a low point yet. Maybe I will just watch TV instead.

Finally fall asleep at 4 a.m., only to be woken up an hour later by the cat, who is demanding I relinquish my pillow so she can nap on it. Attempt to put cat on the floor. Doesn't work, she jumps right back on the bed. End up trying to fit myself on the sofa while the cat stretches out on the bed and falls asleep.

Thursday, May 7, 2012

Headline of the day: 'Big black ghost lands many factory workers in the hospital'

I wake up feeling sick and exhausted from thinking about Saad and Zara. I'm checking my phone for any signs of activity from the two—surely they tweeted about the movie, or posted selfies on Instagram, or shared an in-joke on Facebook—when an e-mail pops up. It's from a girl called Carla at the BBC, who says I was referred to her by Andrea. They're looking for a fixer to work with their correspondent on a story about crime in Karachi next week. It's three days of work, and I'll get paid $150 a day.

Dash off an e-mail to Andrea to say thanks. She has really turned into my fairy news mother. She keeps sending me links to fellowships and ideas for stories that I can do. She's offered to write a recommendation letter for me whenever I do want another job and texts me every other day with snarky comments about Islamabad's social scene: 'Isloo is out of red wine after the cops shut down the Koreans' bootlegging ring. It is a fucking disaster'.

She replies to my e-mail instantly. 'No need to say thanks. I'm frustrated with how limited the work at NBC is. The least I can do is help someone else tell a good story!'

Carla's asked me to line up some interviews, including with someone involved with the criminal justice system. I call up the prosecutor at the anti-terrorism court, who sounds delighted to hear from me. 'Come over. I have a charge sheet you'll find very interesting.' It's vague, but he's passed on gems in the past such as a list of targets from a Lashkar-e-Jhangvi suspect.

When I get to court, the guard greets me so exuberantly I'm almost embarrassed. 'After so long! No, no, no need to give your bag, we know you!' he says, as I hand over my handbag and notebook. 'Chai? Order chai for madam!' he barks to the sentry who is writing my name down in the logbook. 'No, thanks, not right now,' I say, and quickly head out to the courtrooms. The prosecutor is busy in a deposition, so I head to another courtroom and listen to a police officer describing how he led a raid on a kidnapper's hideout.

The judge, who I've never seen before, calls for a recess after the police officer has been cross-examined. 'Shukar, shukar,' the officer says as he hurriedly leaves the dock. The lawyers clutch their stacks of cardboard files and begin walking out, and I spot a lawyer who would probably be a good fit for the BBC interviews. 'Wait, you, the girl in the back,' the judge calls out. The court typist—who I've spent several hours harassing for transcripts in the past—raises an eyebrow. 'Yes?' I say, finally finding my voice.

'What are you doing here?' the judge calls out.

'I am a..'

'NO, NO—come up front.'

I walk up and stand next to the typist. 'No, not there,' the judge says exasperatedly. 'In the dock.'

'Oh. Okay.' I have no idea what is going on here. Am I going to be charged with contempt? There's a mad medley of Pakistani and Indian films playing in my head, the melodramatic Mohammad Ali screaming for insaaf and Sunny Deol's 'tareekh pe tareekh' monologue. I half expect to be asked to swear that I'm telling the truth, the whole truth, so help me god.

'So, what is your name? What are you doing here?'

I stammer my name and profession, and explain how I often come to court to take notes on proceedings. The judge listens, takes off his glasses and then starts cleaning them with his robe. The typist muffles a giggle. 'I see. Well I don't know how the other judges operate, but I really like to know who everyone is in the courtroom. You know this is a very high-profile courtroom, we're not listening to cases of marriage disputes here, but cases involving bomb blasts and extortion.'

'I understand,' I say.

'You're free to go. Don't be offended, I question everyone the same way.'

I head out and bump into the prosecutor. 'What happened? I heard the judge was grilling some journalist! You should have told him I invited you.'

'It's okay,' I say, and follow him into his office. It's a small room filled with filing cabinets, three grimy desks, and the coterie of exhausted prosecutors and clerks who huddle around them, drink endless cups of tea and try and figure out how they're going to deal with suspects who send them death threats from their jail cells. We set a time for his BBC interview, and then he surreptitiously hands me a folder. 'Transcript of a phone conversation from jail. Remember that guy who we found guilty of killing a journalist? His case is up for appeal and he's discussing it with someone from his party. Very interesting stuff.'

I know it's pointless to try and ask how I'm going to verify the information. I'm mentally running through a list of contacts—the press club spy, Saad's uncle who used to be the head of the police—when the prosecutor leans in. 'The jail warden is willing to talk about this. But I can tell you right now that his agenda is very clear. He wants the guy out of his jail and transferred to some small town.'

I stuff the file into my handbag and get up to leave. I

never quite know how to thank someone for leaking a government document. 'This is very kind of you,' I say, and leave.

The guard stops me as I walk by his check post. 'Madam, the traffic is insane outside. Why don't you wait for a bit?'

I really want to get the file away from this maze of government buildings and random security checks. It's a hotchpotch of colonial buildings and grimy concrete blocks that seem like they were transplanted from the former Soviet republics. The mood is as stilted, everyone walks around with the look of the clinically depressed. Even the stray cats and dogs lie around listlessly, clearly having lost their will to live amid the stacks of files full of bureaucratic correspondence and memos.

I hail a rickshaw and as we reach the main road, I realize the guard was right. The traffic is pretty bad, even for rush hour. Horns are blaring fruitlessly, almost as if the collective noise will somehow propel the traffic forward. The driver gets out of the rickshaw angrily. 'I'm going to find out what's wrong.' He confers with a traffic cop sitting on the sidewalk, who has clearly also given up on ever resolving the snarl and walks back. 'There's a protest up ahead, some religious group. These bloody beards never stop.'

The driver has a fairly long beard himself and I'm just about to point that out when there's a loud boom in the distance and a jolt, like an earthquake. The rickshaw

actually shudders as if it's about to topple over. I can hear
a woman screaming from the car next to us. I look up and
there's a plume of smoke in the distance. I look back and
there are cars reversing madly to try and get out of here.
There's a wail of ambulance sirens and the rickshaw driver
looks like he's about to pass out from fear. 'Don't worry,'
I say, even though I have no idea what has happened. 'I'll
be back,' I say and start running in the direction of the
noise. A cop waves me back. 'Bomb blast. At the protest.
It was pretty bad.'

'How do you know?' I say. He gestures to his wireless.
'Just go back, please.'

'I'm a journalist, at least tell me what happened,' I say,
scrambling in my bag for my press card.

'Five dead so far, at least forty injured. They're taking
them to Civil.' He takes out a handkerchief and mops his
forehead. 'God saved us, god saved us, I was supposed to
be there on duty. Just go back, otherwise other people will
start walking too and we don't know whether there'll be
another one.'

I reach for my cell phone to check if I have any alerts
from the hospital. The phone services seem to have gone
down. I walk back slowly. My legs feel like they're made
of jelly and it's like all my organs have been rearranged.
My eyes are stinging from the smoke in the air, combined
with the fumes from the dozens of rickshaws and cars all
stuck on the road. 'AYESHA. AYESHAAAAAAAAAA.' I
look around and it's Kamran, his head out of a car window,

waving madly. 'Hey,' I say.

'I need to get out of here, I can't do this.' Kamran looks ashen and absolutely terrified. 'I can't be here, I think I'm having a fucking panic attack.'

'Kamran! Breathe! We can't go forward, I just asked.' How does he expect me to get him out of here? I don't have a bloody helicopter. I'm about to ask why he doesn't own one when I look at him again. His hands are shaking on the wheel. 'Ok, get out of the car,' I say. He jumps out, slams the door and I take his hand. 'Now just walk with me.'

My plan is to get him some water and calm him down enough so he can get back into his car and drive but he's so panicky he's talking about five hundred words a minute. 'I was in a meeting at the governor's house, the bloody driver decided to take the day off so I'm driving myself around like a bloody pleb. My wife wanted me to take her to the tailor, what does she think I do, run a newspaper stand? I decided to take the longer route back home and Jesus, I could have bloody well died. What the hell is happening? Did you hear that blast? Good god. I thought my car was about to melt. Is it hot? Why is it so hot here?' Kamran is tugging at his tie and I'm convinced he's going to have a heart attack. 'Okay, Kamran, you've got to breathe.' We're standing in the narrow space between my rickshaw and a truck. I dig out a water bottle from my bag. 'Drink this, and just calm down, okay. You're alive, see. We're really, really lucky.'

Drinking water doesn't seem to be helping him. I don't

see a way out of the traffic jam, which has grown even worse. How the hell do people not know that there's been a bomb blast on this route and they should head the other way?! It is at times like this when I wish for a massive, citywide PA system. Kamran is still hyperventilating. We're going to have to get out of here on foot. I pay the rickshaw driver a thousand rupees and tell Kamran to follow me.

Except I have no idea where I'm going. There's a narrow alley squeezed between a shop advertising camel milk—'Health benefits from the finest camels'—and a men's clothing store with a massive set of briefs fluttering outside. 'Let's go.' The alley is full of water dripping from the air conditioners in the shops and houses above and I can see a rat run by. I curse myself for wearing sandals. Kamran and I walk through the alley and reach a lane of shops that I vaguely recognize, but all the shutters are pulled down. Kamran's tugging at his top shirt button and still frantically asking me where we're going. 'Stop, stop!' he gasps. I look around and he suddenly doubles over.

Oh my god, he's having a heart attack, I think. I am reaching for my phone to call an ambulance when Kamran starts throwing up. I crouch beside him and rub his back. 'It'll be okay, just let it out.' I hand him the last dregs of water and dig out a few tissues. He shakes his head and starts hurling again. The smell of the vomit is making me nauseous and I feel like I'm nine again, stuck on a class trip to the Pepsi factory where five kids threw up on the bus ride back to school because they drank too many free drinks. After what seems like a few hours, Kamran reaches for the bottle of water I'm still holding on to. 'Let's go,' he mutters weakly.

'Kamran, just keep walking, we're going to find a way back out.' The lane has been barricaded off but there's another alley up ahead. 'In there,' I say, hoping this will eventually lead somewhere. We walk through a deserted neighbourhood of crumbling apartment buildings and I can see a few rickshaws parked in the distance. 'Oh thank goodness. Kamran, do you think you can walk till there?' he nods and we head towards the rickshaws. If there are no drivers, I'm prepared to find a way to drive one myself. A group of boys suddenly emerge from one of the buildings, their faces covered with scarves. One has a gun.

Oh great. Now we're getting mugged?! Kamran is fumbling for his wallet. 'What are you doing in this neighbourhood?'

What is this? The neighbourhood watch? 'Our people have been slaughtered and you're traipsing around here. Don't you know we're in mourning?'

I realize with a sickening sense of dread that these folks are out for revenge. One of the guys is rubbing a gun in his hand, as if he's warming it up. 'Look guys...' Kamran starts and I interrupt. 'I'm so sorry for your loss, it is the most horrible thing that could have happened,' I say contritely. 'Please accept your sister's condolences.' How am I coming up with this stuff? Have I spent so much time with religious activists that their mannerisms have seeped in through some bizarre personality osmosis? 'I am your sister,' I say and look into the eyes of the guy with the gun. 'Look at my brother here, he works with me. He's very sick. We weren't supposed to be here. We are looking for a clinic. He needs to go to a doctor and the streets are blocked. There is no humanity left in this city, look at what they just did to your brothers.'

The guy with the gun looks at his friends and then at Kamran and I. I can actually hear my blood thrumming in my veins. 'Go,' he says, pointing to the path with his gun.

I touch my hand to my heart and bow my head, trembling slightly. Kamran and I look at each other and start walking towards the rickshaws. He's going to shoot us the moment we turn around. I imagine him training his gun at us, laughing inwardly at these naïve idiots. 'Wait,' I hear him say. This is it. I'm going to be a story in tomorrow's paper. In fact, Kamran will be a story and I'll be lucky if I even get a mention. 'SHEHZADAY!' he yells out and a man pops out of a rickshaw. 'Take these two wherever they want to go.'

I turn around, smile gratefully and shepherd Kamran into the rickshaw. I give the driver the office address and he expertly navigates through lanes and alleys and a park to get onto the bridge that leads to the office. We don't talk at all, in fact, we don't exhale until we're at the office gate. I pay the driver and he trundles off. I call out to the office guard. 'Take Kamran sahib inside,' I say when Kamran suddenly turns and gives me a hug. 'Thank you.

You saved my life. I would have died if it wasn't for you.'

'It's okay, I'm just glad you're not having a heart attack or something.'

'Come into the office. Have some water. I'll get someone to take you home.'

I walk in and Kamran's wife is sitting in the lobby, looking worriedly at the television screens showing visuals of the bomb blast. She jumps up and hugs him. 'I have been calling you for hours,' she says, and Kamran disentangles himself. 'Thank Ayesha. She rescued me from that hellhole.'

Kamran's wife awkwardly hugs me and I cough. 'Let's go to the newsroom,' Kamran says.

An hour later, he's retelling the story for the fifth time to a group of editors and sub-editors and the heads of marketing and sales who've all amassed in the office to check in on him. Each version is more exaggerated than the last one. Someone has ordered lattes from Espresso for us, and I am sipping on mine and smoking—no one, I have realized, dares question the girl who has just saved the boss's life—and listening to Kamran rattling on. 'And then Ayesha so confidently talked to the guys, you should have seen it!' he crows. It's hard to believe he was hurling a short while ago, except my shoes are covered in his puke. 'Ayesha, you're a star. I'm so proud of you. We should talk about you contributing at some point. We'll match whatever the people abroad are paying you.'

'Oh, thanks,' I say. I really need to get out of the office before he eventually talks me into coming back to work.

'Kamran, can someone drop me?'

'Sure, sure,' he says, and jumps to his feet and hugs me again. 'The receptionist will get you a car. Thank you so much once again, you're...'

'A genius, I know,' I say, and smile. Who knew it would take a near-death experience to turn Kamran into a human being?

CHAPTER 13

Thursday, May 7, 2012

9 p.m.: I've thrown out the puke-covered shoes and taken the world's longest shower. News channels are one-upping themselves in the race to show the grisliest visuals possible of the bomb blast. 'And as you can see we were forty seconds ahead of our rivals in reporting the blast,' one anchor crows. Another is shrilly narrating CCTV footage of the blast.

Kamran has sent about a dozen text messages. 'What if I hadn't been stuck in traffic? What if I had just driven into the blast? What if those guys hadn't let us pass?' I want to be annoyed at him but I know he's now in the throes of the guessing game everyone plays when they've had a near-miss like we did. It's the Karachiite version of 'the first time I had sex' story. You'll always remember your first time. Zara is on television. She's standing in front of the hospital's ER sign and patiently replying to questions thrown at her by the news anchor. 'Well, obviously, the injuries are severe, they were caught in a bomb blast,' she says tiredly before the anchor quizzes her on whether the hospital was able to deal with the influx of patients. 'Yes, the hospital was prepared for an emergency, this is, as you can see, the emergency room.' I feel a rush of fondness for her and send her a text: 'So, can you tell me what kind of injuries they are?'

Five minutes later she replies: 'I'd tell you to fuck off, but I've actually been asked that question twice on air. Where are you?'

'Finally home. Don't ask. Got caught in the post-blast madness.'

Most people would offer trite phrases of concern and 'are you holding up okay?' Zara knows better. 'Could be worse. You could be mopping up the blood here. Looks like the aftermath of Bakra Eid.'

I close my laptop. I don't think I'm going to get any writing done tonight. People tend to think living amid bombs and blood is inspiring. It isn't. It just makes me feel exhausted with the sheer pressure of either trying to shrug it off like nothing happened or having to write about it—how many new ways can one come up with to write about blood and gore?

Might as well call Anil. He's in the neighbourhood and five minutes later, I'm standing at the apartment gate collecting a bottle of scotch. 'Hurry up,' he says, as I count out the money. 'The entire city seems to be drinking today. Bomb blast happened in a place they've never heard of, yet *they're* all shaken up.' I'm assuming at least one of the orders is Kamran's, who is probably now regaling his entire family with the story of his brush with death.

As Anil drives away I'm almost tempted to call after him and ask him if he'd like to drink with me. I really don't feel like drinking alone. And Saad hasn't called yet. Should I call him instead? Do the same rules of calling someone after a fight apply to a friendship as they do to a relationship? I don't want to seem like I'm desperately eager to patch things up, especially since he's the one who should be apologetic for being such an ass about Jamie. Even if I did want to talk to Jamie, why is that Saad's problem?

I'm pouring out my third drink and surfing Facebook. Carla, the BBC girl, has added me on Facebook and I'm scrolling through her wall posts to see if she seems like a sane person to work with for three days. I stop at the second post. Dammit. I should have done this before I told her I would be available to work with her. 'James has a fabulous story on a drone attack survivor who is undergoing psychiatric counseling in Peshawar'.

Wish there was a way one could filter all mentions of Jamie online. The Eternal Sunshine of the Tweetless Mind? I'm about to ask Zara what she thinks about this but I put the phone down. She might start ranting again because I know what work Jamie is doing these days. I'm staring at Facebook. It does sound like a good story. Probably won't hurt to click.

The first frame is of the ward at a hospital in Peshawar.

It's dark and dreary and the man is sitting in a corner, curled up on a chair. He's going to have a nightmare, I think, and the screen fills with an image of him thrashing in bed before a nurse wakes him up and increases his sleep medication dosage.

How did I know that? Is this a scene from an all too realistic film I've seen recently? That doesn't seem possible.

I quickly Google 'drone survivor' and five minutes later, I'm watching the same footage of the man thrash around in his bed. It's part of a story smarmy Ali did last week from Peshawar. Andrea had asked me for some help with translating the dialogue because Ali had jetted off to Bangkok for a weekend vacation with his girlfriend.

This seems like far too much of a coincidence. Foreign correspondents routinely do the same story—operating like a wolf pack hunting together—but no one uses the same footage. It seems odd that Ali would have shared his work with Jamie.

Unless.

I send the links to both stories to Andrea, who e-mails me ten minutes later. 'Thanks for letting me know. I'm investigating this.'

Saturday, May 8, 2012

11 a.m.: Saad still hasn't called. I scrolled through Instagram this morning and found photos of Saad having coffee at

Espresso with his ex-girlfriend Nazia, who went to school with us. I cannot believe Saad is socializing with that cow. She had the gall to show up at my mother's funeral and ask me why I hadn't brushed my hair and if that was the only black shalwar kameez I owned? Of all of Saad's girlfriends—and there were many—she's the one I hated the most. There was McSweety, a ditzy girl whose name was actually Samira, who thought everything Saad did was 'soooo cuuuuute' and that he was 'soooooo adorable'. Or Nida, who had treated Saad like a possession for all of the month that they were together. Or Urooj, who wrote him poems.

Why is Saad hanging out with Nazia when his so-called best friend—ME, ME, ME—is a twenty-minute drive away?

Unless he's getting back together with her. The prospect fills me with despair. I don't think I am mentally up to socializing with Nazia. I open up the Instagram photo of them again. Nazia has suspiciously poker straight hair. I bet she's gone in for that ridiculous hair bonding treatment that all the salons are advertising. Zara tried it out last year and ended up buying a curling iron. 'I look like a Barbie doll,' she'd said, mournfully pulling at her hair. 'I spend all day reporting and it doesn't move an inch. It seems unnatural. Like Botox for your hair.'

Ugh. Fuck this. Am going to go get ice cream.

1 p.m.: Am sitting in a booth and eating a double scoop of chocolate chip ice cream, hoping no one is giving me the typical pitying looks and raised eyebrows that are the fate of anyone who decides to go to a café alone. I spot Farrah,

looking completely overdressed for a weekday afternoon in a silk jumpsuit and high heels. I wave at her. 'Models eat ice cream now? Wonders never cease.' She slides into the booth and looks longingly at the bowl in front of me. 'I bet that tastes amazing,' she says.

'What are you having?' I ask, mostly to be polite, as I wonder why she's hanging out at my table instead of at a table of designers, stylists, and other associated folk.

'Oh, a black coffee.'

Farrah's black coffee arrives...along with, of all the people in the world who I would rather never see again, Jamie. He's balancing a cup filled to the brim with coffee and a waffle cone, and freezes at seeing Farrah and me together. 'Join us!' Farrah turns to me and exclaims. Oh bloody hell. 'Actually, I should be leaving soon,' I say, hurriedly finishing my ice cream and hoping my face doesn't register the fact that I now have brain freeze. 'Don't be silly,' she drawls. 'Ayesha, you've met Jamie? He's following me around for a story for CNN.'

'We've met,' Jamie says softly. 'I'd really like to talk to you Ayesha,' he says, and for a moment I am reminded of just how amazing he was in bed, how lonely I feel with Saad clearly out and about and having a great time without me. 'Sure,' I say. 'Look, about what happened,' Jamie starts. 'I just wanted to let you know that I didn't mean to hurt you. It's a story, and this stuff happens.'

'This stuff happens?' I am aware that my jaw is hanging open at his blasé comment. 'What is that even supposed to mean?' Farrah looks completely confused and I'm trying very, very hard to keep my voice low and not scream at the top of my lungs about how this assholic, lying creep broke my heart and my career in one shot. I'm staring at Jamie, wondering how I could have ever let this man touch me, when I hear a voice in the distance. 'Hi Ayesha.'

I can feel my heart sinking to my Bata flip flops. I slowly turn my head around to see Saad and Nazia standing by the door to the café. 'Hi,' I say. 'Oh hi, Nazia.' This is the most awkward moment of my life—how stupid am I to be sitting here with bloody Jamie!??! 'I have to go,' I tell Farrah and Jamie, and run out of the café, brushing past Saad in the process.

An hour later, there's a knock on the door. I open it resignedly, knowing its Saad, who is going to be very, very angry.

'What the hell were you thinking?' he says, as he slams the door behind him.

'Oh, it's nice to see you too,' I say. 'Thanks for asking, I'm perfectly fine.'

'You were having coffee with that despicable human being. I really thought you were better than this. A bloody gora says hello and all is forgiven? Do you have absolutely no self-respect?'

Saad is standing in my room, arms crossed, oozing self-righteousness. 'Saad, it's not what you think. I ran into him and Farrah, they just took over the booth and I was trying to leave.'

'You looked pretty comfortable. I'm sure he told you that it was all just a big misunderstanding or whatever. Right?'

'We didn't even get to that,' I say, wondering what the hell has gotten into Saad. 'What is wrong with you? Why are you acting this way? Do you think I would ever forgive him?'

Saad looks at me and then looks away. I get up and try to hug him, but he's standing like a statue. 'Saad, seriously. You've known me for so long. Why do you think I'm such a naïve idiot?'

Saad moves my arms away from his waist, and stares at me for a long moment. 'I don't think that at all. In fact, I wish I didn't think about you at all.'

'What is that supposed to mean?' I say. There's this sense of panic rising in me. My friendship with Saad is over. He's going to tell me that we should 'take a break', not hang out so often, and the thought is breaking my heart. I need to do something, anything to save it. 'What do you mean, Saad?!' I shout.

'Nothing,' Saad says, and looks down at his feet. 'I have to go. I'll call you later.'

I want to run after Saad but I feel like I'm rooted to the ground. I've lost him and not to a freakishly straight-haired ditz, but because I was stupid enough to try and hear out a guy who was actually just a typical dick. I've been angry and hurt for weeks now, and for what? After all, Jamie did exactly what any opportunistic douchebag would do: he found someone who'd be easily charmed (single, sad, me), praised her (wide-eyed me), and slept with her (sexless for months me) and then, when she handed him the biggest scoop of his career, he used it. In the process, I've basically destroyed my friendship with Saad. He never liked Jamie, he tried to warn me against him, and I still went ahead and screwed myself over royally in the process. And now... I can't even process what this means. Am I going to spend the rest of my life talking about the good ol' times I had with this 'old friend' who I don't see anymore? Will he even invite me to his wedding? Or will I find out through Facebook and spend hours looking at him and some girl posing happily together, all our friends surrounding them, except me? Surely someone will whisper, 'Ayesha isn't here because she and Saad had a huuuuge fight months ago, don't you know?' The hurt tone in Saad's voice when he said he wished he didn't think about me at all is playing incessantly in my head, like a bad Bollywood song I can't shake off. Why can't Saad think about me? Surely what I did—sleeping with Jamie, trying to get him to talk about what happened—can't be so unforgivable?

Tuesday, May 11, 2012

Headline of the day: 'Taliban accuse Pakistani government of using sorcery and black magic'

5 p.m.: Have escaped to the gym. I can't be in my room alone anymore. I've spent the entire weekend working

and rehashing the fight with Saad. I can still picture him screaming at me, telling me he can't think about me anymore, that horrible moment when I turned around at the café and saw him standing there with Nazia, who he probably spent the weekend having sex with while I stayed under the comforter and watched episodes of *Sex and the City*.

I am running manically on the treadmill when my phone rings. How is one supposed to answer the phone when out of breath? I haven't been able to wean myself off answering calls on the first ring, a habit ingrained by years of being in a newsroom where not answering your phone means missing out on scoops and assignments and led Kamran to tell the finance department to stop paying employees' phone bills as revenge for not answering his calls. Must ignore, must ignore... Maybe it's Saad? Push 'stop' on the treadmill and grab my phone. 'Hello?' I say, trying to calm myself down.

'Hi, it's Andrea.'

'Oh hello. What's up?'

'Nothing. Is this a bad time? You sound busy.'

'No, no, absolutely not, I say, and sit down on the treadmill. My trainer walks by and is about to say something when I point to my phone. 'Very important,' I mouth and she shakes her head in disappointment.

'Well, I wanted to tell you that I have some good news for you. Jamie won't be stealing anyone's stories any time soon.'

'What?'

'I think there's a bad connection,' Andrea says. 'Let me call you back.'

'No no. I can hear you FINE! What exactly do you mean?'

'All I can say is, have a look at MediaMatters in about ten minutes.'

MediaMatters is an American website that covers media news, reports on gossip in the newsroom, and on new hires and layoffs. I remember using it to find out where Jamie had reported from. I grab my stuff from the locker and head outside and light up a cigarette. There's nothing up on MediaMatters yet so I check Jamie's Twitter account. He's posted a selfie with Farrah. Ugh. I hope Farrah maces him with a can of hairspray or something.

Refresh the page again.

Holy cow.

'A CNN spokesperson announced today that James Maxwell—who reported for the news network from Beirut, Baghdad and most recently, from Islamabad—is no longer associated with CNN. While the spokesperson declined to comment, a source in CNN's Dubai bureau told MediaMatters that Maxwell had been informed over the weekend about an internal investigation on a story that aired on CNN last week. Maxwell has reportedly plagiarized content from NBC for the story, including paying off a stringer attached to the story to give him the same footage used by NBC.

The source also said that questions were raised regarding Maxwell's last story, an exclusive interview of a recently released detainee from Guantanamo Bay that had generated early Pulitzer buzz. MediaMatters learnt that the profile had been pitched by a Pakistani reporter to a UK-based news website days before Maxwell's story went on-air.'

Oh my god in heaven above.

I check Twitter. Every single foreign correspondent on my timeline seems to be in a state of shock at what's happened. One guy has tweeted: 'Disgusting if true. James's career seems effectively dead. Quite sad.'

Andrea is a bloody genius. In this moment, I could erect a shrine to her and offer a pint of my blood to her every single day to express my gratitude. She's managed to get Jamie fired AND has exacted revenge on my behalf by questioning his source for the story. I try to call her but she cancels. 'I'm in a meeting with Ali, but you saw the link?'

'YESSSS!' I reply back. 'Thank you, this is absolutely amazing.'

She sends a wink emoticon back. The cigarette I'm smoking seems more potent, the knot of tension in my stomach that's been omnipresent since the day CNN scooped me is gone, and even my achy muscles feel more relaxed. There's a jolt of energy coursing through me. I need to tell Saad. I need to fix things with Saad. I need to do something to save what we have.

I run out of the gates and jump into the first empty

rickshaw I see. Where will Saad be? Its 5.45 p.m., so he's probably leaving work. I should go to his house and wait for him.

Saad's mother looks fairly confused to see me at the door in sweaty track pants and an old shirt with an 'I hate running' slogan. 'What's wrong, beta?' she says, waving me in. 'Are you doing okay?'

'Yes, yes, aunty. Is Saad back from work yet?'

She looks like I've asked her if Saad has committed a dozen murders. 'Oh beta,' she says, sitting down on her armchair. 'I knew you and Saad had had a fight, he's been so upset all weekend, but I didn't realize he left without telling you.'

'Left?! Where is he?'

'Beta the driver left to pick him up from work—he's going to the airport. He's set up a meeting with his boss in Dubai to see if he can move back.'

'What?!' I scream. 'When did this happen? Oh my god, aunty, I need to see him now.'

'Oh,' she says, 'I think the driver should have picked him up already, and the idiot left his phone at home so I can't even call to see where he is. And Saad's left his Pakistani SIM here too, he said he didn't need it there.'

I don't know what to do. It's rush hour, so there's a good chance Saad isn't at the airport yet. Should I go to his office? Should I make the trek to the airport? I'm standing outside Saad's house, which isn't anywhere close to a main road from where I can hail a rickshaw or cab. A cabbie drives by, ignoring me waving frantically. I start walking when he reverses. 'Where to?'

'The airport,' I say. 'I'll pay you two hundred rupees more if you can get me there in twenty minutes.'

He looks at me and then revs up the car. We're speeding through a maze of small houses on what used to be railway tracks, land that people have been squatting on for decades now. The cab splashes through a stream of muddy water and drives through a patch of bushes. 'Do you know what you're doing?' I ask. 'I swear to God, stop worrying. This is the route I use when there is violence in the city. Best way to get there.'

I look at my phone. Fifteen minutes gone. If Saad left ten minutes before I did… God, why did we have to have that fight? I don't know why I want to see Saad so desperately, it just feels like I am going to lose everything if I don't. 'Hurry up, please,' I beg the driver, who has slowed down to light a cigarette. 'Acha acha, don't worry, we'll get you on that flight.' I want to correct him but there's a better chance he'll continue speeding if he thinks I need to catch a plane. The cab suddenly smells rather odd. The driver is smoking a fucking joint.

The turn-off for the airport suddenly emerges out of nowhere. 'We're here!' I exclaim. 'Of course,' the cabbie says proudly. 'I told you na, I've done this before.'

I get off at the international departures gate and look around frantically for Saad. He isn't here. The signboard says the flight for Dubai hasn't even opened for check-in

yet. I race from one end of the hall to the other. No sign of
Saad. A guy in his fifties stops me. 'Beta, whoever you're
looking for, I'm sure they're looking for you too. Stop
running around.'

I'm just about to tell the guy to mind his own bloody
business when I hear a voice behind me. 'Yeah, Ayesha,
you really shouldn't run around.'

It's Saad, clutching a cup of takeaway coffee from
McDonald's. I throw my arms around him.

'How did you even get here?!' he says, as he sets his
coffee down on the floor. 'I literally just got to the airport.
How'd you know I was here?'

'Your mother. You idiot. Were you really leaving?'

Saad doesn't reply. Shit. I should have phrased this
better. 'I'm sorry...' I start.

'No, I am,' he says, running his hand through his hair.
'I've been a bloody idiot and I was trying to escape having
to deal with this.'

'Deal with what, Saad? It's us. We got over the fact that
you had to give me your sweater when I got my period at
school. Seriously...'

'I can't really think straight,' he says, and sighs. 'I think
I may be in love with you.'

I feel like I'm standing on the edge of a pit and if I take
one wrong step I'm going to fall in. Saad starts talking
hurriedly. 'Clearly you don't feel the same way, and that's
okay, we'll still be friends. I just need to get you out of my

head, which is kind of impossible when you've been in my head since we were fourteen...'

I take a step and wrap my arms around Saad. I can feel a jolt of electricity go through me. He leans down, brushes my hair away, and is about to kiss me when I hear someone clear his throat right behind us.

'Is this man bothering you?', asks the guy, shooting daggers at Saad.

I'm shocked out of the haze and suddenly very, very aware of where I am. 'Saad, bloody hell, we're at the airport!' I say and wrest his arm away.

'Oh, seriously!?' Saad says, exasperated.

'Is he bothering you?' asks the concerned bystander again, while we're frozen in motion.

'YES!' Saad and I shout in unison.

'I hope you bother me forever,' Saad says, smirking. And for the first time in years, I can feel pure, unadulterated happiness.

'Uff ho, jumma chummaaa dee dayyyyyyyyyy,' sings a boy as he passes by.

Saad and I burst out laughing and he holds my hand. 'Let's go home.'

ACKNOWLEDGEMENTS

I'd like to thank Faiza S. Khan; she didn't just commission and edit this book, she quite literally made it happen. Without her, I'd still be on my couch staring at the first three hundred words. Faiza and Random House took a chance on a snarky, cynical journalist who'd never written fiction before—I am forever indebted to them.

Mohammed Hanif was incredibly encouraging and gave great advice and suggestions on the manuscript.

Thank you to my family: my father Imtiaz Ali and sister Huma, and my cat, who stayed up most nights while I hunched over the laptop and took naps on drafts.

Alex Strick van Linschoten, Alexander Lobov, Amna Iqbal, Nefer Sehgal and Misha Rezvi attempted to keep me sane, though I doubt their efforts worked.

And lastly, thank you to the Karachiites who inspired the characters and are presumably writing me up in their burn books.

A NOTE ON THE AUTHOR

Photograph © Nefer Sehgal

Saba Imtiaz is a journalist based in Karachi. Her work has appeared in the *Guardian* and the *Christian Science Monitor*. This is her first novel.